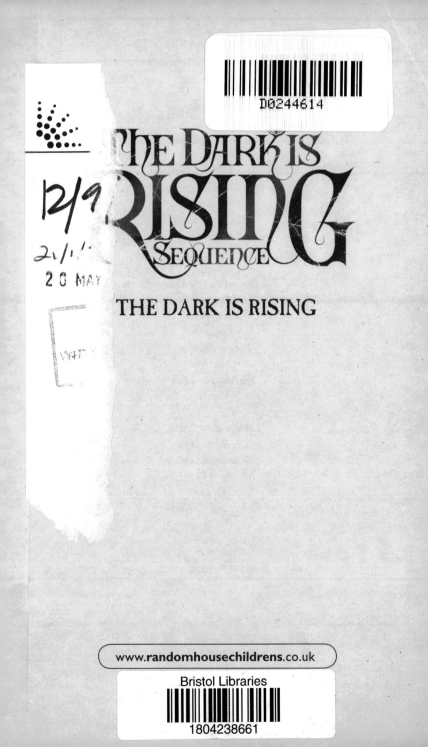

THE DARK IS
RISING
SEQUENCE

THE DARK IS RISING

D0244614

www.**randomhousechildrens**.co.uk

Also by Susan Cooper

THE DARK IS RISING SEQUENCE

THE DARK IS RISING

SUSAN COOPER

RED FOX

THE DARK IS RISING
A RED FOX BOOK 978 1 849 41270 4

Published by Red Fox,
An imprint of Random House Children's Publishers UK
A Random House Group Company

First published in Great Britain by Chatto and Windus Ltd 1973
Puffin Books edition published 1976
This edition published 2010

5 7 9 10 8 6

The poem 'White in the moon the long road lies', one of ten from A. E. Housman's
A Shropshire Lad which have been set to music by Arthur Somervell, is quoted on
pages 283 & 284 by permission of the Society of Authors and Jonathan Cape Ltd.

Copyright © Susan Cooper, 1973

The Random House Group Limited supports the Forest Stewardship Council® (FSC®), the leading
international forest-certification organisation. Our books carrying the FSC label are printed on FSC®-certified
paper. FSC is the only forest-certification scheme supported by the leading environmental organisations,
including Greenpeace. Our paper procurement policy can be found at www.randomhouse.co.uk/environment

MIX
Paper from
responsible sources
FSC® C016897

Set in Adobe Caslon

Red Fox Books are published by Random House Children's Publishers UK
61-63 Uxbridge Road, London W5 5SA

www.randomhousechildrens.co.uk
www.randomhouse.co.uk

Addresses for companies within The Random House Group Limited can be found at:
www.randomhouse.co.uk/offices.htm

THE RANDOM HOUSE GROUP Limited Reg. No. 954009

A CIP catalogue record for this book is available from the British Library.

Printed and bound by CPI Group
(UK) Ltd, Croydon, CR0 4YY

For Jonathan

Part One: *The Finding*

Midwinter's Eve

'Too many!' James shouted, and slammed the door behind him.

'What?' said Will.

'Too many kids in this family, that's what. Just *too many*.' James stood fuming on the landing like a small angry locomotive, then stumped across to the window-seat and stared out at the garden. Will put aside his book and pulled up his legs to make room. 'I could hear all the yelling,' he said, chin on knees.

'Wasn't anything,' James said. 'Just stupid Barbara again. Bossing. Pick up this, don't touch that. And Mary joining in, twitter twitter twitter. You'd think this house was big enough, but there's always *people*.'

They both looked out of the window. The snow lay thin and apologetic over the world. That wide grey sweep was the lawn, with the straggling trees of the orchard still dark beyond; the white squares were the roofs of the garage, the old barn, the rabbit hutches, the chicken coops. Further back there were only the flat fields of Dawsons' Farm, dimly white-striped. All the broad sky was grey, full of more snow that refused to fall. There was no colour anywhere.

'Four days to Christmas,' Will said. 'I wish it would snow properly.'

'And your birthday tomorrow.'

'Mmm.' He had been going to say that too, but it would have been too much like a reminder. And the gift he most wished for on his birthday was some-thing nobody could give him: it was snow, beautiful, deep, blanketing snow, and it never came. At least this year there was the grey sprinkle, better than nothing.

He said, remembering a duty: 'I haven't fed the rabbits yet. Want to come?' Booted and muffled, they clumped out through the sprawling kitchen. A full symphony orchestra was swelling out of the radio; their eldest sister Gwen was slicing onions and singing; their mother was bent broad-beamed and red-faced over an oven. 'Rabbits!' she shouted, when she caught sight of them. 'And some more hay from the farm!'

'We're going!' Will shouted back. The radio let out a sudden hideous crackle of static as he passed the table. He jumped. Mrs Stanton shrieked, 'Turn that thing DOWN.'

Outdoors, it was suddenly very quiet. Will dipped out a pail of pellets from the bin in the farm-smelling barn, which was not really a barn at all, but a long, low building with a tiled roof, once a stable. They tramped through the thin snow to the row of heavy wooden hutches, leaving dark foot-marks on the hard frozen ground.

Opening doors to fill the feed-boxes, Will paused, frowning. Normally the rabbits would be huddled sleepily in corners, only the greedy ones coming twitch-nosed forward to eat. Today they seemed restless and uneasy, rustling to and fro, banging against their wooden walls; one or two even leapt back in alarm when he opened their doors. He came to his favourite rabbit, named Chelsea, and reached in as usual to rub him affectionately behind the ears, but the animal scuffled back away from him and cringed into a corner, the pink-rimmed eyes staring up blank and terrified.

'Hey!' Will said, disturbed. 'Hey James, look at that. What's the matter with him? And all of them?'

'They seem all right to me.'

'Well, they don't to me. They're all jumpy. Even Chelsea. Hey, come on, boy—' But it was no good.

'Funny,' James said with mild interest, watching. 'I dare say your hands smell wrong. You must have touched something they don't like. Same as dogs and aniseed, but the other way round.'

'I haven't touched anything. Matter of fact, I'd just washed my hands when I saw you.'

'There you are then,' James said promptly. 'That's the trouble. They've never smelt you clean before. Probably all die of shock.'

'Ha very ha.' Will attacked him, and they scuffled together, grinning, while the empty pail toppled rattling on the hard ground. But when he glanced back as they left, the animals were still moving distractedly, not eating yet, staring after him with those strange frightened wide eyes.

'There might be a fox about again, I suppose,' James said. 'Remind me to tell Mum.' No fox could get at the rabbits, in their sturdy row, but the chickens were more vulnerable; a family of foxes had broken into one of the henhouses the previous winter and carried off six nicely-fattened birds just before marketing-time. Mrs Stanton, who relied on the chicken-money each year to help pay for eleven Christmas presents, had been so furious she had kept watch afterwards in the cold barn two nights running, but the villains had not come back. Will thought that if he were a fox he would have kept clear too; his mother might be married to a jeweller, but with generations of Buckinghamshire farmers behind her, she was no joke when the old instincts were roused.

Tugging the handcart, a home-made contraption with a bar joining its shafts, he and James made their way down the curve of the overgrown drive and out along the road to Dawsons' Farm. Quickly past the churchyard, its great dark yew trees leaning out over the crumbling wall; more slowly by Rooks' Wood, on the corner of Church Lane. The tall spinney of horse-chestnut trees, raucous with the calling of the rooks and rubbish-roofed with the clutter of their sprawling nests, was one of their familiar places.

'Hark at the rooks! Something's disturbed them.' The harsh irregular chorus was deafening, and when Will looked up at the tree-tops he saw the sky dark with wheeling birds. They flapped and drifted to and fro; there were no flurries of sudden movement, only this clamorous interweaving throng of rooks.

'An owl?'

'They're not chasing anything. Come on, Will, it'll be getting dark soon.'

'That's why it's so odd for the rooks to be in a fuss. They all ought to be roosting by now.' Will turned his head reluctantly down again, but then jumped and clutched his brother's arm, his eye caught by a movement in the darkening lane that led away from the road where they stood. Church Lane: it ran between Rooks' Wood and the churchyard to the tiny local church, and then on to the River Thames.

'Hey!'

'What's up?'

'There's someone over there. Or there was. Looking at us.'

James sighed. 'So what? Just someone out for a walk.'

'No, he wasn't.' Will screwed up his eyes nervously, peering down the little side road. 'It was a weird-looking man all hunched over, and when he saw me looking he ran off behind a tree. *Scuttled*, like a beetle.'

James heaved at the handcart and set off up the road, making Will run to keep up. 'It's just a tramp, then. I dunno, everyone seems to be going batty today – Barb and the rabbits and the rooks and now you, all yak-twitchetty-yakking. Come on, let's get that hay. I want my tea.'

The handcart bumped through the frozen ruts into Dawsons' yard, the great earthen square enclosed by buildings on three sides, and they smelt the familiar farm-smell. The cowshed must have been mucked out that day; Old George, the toothless cattleman, was piling dung across the yard. He raised a hand to them. Nothing missed Old George; he could see a hawk drop from a mile away. Mr Dawson came out of a barn.

'Ah,' he said. 'Hay for Stantons' Farm?' It was his joke with their mother, because of the rabbits and the hens.

James said, 'Yes, please.'

'It's coming,' Mr Dawson said. Old George had disappeared into the barn. 'Keeping well, then? Tell your mum I'll have ten birds off her tomorrow. And four rabbits. Don't look like that, young Will. If it's not their happy Christmas, it's one for the folks as'll have them.' He glanced up at the sky, and Will thought a strange look came over his lined brown face. Up against the lowering grey clouds, two black rooks were flapping slowly over the farm in a wide circle.

'The rooks are making an awful din today,' James said. 'Will saw a tramp up by the wood.'

Mr Dawson looked at Will sharply. 'What was he like?'

'Just a little old man. He dodged away.'

'So the Walker is abroad,' the farmer said softly to himself. 'Ah. He would be.'

'Nasty weather for walking,' James said cheerfully. He nodded at the northern sky over the farmhouse roof; the clouds there seemed to be growing darker, massing in ominous grey mounds with a yellowish tinge. The wind was rising too; it stirred their hair, and they could hear a distant rustling from the tops of the trees.

'More snow coming,' said Mr Dawson.

'It's a horrible day,' said Will suddenly, surprised by his own violence; after all, he had wanted snow. But somehow uneasiness was growing in him. 'It's – creepy, somehow.'

'It will be a bad night,' said Mr Dawson.

'There's Old George with the hay,' said James. 'Come on, Will.'

'You go,' the farmer said. 'I want Will to pick up something for your mother from the house.' But he did not move, as James pushed the handcart off towards the barn; he stood with his hands thrust deep into the pockets of his old tweed jacket, looking at the darkening sky.

'The Walker is abroad,' he said again. 'And this night will be bad, and tomorrow will be beyond imagining.' He looked at Will, and Will looked back in growing alarm into the weathered face, the bright dark eyes creased narrow by decades of peering into sun and rain and wind. He had never noticed before how dark Farmer Dawson's eyes were: strange, in their blue-eyed county.

'You have a birthday coming,' the farmer said.

'Mmm,' said Will.

'I have something for you.' He glanced briefly round the yard, and withdrew one hand from his pocket; in it, Will saw what looked like a kind of ornament, made of black metal, a flat circle quartered by two crossed lines. He took it, fingering it curiously. It was about the size of his palm, and quite heavy; roughly forged out of iron, he guessed, though with no sharp points or edges. The iron was cold to his hand.

'What is it?' he said.

'For the moment,' Mr Dawson said, 'just call it something to keep. To keep with you always, all the time. Put it in your pocket, now. And later on, loop your belt through it and wear it like an extra buckle.'

Will slipped the iron circle into his pocket. 'Thank you very much,' he said, rather shakily. Mr Dawson, usually a comforting man, was not improving the day at all.

The farmer looked at him in the same intent,

unnerving way, until Will felt the hair die on the back of his neck; then he gave a twisted half-smile, with no amusement in it but a kind of anxiety. 'Keep it safe, Will. And the less you happen to talk about it, the better. You will need it after the snow comes.' He became brisk. 'Come on, now, Mrs Dawson has a jar of her mincemeat for your mother.'

They moved off towards the farmhouse. The farmer's wife was not there, but waiting in the doorway was Maggie Barnes, the farm's round-faced, red-cheeked dairymaid, who always reminded Will of an apple. She beamed at them both, holding out a big white crockery jar tied with a red ribbon.

'Thank you, Maggie,' Farmer Dawson said.

'Missus said you'd be wanting it for young Will here,' Maggie said. 'She went down the village to see the vicar for something. How's your big brother, then, Will?'

She always said this, whenever she saw him; she meant Will's next-to-oldest brother Max. It was a Stanton family joke that Maggie Barnes at Dawsons' had a thing about Max.

'Fine, thank you,' Will said politely. 'Grown his hair long. Looks like a girl.'

Maggie shrieked with delight. 'Get away with you!' She giggled and waved her farewell, and just at the last moment Will noticed her gaze slip upward past his head. Out of the corner of his eye as he turned, he thought he saw a flicker of movement by the farmyard gate, as if someone were dodging quickly out of sight. But when he looked, no one was there.

With the big pot of mincemeat wedged between two bales of hay, Will and James pushed the hand-cart out of the yard. The farmer stood in his doorway behind them; Will could feel his eyes, watching. He glanced up uneasily at the looming, growing clouds, and half-unwillingly slipped a hand into his pocket to finger the strange iron circle. '*After the snow comes.*' The sky looked as if it were about to fall on them. He thought: *what's happening?*

One of the farm dogs came bounding up, tail waving; then it stopped abruptly a few yards away, looking at them.

'Hey, Racer!' Will called.

The dog's tail went down, and it snarled, show-ing its teeth.

'James!' said Will.

'He won't hurt you. What's the matter?'

They went on, and turned into the road.

'It's not that. Something's wrong, that's all. Something's awful. Racer, Chelsea – the animals are all scared of me.' He was beginning to be really frightened now.

The noise from the rookery was louder, even though the daylight was beginning to die. They could see the dark birds thronging over the treetops, more agitated than before, flapping and turning to and fro. And Will had been right; there was a stranger in the lane, standing beside the churchyard.

He was a shambling, tattered figure, more like a bundle of old clothes than a man, and at the sight of him the boys slowed their pace and drew instinctively closer to the cart and to one another. He turned his shaggy head to look at them.

Then suddenly, in a dreadful blur of unreality, a hoarse, shrieking flurry was rushing dark down out of the sky, and two huge rooks swooped at the man. He staggered back, shouting, his hands thrust up to protect his face, and the birds flapped their great wings in a black vicious whirl and were gone, swooping up past the boys and into the sky.

Will and James stood frozen, staring, pressed against the bales of hay.

The stranger cowered back against the gate.

'Kaaaaaak . . . kaaaaaak . . .' came the head-splitting racket from the frenzied flock over the wood, and then three more whirling black shapes were swooping after the first two, diving wildly at the man and then away. This time he screamed in terror and stumbled out into the road, his arms still wrapped in defence round his head, his face down; and he ran. The boys heard the frightened gasps for breath as he dashed headlong past them, and up the road past the gates of Dawsons' Farm and on towards the village. They saw bushy, greasy grey hair below a dirty old cap; a torn brown overcoat tied with string, and some other garment flapping beneath it; old boots, one with a loose sole that made him kick his leg oddly sideways, half-hopping, as he ran. But they did not see his face.

The high whirling above their heads was dwindling into loops of slow flight, and the rooks began to settle one by one into the trees. They were still talking loudly to one another in a long cawing jumble, but the madness and the violence were not in it now. Dazed, moving his head for the first time, Will felt his cheek brush against something, and putting his hand to his shoulder, he found a long black feather there. He pushed it into his jacket pocket, moving slowly, like someone half-awake.

Together they pushed the loaded cart down the road to the house, and the cawing behind them died to an ominous murmur, like the swollen Thames in spring.

James said at last, 'Rooks don't do that sort of thing. They don't attack people. And they don't come down low when there's not much space. They just don't.'

'No,' Will said. He was still moving in a detached half-dream, not fully aware of anything except a curious vague groping in his mind. In the midst of all the din and the flurry, he had suddenly had a strange feeling stronger than any he had ever known: he had been aware that someone was trying to tell him something, something that had missed him because he could not understand the words. Not words exactly; it had been like a kind of silent shout. But he had not been able to pick up the message, because he had not known how.

'Like not having the radio on the right station,' he said aloud.

'What?' said James, but he wasn't really listening. 'What a thing,' he said. 'I s'pose the tramp must have been trying to catch a rook. And they got wild. He'll be snooping around after the hens and the rabbits, I bet you. Funny he didn't have a gun. Better tell Mum to leave the dogs in the barn tonight.' He chattered amiably on as they reached home and unloaded the hay. Gradually Will realized in amazement that all the shock of the wild, savage attack was running out of James's mind like water, and that in a matter of minutes even the very fact of its happening had gone.

Something had neatly wiped the whole incident from James's memory; something that did not want it reported. Something that knew this would stop Will from reporting it too.

'Here, take Mum's mincemeat,' James said. 'Let's go in before we freeze. The wind's really getting up – good job we hurried back.'

'Yes,' said Will. He felt cold, but it was not from the rising wind. His fingers closed round the iron circle in his pocket and held it lightly. This time, the iron felt warm.

The grey world had slipped into the dark by the time they went back to the kitchen. Outside the window, their father's battered little van stood in a yellow cave of light. The kitchen was even noisier and hotter than before. Gwen was setting the table, patiently steering her way round a trio of bent figures where Mr Stanton was peering at some small, nameless piece of machinery with the twins, Robin and Paul; and with Mary's plump form now guarding it, the radio was blasting out pop music at enormous volume. As Will approached, it erupted again into a high-pitched screech, so that everyone broke off with grimaces and howls.

'Turn that thing OFF!' Mrs Stanton yelled desperately from the sink. But though Mary, pouting, shut off the crackle and the buried music, the noise level changed very little. Somehow it never did when more than half the family was at home. Voices and laughter filled the long stone-floored kitchen as they sat round the scrubbed wooden table; the two Welsh collies, Raq and Ci, lay dozing at the far end of the room beside the fire. Will kept away from them; he could not have borne it if their own dogs had snarled at him. He sat quietly at tea – it was called tea if Mrs Stanton managed to produce it before five o'clock, supper if it was later, but it was always the same hearty kind of meal – and kept his plate and his mouth full of sausage to avoid having to talk. Not that anyone was likely to miss your talk in the cheerful babble of the Stanton family, especially when you were its youngest member.

Waving at him from the end of the table, his mother called, 'What shall we have for tea tomorrow, Will?'

He said indistinctly, 'Liver and bacon, please.'

James gave a loud groan.

'Shut up,' said Barbara, superior and sixteen. 'It's his birthday, he can choose.'

'But *liver*,' said James.

'Serves you right,' Robin said. 'On your last birthday, if I remember right, we all had to eat that revolting cauliflower cheese.'

'I made it,' said Gwen, 'and it wasn't revolting.'

'No offence,' said Robin mildly. 'I just can't bear cauliflower. Anyway you take my point.'

'I do. I don't know whether James does.'

Robin, large and deep-voiced, was the more muscular of the twins and not to be trifled with. James said hastily, 'Okay, okay.'

'Double-ones tomorrow, Will,' said Mr Stanton from the head of the table. 'We should have some special kind of ceremony. A tribal rite.' He smiled at his youngest son, his round, rather chubby face crinkling in affection.

Mary sniffed. 'On my eleventh birthday, I was beaten and sent to bed.'

'Good heavens,' said her mother, 'fancy you remembering that. And what a way to describe it. In point of fact you got one hard wallop on the bottom, and well-deserved, too, as far as I can recollect.'

'It was my birthday,' Mary said, tossing her pony-tail. 'And I've never forgotten.'

'Give yourself time,' Robin said cheerfully. 'Three years isn't much.'

'And you were a very young eleven,' Mrs Stanton said, chewing reflectively.

'Huh!' said Mary. 'And I suppose Will isn't?'

For a moment everyone looked at Will. He blinked in alarm at the ring of contemplating faces, and scowled down into his plate so that nothing of him was visible except a thick slanting curtain of brown hair. It was most disturbing to be looked at by so many people all at once, or at any rate by more people than one could look at in return. He felt almost as if he were being attacked. And he was suddenly convinced that it could in some way be dangerous to have so many people thinking about him, all at the same time. As if someone unfriendly might *hear* . . .

'Will,' Gwen said at length, 'is rather an old eleven.'

'Ageless, almost,' Robin said. They both sounded solemn and detached, as if they were discussing some far-off stranger.'

'Let up, now,' said Paul unexpectedly. He was the quiet twin, and the family genius, perhaps a real one: he played the flute and thought about little else. 'Anyone coming to tea tomorrow, Will?'

'No. Angus Macdonald's gone to Scotland for Christmas, and Mike's staying with his grannie in Southall. I don't mind.'

There was a sudden commotion at the back door, and a blast of cold air; much stamping, and noises of loud shivering. Max stuck his head into the room from the passage; his long hair was wet and white-starred. 'Sorry I'm late, Mum, had to walk from the Common. Wow, you should see it out there – like a blizzard.' He looked at the blank row of faces, and grinned. 'Don't you know it's snowing?'

Forgetting everything for a moment, Will gave a joyful yell and scrambled with James for the door. 'Real snow? Heavy?'

'I'll say,' said Max, scattering drops of water over them as he unwound his scarf. He was the eldest brother, not counting Stephen, who had been in the Navy for years and seldom came home. 'Here.' He opened the door a crack, and the wind whistled through again; outside, Will saw a glittering white fog of fat snowflakes – no trees or bushes visible, nothing but the whirling snow. A chorus of protest came from the kitchen: 'SHUT THAT DOOR!'

'There's your ceremony, Will,' said his father. 'Right on time.'

* * *

Much later, when he went to bed, Will opened the bedroom curtain and pressed his nose against the cold windowpane, and he saw the snow tumbling down even thicker than before. Two or three inches already lay on the sill, and he could almost watch the level rising as the wind drove more against the house. He could hear the wind, too, whining round the roof close above him, and in all the chimneys. Will slept in a slant-roofed attic at the top of the house; he had moved into it only a few months before, when Stephen, whose room it had always been, had gone back to his ship after a leave. Until then Will had always shared a room with James – everyone in the family shared with someone else. 'But my attic ought to be lived in,' his eldest brother had said, knowing how Will loved it.

On a bookcase in one corner of the room now stood a portrait of Lieutenant Stephen Stanton, R.N., looking rather uncomfortable in dress uniform, and beside it a carved wooden box with a dragon on the lid, filled with the letters he sent Will sometimes from unthinkably distant parts of the world. They made a kind of private shrine.

The snow flurried against the window, with a sound like fingers brushing the pane. Again Will heard the wind moaning in the roof, louder than before; it was rising into a real storm. He thought of the tramp, and wondered where he had taken shelter. '*The Walker is abroad . . . this night will be bad . . .*' He picked up his jacket and took the strange iron ornament from it, running his fingers round the circle, up and down the inner cross that quartered it. The surface of the iron was irregular, but though it showed no sign of having been polished it was completely smooth – smooth in a way that reminded him of a certain place in the rough stone floor of the kitchen, where all the roughness had been worn away by generations of feet turning to come round the corner from the door. It was an odd kind of iron: deep, absolute black, with no shine to it but no spot anywhere of discoloration or rust. And once more now it was cold to the touch; so cold this time that Will was startled to find it numbing his fingertips. Hastily he put it down. Then he pulled his belt out of his trousers, slung untidily as usual over the back of a chair, took the circle, and threaded it through like an extra buckle, as Mr Dawson had told him. The wind sang in the window-frame. Will put the belt back in his trousers and dropped them on the chair.

It was then, without warning, that the fear came.

The first wave caught him as he was crossing the room to his bed. It halted him stock-still in the middle of the room, the howl of the wind outside filling his ears. The snow lashed against the window. Will was suddenly deadly cold, yet tingling all over. He was so frightened that he could not move a finger. In a flash of memory he saw again the lowering sky over the spinney, dark with rooks, the big black birds wheeling and circling overhead. Then that was gone, and he saw only the tramp's terrified face and heard his scream as he ran. For a moment, then, there was only a dreadful darkness in his mind, a sense of looking into a great black pit. Then the high howl of the wind died, and he was released.

He stood shaking, looking wildly round the room. Nothing was wrong. Everything was just as usual. The trouble, he told himself, came from thinking. It would be all right if only he could stop thinking and go to sleep. He pulled off his dressing-gown, climbed into bed, and lay there looking up at the skylight in the slanting roof. It was covered grey with snow.

He switched off the small bedside lamp, and the night swallowed the room. There was no hint of light even when his eyes had grown accustomed to the dark. Time to sleep. Go on, go to sleep. But although he turned on his side, pulled the blankets up to his chin, and lay there relaxed; contemplating the cheerful fact that it would be his birthday when he woke up, nothing happened. It was no good. Something was wrong.

Will tossed uneasily. He had never known a feeling like this before. It was growing worse every minute. As if some huge weight were pushing at his mind, threatening, trying to take him over, turn him into something he didn't want to be. That's it, he thought make me into someone else. But that's stupid. Who'd want to? And make me into what? Something creaked outside the half-open door, and he jumped. Then it creaked again, and he knew what it was: a certain floorboard that often talked to itself at night, with a sound so familiar that usually he never noticed it at all. In spite of himself, he still lay listening. A different kind of creak came from further away, in the other attic, and he twitched again, jerking so that the blanket rubbed against his chin. You're just jumpy, he said to himself; you're remembering this afternoon, but really there isn't much to remember. He tried to think of the tramp as someone unremarkable, just an ordinary man with a dirty overcoat and worn-out boots; but instead all he could see once more was the vicious diving of the rooks. '*The Walker is abroad* . . .' Another strange crackling noise came, this time above his head in the ceiling, and the wind whined suddenly loud, and Will sat bolt upright in bed and reached in panic for the lamp.

The room was at once a cosy cave of yellow light, and he lay back in shame, feeling stupid. Frightened of the dark, he thought: how awful. Just like a baby. Stephen would never have been frightened of the dark, up here. Look, there's the bookcase and the table, the two chairs and the window seat; look, there are the six little square-riggers of the mobile hanging from the ceiling, and their shadows sailing over there on the wall. Everything's ordinary. Go to sleep.

He switched off the light again, and instantly everything was even worse than before. The fear jumped at him for the third time like a great animal that had been waiting to spring. Will lay terrified, shaking, feeling himself shake, and yet unable to move. He felt he must be going mad. Outside, the wind moaned, paused, rose into a sudden howl, and there was a noise, a muffled scraping thump, against the skylight in the ceiling of his room. And then in a dreadful furious moment, horror seized him like a nightmare made real; there came a wrenching crash, with the howling of the wind suddenly much louder and closer, and a great blast of cold; and the Feeling came hurtling against him with such force of dread that it flung him cowering away.

Will shrieked. He only knew it afterwards; he was far too deep in fear to hear the sound of his own voice. For an appalling pitch-black moment he lay scarcely conscious, lost somewhere out of the world, out in black space. And then there were quick footsteps up the stairs outside his door, and a voice calling in concern, and blessed light warming the room and bringing him back into life again.

It was Paul's voice. 'Will? What is it? Are you all right?'

Slowly Will opened his eyes. He found that he was clenched into the shape of a ball, with his knees drawn up tight against his chin. He saw Paul standing over him, blinking anxiously behind his dark-rimmed spectacles. He nodded, without finding his voice. Then Paul turned his head, and Will followed his looking and saw that the skylight in the roof was hanging open, still swaying with the force of its fall; there was a black square of empty night in the roof, and through it the wind was bringing in a bitter midwinter cold. On the carpet below the skylight lay a heap of snow.

Paul peered at the edge of the skylight frame.

'Catch is broken – I suppose the snow was too heavy for it. Must have been pretty old anyway, the metal's all rusted. I'll get some wire and fix it up till tomorrow. Did it wake you? Lord, what a horrible shock. If I woke up like that, you'd find me somewhere under the bed.'

Will looked at him in speechless gratitude, and managed a watery smile. Every word in Paul's soothing, deep voice brought him closer back to reality. He sat up in bed and pulled back the covers.

'Dad must have some wire with that junk in the other attic,' Paul said. 'But let's get this snow out before it melts. Look, there's more coming in. I bet there aren't many houses where you can watch the snow coming down on the carpet.'

He was right: snowflakes were whirling in through the black space in the ceiling, scattering everywhere. Together they gathered what they could into a misshapen snowball on an old magazine, and Will scuttled downstairs to drop it in the bath. Paul wired the skylight back to its catch.

'There now,' he said briskly, and though he did not look at Will, for an instant they understood one another very well. 'Tell you what, Will, it's freezing up here – why don't you go down to our room and sleep in my bed? And I'll wake you when I come up later – or I might even sleep up here if you can survive Robin's snoring. All right?'

'All right,' Will said huskily. 'Thanks.'

He picked up his discarded clothes – with the belt and its new ornament – and bundled them under his arm, then paused at the door as they went out, and looked back. There was nothing to see, now, except a dark damp patch on the carpet where the heap of snow had been. But he felt colder than the cold air had made him, and the sick, empty feeling of fear still lay in his chest. If there had been nothing wrong beyond being frightened of the dark, he would not for the world have gone down to take refuge in Paul's room. But as things were, he knew he could not stay alone in the room where he belonged. For when they were clearing up that heap of fallen snow, he had seen something that Paul had not. It was impossible, in a howling snow-storm, for anything living to have made that soft unmistakable thud against the glass that he had heard just before the skylight fell. But buried the heap of snow, he had found the fresh black wing-feather of a rook.

He heard the farmer's voice again: *This night will be bad. And tomorrow will be beyond imagining.*

Midwinter Day

He was woken by music. It beckoned him, lilting and insistent; delicate music, played by delicate instruments that he could not identify, with one rippling, bell-like phrase running through it in a gold thread of delight. There was in this music so much of the deepest enchantment of all his dreams and imaginings that he woke smiling in pure happiness at the sound. In the moment of his waking, it began to fade, beckoning as it went, and then as he opened his eyes it was gone. He had only the memory of that one rippling phrase still echoing in his head, and itself fading so fast that he sat up abruptly in bed and reached his arm out to the air, as if he could bring it back.

The room was very still, and there was no music, and yet Will knew that it had not been a dream.

He was in the twins' room still; he could hear Robin's breathing, slow and deep, from the other bed. Cold light glimmered round the edge of the curtains, but no one was stirring anywhere; it was very early. Will pulled on his rumpled clothes from the day before, and slipped out of the room. He crossed the landing to the central window, and looked down.

In the first shining moment he saw the whole strange-familiar world, glistening white; the roof of the outbuildings mounded into square towers of snow, and beyond them all the fields and hedges buried, merged into one great flat expanse, unbroken white to the horizon's brim. Will drew in a long, happy breath, silently rejoicing. Then, very faintly, he heard the music again, the same phrase. He swung round vainly searching for it in the air, as if he might see it somewhere like a flickering light.

'Where are you?'

It had gone again. And when he looked back through the window, he saw that his own world had gone with it. In that flash, everything had changed. The snow was there as it had been a moment before, but not piled now on roofs or stretching flat over lawns and fields. There were no roofs, there were no fields. There were only trees. Will was looking over a great white forest: a forest of massive trees, sturdy as towers and ancient as rock. They were bare of leaves, clad only in the deep snow that lay untouched along every branch, each smallest twig. They were everywhere. They began so close to the house that he was looking out through the topmost branches of the nearest tree, could have reached out and shaken them if he had dared to open the window. All around him the trees stretched to the flat horizon of the valley. The only break in that white world of branches was away over to the south, where the Thames ran; he could see the bend in the river marked like a single stilled wave in this white ocean of forest, and the shape of it looked as though the river were wider than it should have been.

Will gazed and gazed, and when at last he stirred he found that he was clutching the smooth iron circle threaded on to his belt. The iron was warm to his touch.

He went back into the bedroom.

'Robin!' he said loudly. 'Wake up!' But Robin breathed slowly and rhythmically as before, and did not stir.

He ran into the bedroom next-door, the familiar small room that he had once shared with James, and shook James roughly by the shoulder. But when the shaking was done, James lay motionless, deeply asleep.

Will went out on to the landing again and took a long breath, and he shouted with all his might: 'Wake up! Wake up, everyone!'

He did not now expect any response, and none came. There was a total silence, as deep and timeless as the blanketing snow; the house and everyone in it lay in a sleep that would not be broken.

Will went downstairs to pull on his boots, and the old sheepskin jacket that had belonged, before him, to two or three of his brothers in turn. Then he went out of the back door, closing it quietly behind him, and stood looking out through the quick white vapour of his breath.

The strange white world lay stroked by silence. No birds sang. The garden was no longer there, in this forested land. Nor were the outbuildings nor the old crumbling walls. There lay only a narrow clearing round the house now, hummocked with unbroken snowdrifts, before the trees began, with a narrow path leading away. Will set out down the white tunnel of the path, slowly, stepping high to keep the snow out of his boots. As soon as he moved away from the house, he felt very much alone, and he made himself go on without looking back over his shoulder, because he knew that when he looked, he would find that the house was gone.

He accepted everything that came into his mind, without thought or question, as if he were moving through a dream. But a deeper part of him knew that he was not dreaming. He was crystal-clear awake, in a Midwinter Day that had been waiting for him to wake into it since the day he had been born, and, he somehow knew, for centuries before that. *Tomorrow will be beyond imagining* . . . Will came out of the white-arched path into the road, paved smooth with snow and edged everywhere by the great trees, and he looked up between the branches and saw a single black rook flap slowly past, high in the early sky.

Turning to the right, he walked up the narrow road that in his own time was called Huntercombe Lane. It was the way that he and James had taken to Dawsons' Farm, the same road that he had trodden almost every day of his life, but it was very different now. Now, it was no more than a track through a forest, great snow-burdened trees enclosing it on both sides. Will moved bright-eyed and watchful through the silence, until, suddenly, he heard a faint noise ahead of him.

He stood still. The sound came again, through the muffling trees: a rhythmical, off-key tapping, like a hammer striking metal. It came in short irregular bursts, as though someone were hammering nails. As he stood listening, the world around him seemed to brighten a little; the woods seemed less dense, the snow glittered, and when he looked upward, the strip of sky over Huntercombe Lane was a clear blue. He realized that the sun had risen at last out of the sullen bank of grey cloud.

He trudged on towards the sound of hammering, and soon came to a clearing. There was no village of Huntercombe any more, only this. All his senses sprang to life at once, under a shower of unexpected sounds, sights, smells. He saw two or three low stone buildings thick-roofed with snow; he saw blue wood-smoke rising, and smelt it too, and smelt at the same time a voluptuous scent of new-baked bread that brought the water springing in his mouth. He saw that the nearest of the three buildings was three-walled, open to the track, with a yellow fire burning bright inside like a captive sun. Great showers of sparks were spraying out from an anvil where a man was hammering. Beside the anvil stood a tall black horse, a beautiful gleaming animal; Will had never seen a horse so splendidly midnight in colour, with no white markings anywhere.

The horse raised its head and looked full at him, pawed the ground, and gave a low whinny. The smith's voice rumbled in protest, and another figure moved out of the shadows behind the horse. Will's breath came faster at the sight of him, and he felt a hollowness in his throat. He did not know why.

The man was tall, and wore a dark cloak that fell straight like a robe; his hair, which grew low over his neck, shone with a curious reddish tinge. He patted the horse's neck, murmuring in its ear; then he seemed to sense the cause of its restlessness, and he turned and saw Will. His arms dropped abruptly. He took a step forward and stood there, waiting.

The brightness went out of the snow and the sky, and the morning darkened a little, as an extra layer of the distant cloudbank swallowed the sun.

Will crossed the road through the snow, his hands thrust deep into his pockets. He did not look at the tall cloaked figure facing him. Instead he stared resolutely at the other man, bent again now over the anvil, and realized that he knew him; it was one of the men from Dawsons' Farm. John Smith, Old George's son.

'Morning, John,' he said.

The broad-shouldered man in the leather apron glanced up. He frowned briefly, then nodded in welcome. 'Eh, Will. You're out early.'

'It's my birthday,' Will said.

'A Midwinter birthday,' said the strange man in the cloak. 'Auspicious, indeed. And you will be eleven years grown.' It was a statement, not a question. Now Will had to look. Bright blue eyes went with the red-brown hair, and the man spoke with a curious accent that was not of the South-East.

'That's right,' Will said.

A woman came out of one of the nearby cottages, carrying a basket of small loaves of bread, and with them the new-baked smell that had so tantalized Will before. He sniffed, his stomach reminding him that he had eaten no breakfast. The red-haired man took a loaf, wrenched it apart, and held out a half towards him.

'Here. You're hungry. Break your birthday fast with me, young Will.' He bit into the remaining half of the loaf, and Will heard the crust crackle invitingly. He reached forward, but as he did so the smith swung a hot horseshoe out of his fire and clapped it briefly on the hoof clenched between his knees. There was a quick smoky smell of burning, killing the scent of the new bread; then the shoe was back in the fire and the smith peering at the hoof. The black horse stood patient and unmoving, but Will stepped back, dropping his arm.

'No, thank you,' he said.

The man shrugged, tearing wolfishly at his bread, and the woman, her face invisible behind the edge of an enveloping shawl, went away again with her basket. John Smith swung the horseshoe out of the fire to sizzle and steam in a bucket of water.

'Get on, get on,' said the rider irritably, raising his head. 'The day grows. How much longer?'

'Your iron will not be hurried,' said the smith, but he was hammering the shoe in place now with quick, sure strokes. 'Done!' he said at last, trimming the hoof with a knife.

The red-haired man led his horse round, tightened the girths, and slid upwards, quick as a jumping cat, into his saddle. Towering there, with the folds of his dark robe flowing over the flanks of the black horse, he looked like a statue carved out of night. But the blue eyes were staring compellingly down at Will. 'Come up, boy. I'll take you where you want to go. Riding is the only way, in snow as thick as this.'

'No, thank you,' Will said. 'I am out to find the Walker.' He heard his own words with amazement. *So that's it*, he thought.

'But now the Rider is abroad,' the man said, and all in one quick movement he twitched his horse's head around, bent in the saddle, and made a sweeping grab at Will's arm. Will jerked sideways, but he would have been seized if the smith, standing at the open wall of the forge, had not leapt forward and dragged him out of reach. For so broad a man, he moved with astonishing speed.

The midnight stallion reared, and the cloaked rider was almost thrown. He shouted in fury, then recovered himself, and sat looking down in a cold contemplation that was more terrible than rage. 'That was a foolish move, my friend smith,' he said softly. 'We shall not forget.' Then he swung the stallion round and rode out in the direction from which Will had come, and the hooves of his great horse made only a muffled whisper in the snow.

John Smith spat, derisively, and began hanging up his tools.

'Thank you,' Will said. 'I hope—' He stopped.

'They can do me no harm,' the smith said. 'I come of the wrong breed for that. And in this time I belong to the road, as my craft belongs to all who use the road. Their power can work no harm on the road through Hunter's Combe. Remember that, for yourself.'

The dream-state flickered, and Will felt his thoughts begin to stir. 'John,' he said. 'I know it's true

I must find the Walker, but I don't know why. Will you tell me?'

The smith turned and looked directly at him for the first time, with a kind of compassion in his weathered face. 'Ah no, young Will. Are you so newly awake? That you must learn for yourself. And much more, this your first day.'

'First day?' said Will.

'Eat,' said the smith. 'There is no danger in it now that you will not be breaking bread with the Rider. You see how quickly you saw the peril of that. Just as you knew there would be greater peril in riding with him. Follow your nose through the day, boy, just follow your nose.' He called to the house, 'Martha!'

The woman came out again with her basket. This time she drew back her shawl and smiled at Will, and he saw blue eyes like the Rider's but with a softer light in them. Gratefully, he munched at the warm crusty bread, which had been split now and spread with honey. Then beyond the clearing there was a new sound of muffled footfalls in the road, and he spun fearfully round.

A white mare, without rider or harness, trotted into the clearing towards them: a reverse image of the Rider's midnight-black stallion, tall and splendid and without marking of any kind. Against the dazzle of the snow, glittering now as the sun re-emerged from cloud, there seemed a faint golden glow in its whiteness and in the long mane falling over the arched neck. The horse came to stand beside Will, bent its nose briefly and touched his shoulder as if in greeting, then tossed its great white head, blowing a cloud of misty breath into the cold air. Will reached out and laid a reverent hand on its neck.

'You come in good time,' John Smith said. 'The fire is hot.'

He went back into the forge and pumped once or twice at the bellows-arm, so that the fire roared; then he hooked down a shoe from the shadowed wall beyond and thrust it into the heat. 'Look well,' he said, studying Will's face. 'You've not seen a horse like this ever before. But this will not be the last time.'

'She's beautiful,' Will said, and the mare nuzzled again gently at his neck.

'Mount,' said the smith.

Will laughed. It was so obviously impossible; his head reached scarcely to the horse's shoulder, and even if there had been a stirrup it would have been far out of reach of his foot.

'I am not joking,' said the smith, and indeed he

did not look the kind of man who often smiled, let alone made a joke. 'It is your privilege. Take hold of her mane where you can reach it, and you will see.'

To humour him, Will reached up and wound the fingers of both hands in the long coarse hair of the white horse's mane, low on the neck. In the same instant, he felt giddy; his head hummed like a spinning-top, and behind the sound he heard quite plainly, but very far off, the haunting, bell-like phrase of music that he had heard before waking that morning. He cried out. His arms jerked strangely; the world spun; and the music was gone. His mind was still groping desperately to recover it when he realized that he was closer to the snow-thick branches of the trees than he had been before, sitting high on the white mare's broad back. He looked down at the smith and laughed aloud in delight.

'When she is shod,' the smith said, 'she will carry you, if you ask.'

Will sobered suddenly, thinking. Then something drew his gaze up through the arching trees to the sky, and he saw two black rooks flapping lazily past, high up. 'No,' he said. 'I think I am supposed to go alone.' He stroked the mare's neck, swung his legs to one side, and slid the long way down, bracing himself for a jolt. But he found that he landed lightly on his toes in the snow. 'Thank you, John. Thank you very much. Good-bye.'

The smith nodded briefly, then busied himself with the horse, and Will trudged off in some disappointment; he had expected a word of farewell at least. From the edge of the trees, he glanced back. John Smith had one of the mare's hind feet clenched between his knees, and was reaching his gloved hand for his tongs. And what Will saw then made him forget any thought of words or farewells. The smith had done no removing of old horseshoes, or trimming of a shoe-torn foot; this horse had never been shod before. And the shoe that was now being fitted to its foot, like the line of three other shoes he could now see glinting on the far smithy wall, was not a horseshoe at all but another shape, a shape he knew very well. All four of the white mare's shoes were replicas of the cross-quartered circle that he wore on his own belt. Will walked a little way down the road, beneath its narrow roof of blue sky. He put a hand inside his jacket to touch the circle on his belt, and the iron was icy cold. He was beginning to know what that meant by now. But there was no sign of the Rider; he could not even see any tracks left by the black horse's feet. And he was not thinking of evil encounters. He could feel only that something was drawing him, more and more strongly, towards the place where in his own time Dawsons' Farm would stand.

He found the narrow side-lane and turned down it. The track went on a long way, winding in gentle turns. There seemed to be a lot of scrub in this part of the forest; the branching tops of small trees and bushes jutted snow-laden from the mounding drifts, like white antlers from white rounded heads. And then round the next bend, Will saw before him a low square hut with rough-daubed clay walls and a roof high with a hat of snow like a thick-iced cake. In the doorway, paused irresolute with one hand on the rickety door, stood the shambling old tramp of the day before. The long grey hair was the same, and so were the clothes and the wizened, crafty face.

Will came close to the old man and said, as Farmer Dawson had said the day before: 'So the Walker is abroad.'

'Only the one,' said the old man. 'Only me. And what's it to you?' He sniffed, squinting sideways at Will, and rubbed his nose on one greasy sleeve.

'I want you to tell me some things,' Will said, more boldly than he felt. 'I want to know why you were hanging around yesterday. Why you were watching. Why the rooks came after you. I want to know,' he said in a sudden honest rush, 'what it means that you are the Walker.'

At the mention of the rooks the old man had flinched closer to the hut, his eyes flickering nervously up at the tree-tops; but now he looked at Will in sharper suspicion than before. 'You can't be the one!' he said.

'I can't be what?'

'You can't be . . . you ought to know all this. Specially about those hellish birds. Trying to trick me, eh? Trying to trick a poor old man. You're out with the Rider, ain't you? You're his boy, ain't you, eh?'

'Of course not,' Will said. 'I don't know what you mean.' He looked at the wretched hut; the lane ended here, but there was scarcely even a proper clearing. The trees stood close all round them, shutting out much of the sun. He said, suddenly desolate, 'Where's the farm?'

'There isn't any farm,' said the old tramp impatiently. 'Not yet. You ought to know . . .' He sniffed again violently, and mumbled to himself; then his eyes narrowed and he came close to Will, peering into his face and giving off a strong repellent smell of ancient sweat and unwashed skin. 'But you might be the one, you might. If you're carrying the first sign that the Old One gave you. Have you got it there, then? Show us. Show the old Walker the sign.'

Trying hard not to back away in disgust, Will fumbled with the buttons of his jacket. He knew what the sign must be. But as he pushed the sheepskin aside to show the circle looped on his belt, his hand brushed against the smooth iron and felt it burning, biting with icy cold; at the same moment he saw the old man leap backwards, cringing, staring not at him but behind him, over his shoulder. Will swung round, and saw the cloaked Rider on his midnight horse.

'Well met,' said the Rider softly.

The old man squealed like a frightened rabbit and turned and ran, blundering through the snow-drifts into the trees. Will stood where he was, looking at the Rider, his heart thumping so fiercely that it was hard to breathe.

'It was unwise to leave the road, Will Stanton,' said the man in the cloak, and his eyes blazed like blue stars. The black horse edged forward, forward; Will shrank back against the side of the flimsy hut, staring into the eyes, and then with a great effort he made his slow arm pull aside his jacket so that the iron circle on his belt showed clear. He gripped the belt at its side; the coldness of the sign was so intense that he could feel the force from it, like the radiation of a fierce, burning heat. And the Rider paused, and his eyes flickered.

'So you have one of them already.' He hunched his shoulders strangely, and the horse tossed its head; both seemed to be gaining strength, to be growing taller. 'One will not help you, not alone, not yet,' said the Rider, and he grew and grew, looming against the white world, while his stallion neighed triumphantly, rearing up, its forefeet lashing the air so that Will could only press himself helpless against the wall. Horse and rider towered over him like a dark cloud, blotting out both snow and sun.

And then dimly he heard new sounds, and the rearing black shapes seemed to fall to one side, swept away by a blazing golden light, brilliant with fierce patterns of white-hot circles, suns, stars – Will blinked, and saw suddenly that it was the white mare from the smithy, rearing over him in turn. He grabbed frantically at the waving mane, and just as before he found himself jerked up on to the broad back, bent low over the mare's neck, clutching for his life. The great white horse let out a shrieking cry and leapt for the track through the trees, passing the shapeless black cloud that hung motionless in the clearing like smoke; passing everything in a rising gallop, until they came at last to the road, Huntercombe Lane, the road through Hunter's Combe.

The movement of the great horse changed to a slow-rising, powerful lope, and Will heard the beating of his own heart in his ears as the world flashed by in a white blur. Then all at once greyness came around them, and the sun was blacked out. The wind wrenched into Will's collar and sleeves and boot-tops, ripping at his hair. Great clouds rushed towards them out of the north, closing in, huge grey-black thunderheads; the sky rumbled and growled. One white-misted gap remained, with a faint hint of blue behind it still, but it too was closing, closing. The white horse leapt at it desperately. Over his shoulder Will saw swooping towards them a darker shape even than the giant clouds: the Rider, towering immense, his eyes two dreadful points of blue-white fire. Lightning flashed, thunder split the sky, and the mare leapt at the crashing clouds as the last gap closed.

And they were safe. The sky was blue before and above them; the sun blazing, warming Will's skin. He saw that they had left his Thames Valley behind. Now they were among the curving slopes of the Chiltern Hills, capped with great trees, beech and oak and ash. And running like threads through the snow along the lines of the hills were the hedges that were the marks of ancient fields – very ancient, as Will had always known; more ancient than anything in his world except the hills themselves, and the trees. Then on one white hill, he saw a different mark. The shape was cut through snow and turf into the chalk beneath the soil; it would have been hard to make out if it had not been familiar. But Will knew it. The mark was a circle, quartered by a cross.

Then his hands were jerked away from their tight clutch on the thick mane, and the white mare gave a long shrill whinnying cry that was loud in his ears and then strangely died away into a far distance. And Will was falling, falling; yet he knew no shock of a fall, but knew only that he was lying face down on cold snow. He stumbled to his feet, shaking him- self. The white horse was gone. The sky was clear, and the sunshine warm on the back of his neck. He stood on a snow-mounded hill, with a copse of tall trees capping it far beyond, and two black birds drift- ing tiny to and fro above the trees.

And before him, standing alone and tall on the white slope, leading to nowhere, were two great carved wooden doors.

The Sign-seeker

Will thrust his cold hands into his pockets, and stood staring up at the carved panels of the two closed doors towering before him. They told him nothing. He could find no meaning in the zigzag symbols repeated over and over, in endless variation, on every panel. The wood of the doors was like no wood he had ever seen; it was cracked and pitted and yet polished by age, so that you could scarcely tell it was wood at all except by a rounding here and there, where someone had not quite been able to avoid leaving the trace of a knot-hole. If it had not been for signs like those, Will would have taken the doors to be stone.

His eyes slid beyond their outline as he looked, and he saw that all around them was a quivering of things, a movement like the shaking of the air over a bonfire or over a paved road baked by a summer sun. Yet there was no difference in heat to explain it here.

There were no handles on the doors. Will stretched his arms forward, with the palm of each hand flat against the wood, and he pushed. As the doors swung open beneath his hands, he thought that he caught a phrase of the fleeting bell-like music again; but then it was gone, into the misty gap between memory and imagining. And he was through the doorway, and without a murmur of sound the two huge doors swung shut behind him, and the light and the day and the world changed so that he forgot utterly what they had been.

He stood now in a great hall. There was no sunlight here. Indeed there were no real windows in the lofty stone walls, but only a series of thin slits. Between these, on both sides, hung a series of tapestries so strange and beautiful that they seemed to glow in the half-light. Will was dazzled by the brilliant animals and flowers and birds, woven or embroidered there in rich colours like sunlit stained glass.

Images leapt at him; he saw a silver unicorn, a field of red roses, a glowing golden sun. Above his head the high vaulted beams of the roof arched up into shadow; other shadows masked the far end of the room. He moved dreamily a few paces forward, his feet making no sound on the sheepskin rugs that covered the stone floor, and he peered ahead. All at once sparks leapt and fire flared in the darkness, lighting up an enormous fireplace in the far wall, and he saw doors and high-backed chairs and a heavy carved table. On either side of the fireplace two figures stood waiting for him: an old lady leaning on a stick, and a tall man.

'Welcome, Will,' the old lady said, in a voice that was soft and gentle, yet rang through the vaulted hall like a treble bell. She put out one thin hand towards him, and the firelight glinted on a huge ring that rose round as a marble above her finger. She was very small, fragile as a bird, and though she was upright and alert, Will, looking at her, had an impression of immense age.

He could not see her face. He paused where he stood, and unconsciously his hand crept to his belt. Then the tall figure on the other side of the fireplace moved, bent, and lighted a long taper at the fire, and coming forward to the table, began putting the taper to a ring of tall candles there. Light from the smoking yellow flame played on his face. Will saw a strong, bony head, with deep-set eyes and an arched nose fierce as a hawk's beak; a sweep of wiry white hair springing back from the high forehead; bristling brows and a jutting chin. And though he did not know why, as he stared at the fierce, secret lines of that face, the world he had inhabited since he was born seemed to whirl and break and come down again in a pattern that was not the same as before.

Straightening, the tall man looked at him, across the circle of lighted candles that stood on the table in a frame like the rim of a flat-resting wheel. He smiled slightly, the grim mouth slanting up at its edges, and a sudden fan of lines wrinkling each side of the deep-set eyes. He blew out the burning taper with a quick breath.

'Come in, Will Stanton,' he said, and the deep voice too seemed to leap in Will's memory. 'Come and learn. And bring that candle with you.'

Puzzled, Will glanced around him. Close to his right hand, he found a black wrought-iron stand as tall as himself, rising to three points; two of the points were tipped by a five-pointed iron star and the third by a candlestick holding a thick white candle. He lifted out the candle, which was heavy enough to need both hands, and crossed the hall to the two figures waiting at the other end. Blinking through the light, he saw as he approached them that the circle of candles on the table was not a complete circle after all; one holder in the ring was empty. He leaned across the table, gripping the hard smooth sides of the candle, lighted it from one of the others, and fitted it carefully into the empty socket. It was identical with the rest. They were very strange candles, uneven in width but cold and hard as white marble; they burned with a long bright flame and no smoke, and smelled faintly resinous, like pine trees.

It was only as he leaned back to stand upright that Will noticed the two crossed arms of iron inside the candlestick ring. Here again, as everywhere, was the sign: the cross within the circle, the quartered sphere. There were other sockets for candles within the frame, he saw now: two along each arm of the cross, and one at the central point where they met. But these were still empty.

The old lady relaxed, and sat down in the high-backed chair beside the hearth. 'Very good,' she said comfortably in that same musical voice. 'Thank you, Will.'

She smiled, her face folding into a cobweb of wrinkles, and Will grinned whole-heartedly back. He had no idea why he was suddenly so happy; it seemed too natural to be questioned. He sat down on a stool which was clearly waiting for him in front of the fire, between the two chairs.

'The doors,' he said, 'the great doors I came through. How do they just stand there on their own?'

'The doors?' the lady said.

Something in her voice made Will look back over his shoulder at the far wall from which he had just come: the wall with the two high doors, and the holder from which he had taken the candle. He stared; there was something wrong. The great wooden doors had vanished. The grey wall stretched blank, its massive square stones quite featureless except for one round golden shield, alone, hanging high up and glinting dully in the light from the fire.

The tall man laughed softly. 'Nothing is what it seems, boy. Expect nothing and fear nothing, here or anywhere. There's your first lesson. And here's your first exercise. We have before us Will Stanton – tell us what has been happening to him, this last day or two.'

Will looked into the urgent flames, warm and welcome on his face in the chill room. It took much effort to wrench his mind back to the moment when he and James had left home for Dawsons' Farm to collect hay – hay! – the previous afternoon. He thought, bemused, about everything that stood between that moment and his present self. After a while he said: 'The sign. The circle with the cross. Yesterday Mr Dawson gave me the sign. Then the Walker came after me, or tried to, and afterwards they – whoever they are – they tried to get me.' He swallowed, cold at the memory of his night's fear. 'To get the sign. They want it, that's what everything is about. That's what today is about too, even though it's so much more complicated because now isn't now, it's some other time, I don't know when. With everything like a dream, but real . . . They're still after it. I don't know who they are, except for the Rider and the Walker. I don't know you either, only I know you are against them. You and Mr Dawson and John Wayland Smith.'

He stopped.

'Go on,' said the deep voice.

'Wayland?' Will said, perplexed. 'That's an odd name. That's not part of John's name. What made me say that?'

'Minds hold more than they know,' the tall man said. 'Particularly yours. And what else have you to say?'

'I don't know,' Will said. He looked down and ran a finger along the edge of his stool; it was carved in gentle regular waves, like a peaceful sea. 'Well, yes I do. Two things. One is that there's something funny about the Walker. I don't really think he's one of them, because he was scared stiff of the Rider when he saw him, and ran away.'

'And the other thing?' the big man said.

Somewhere in the shadows of the great room a clock struck, with a deep note like a muffled bell: a single note, a half-hour.

'The Rider,' Will said. 'When the Rider saw the sign, he said: "So you have one of them already." He didn't know I had it. But he had come after me. Chasing me. Why?'

'Yes,' said the old lady. She was looking at him rather sadly. 'He was chasing you. I'm afraid the guess that is in your mind is right, Will. It isn't the sign they want most of all. It's you.'

The big man stood up, and crossed behind Will so that he stood with one hand on the back of the old lady's chair and the other in the pocket of the dark, high-necked jacket he wore. 'Look at me, Will,' he said. Light from the burning ring of candles on the table glinted on his springing white hair, and put his strange, shadowed eyes into even deeper shadows, pools of darkness in the bony face. 'My name is Merriman Lyon,' he said. 'I greet you, Will Stanton. We have been waiting for you for a long time.'

'I know you,' Will said. 'I mean . . . you look . . . I felt . . . don't I know you?'

'In a sense,' Merriman said. 'You and I are, shall we say, similar. We were born with the same gift, and for the same high purpose And you are in this place at this moment, Will, to begin to understand what that purpose is. But first you must be taught about the gift.'

Everything seemed to be running too far, too fast. 'I don't understand,' Will said, looking at the strong, intent face in alarm. 'I haven't any gift, really I haven't. I mean there's nothing special about me.' He looked from one to the other of them, figures alternately lit and shadowed by the dancing flames of candles and fire, and he began to feel a rising fear, a sense of being trapped. He said, 'It's just the things that have been happening to me, that's all.'

'Think back, and remember some of those things,' the old lady said. 'Today is your birthday. Midwinter Day, your eleventh Midwinter's Day. Think back to yesterday, your tenth Midwinter's Eve, before you first saw the sign. Was there nothing special at all, then? Nothing new?'

Will thought. 'The animals were scared of me,' he said reluctantly. 'And the birds perhaps. But it didn't seem to mean anything at the time.'

'And if you had a radio or a television set switched on in the house,' Merriman said, 'it behaved oddly whenever you went near it.'

Will stared at him. 'The radio did keep making

noises. How did you know that? I thought it was sunspots or something.'

Merriman smiled. 'In a way. In a way.' Then he was sombre again. 'Listen now. The gift I speak of, it is a power, that I will show you. It is the power of the Old Ones, who are as old as this land and older even than that. You were born to inherit it, Will, when you came to the end of your tenth year. On the night before your birthday, it was beginning to wake, and now on the day of your birth it is free, flowering, fully grown. But it is still confused and unchannelled because you are not in proper control of it yet. You must be trained to handle it, before it can fall into its true pattern and accomplish the quest for which you are here. Don't look so prickly, boy. Stand up. I'll show you what it can do.'

Will stood up, and the old lady smiled encouragingly at him. He said to her suddenly, 'Who are you?'

'The lady—' Merriman began.

'The lady is very old,' she said in her clear young voice, 'and has in her time had many, many names. Perhaps it would be best for now, Will, if you were to go on thinking of me as – the old lady.'

'Yes, ma'am,' Will said, and at the sound of her voice his happiness came flooding back, the rising alarm dropped away, and he stood up erect and eager, peering into the shadow behind her chair where Merriman had moved a few paces back. He could see the glint of white hair on the tall figure, but no more.

Merriman's deep voice came out of the shadow. 'Stand still. Look at whatever you like, but not hard, concentrate on nothing. Let your mind wander, pretend you are in a boring class at school.'

Will laughed, and stood there relaxed, tilting his head back. He squinted up, idly trying to distinguish between the dark criss-crossing beams in the high roof and the black lines that were their shadows. Merriman said casually, 'I am putting a picture into your mind. Tell me what you see.'

The image formed itself in Will's mind as naturally as if he had decided to paint an imaginary landscape and were making up the look of it before putting it on paper. He said, describing the details as they came to him: 'There's a grassy hillside, over the sea, like a sort of gentle cliff. Lots of blue sky, and the sea a darker blue underneath. A long way down, right down there where the sea meets the land, there's a strip of sand, lovely glowing golden sand. And inland from the grassy headland – you can't really see it from here except out of the corner of your eye – hills, misty hills. They're a sort of soft purple, and their edges dissolve into a blue mist, the way the colours in a painting dissolve into one another if you keep it wet. And' – he came out of his half-trance of seeing and looked hard at Merriman, peering into the shadow with inquisitive interest – 'and it's a sad picture. You miss it, you're homesick for wherever it is. Where is it?'

'Enough,' Merriman said hastily, but he sounded pleased. 'You do well. Now it is your turn. Give me a picture, Will. Just choose some ordinary scene, anything, and think of the way it looks, as if you were standing looking at it.'

Will thought of the first image that came into his head. It was one which he realized now had been worrying away at the back of his thoughts all this while: the picture of the two great doors, isolated on the snowy hillside, with all their intricate carving, and the strange blue at their edges.

Merriman said at once: 'Not the doors. Nothing so close. Somewhere from your life before this winter came.'

For a second Will stared at him disconcerted; then he swallowed hard, closed his eyes and thought of the jeweller's shop his father ran in the little town of Eton.

Merriman said, slowly, 'The door-handle is of the lever kind, like a round bar, to be pushed downward perhaps ten degrees on opening. A small hanging-bell rings as the door moves. You step down a few inches to reach the floor, and the jolt of the drop is startling without being dangerous. There are glass showcases all round the walls, and beneath the glass counter – of course, this must be your father's shop. With some beautiful things inside it. A grandfather clock, very old, in the back corner, with a painted face and a deep, slow tick. A turquoise necklet in the central showcase with a setting of silver serpents: Zuni work, I think, a very long way from home. An emerald pendant like a great green tear. A small enchanting model of a Crusader castle, in gold – perhaps a salt-cellar – that you have loved, I think, since you were a small boy. And that man behind the counter, short and content and gentle, must be your father, Roger Stanton. Interesting to see him clearly at last, free of the mist . . . He has a jeweller's glass in his eye, and he is looking at a ring: an old gold ring with nine tiny stones set in three rows, three diamond chips in the centre and three rubies at either side, and some curious runic lines edging those that I think I must look at more closely one day soon—'

'You even got the ring!' Will said, fascinated. 'That's Mother's ring, Dad was looking at it last time

I was in the shop. She thought one of the stones was loose, but he said it was an optical illusion ... However do you do it?'

'Do what?' There was an ominous softness in the deep voice.

'Well – that. Put a picture in my head. And then see the one I had there myself. Telepathy, isn't it called? It's tremendous.' But an uneasiness was beginning in his mind.

'Very well,' Merriman said patiently. 'I will show you in another way. There is a circle of candle flames beside you there on the table, Will Stanton. Now – do you know of any possible way of putting out one of those flames, other than blowing it out or quenching it with water or snuffer or hand?'

'No.'

'No. There is none. But now, I tell you that you, because you are who you are, can do that simply by wishing it. For the gift that you have, this is a very small task indeed. If in your mind you choose one of those flames and think of it without even looking, think of it and tell it to go out, then that flame will go out. And is that a possible thing for any normal boy to do?'

'No,' Will said unhappily.

'Do it,' Merriman said. 'Now.'

There was a sudden thick silence in the room, like velvet. Will could feel them both watching him. He thought desperately: I'll get out of it, I'll think of a flame, but it won't be one of those; it'll be something much bigger, something that couldn't be put out except by some tremendous impossible magic even Merriman doesn't know ... He looked across the room at the light and shadow dancing side by side across the rich tapestries on the stone walls, and he thought hard, in furious concentration, of the image of the blazing log fire in the huge fireplace behind him. He felt the warmth of it on the back of his neck, and thought of the glowing orange heart of the big pile of logs and the leaping yellow tongues of flame. *Go out, fire,* he said to it in his mind, feeling suddenly safe and free from the dangers of power, because of course no fire as big as that could possibly go out without a real reason. *Stop burning, fire. Go out.*

And the fire went out.

All at once the room was chill – and darker. The ring of candle flames on the table burned on, in a small cold pool of their own light only. Will spun round, staring in consternation at the hearth; there was no hint of smoke, or water, or of any way in which the fire could possibly have died. But dead it was, cold and black, without a spark. He moved towards it slowly. Merriman and the old lady said no word, and did not stir. Will bent and touched the blackened logs in the hearth, and they were cold as stone – yet furred with a layer of new ash that fell away under his fingers into a white dust. He stood up, rubbing his hand slowly up and down his trouser-leg, and looked helplessly at Merriman. The man's deep eyes burned like black candle flames, but there was compassion in them, and as Will glanced nervously across at the old lady, he saw a kind of tenderness in her face too. She said gently: 'It's a little cold, Will.'

For a timeless interval that was no more than the flicker of a nerve, Will felt a screaming flash of panic, a memory of the fear he had felt in the dark nightmare of the snowstorm; then it was gone, and in the peace of its vanishing he felt somehow stronger, taller, more relaxed. He knew that in some way he had accepted the power, whatever it was, that he had been resisting, and he knew what he must do. Taking a deep breath, he squared his shoulders and stood straight and firm there in the great hall. He smiled at the old lady; then looked past her, at nothing, and concentrated on the image of the fire. *Come back, fire*, he said in his mind. *Burn again*. And the light was dancing over the tapestried walls once more, and the warmth of the flames was back on his neck, and the fire burned.

'Thank you,' the old lady said.

'Well done,' said Merriman softly, and Will knew that he was not speaking merely of the extinguishing and relighting of a fire.

'It is a burden,' Merriman said. ' Make no mistake about that. Any great gift of power or talent is a burden, and this more than any, and you will often long to be free of it. But there is nothing to be done. If you were born with the gift, then you must serve it, and nothing in this world or out of it may stand in the way of that service, because that is why you were born and that is the Law. And it is just as well, young Will, that you have only a glimmering of an idea of the gift that is in you, for until the first ordeals of learning are over, you will be in great danger. And the less you know of the meaning of your power, the better able it will be to protect you as it has done for the last ten years.'

He gazed at the fire for a moment, frowning. 'I will tell you only this: that you are one of the Old Ones, the first to have been born for five hundred years, and the last. And like all such, you are bound by nature to devote yourself to the long conflict between the Light and the Dark. Your birth, Will, completed a circle that has been growing for four thousand years in every oldest part of this land: the circle of the Old Ones. Now that you have come into your power, your task is to make that circle indestructible. It is your quest to find and to guard the six great Signs of the Light, made over the centuries by the Old Ones, to be joined in power only when the circle is complete. The first Sign hangs on your belt already, but to find the rest will not be easy. You are the Sign-seeker, Will Stanton. That is your destiny, your first quest. If you can accomplish that, you will have brought to life one of the three great forces that the Old Ones must turn soon towards vanquishing the powers of the Dark, which are reaching out now steadily and stealthily over all this world.'

The rhythms of his voice, which had been rising and falling in an increasingly formal pattern, changed subtly into a kind of chanted battle cry; a call, Will thought suddenly, with a chill tightening his skin, to things beyond the great hall and beyond the time of the calling. 'For the Dark, the Dark is rising. The Walker is abroad, the Rider is riding; they have woken, the Dark is rising. And the last of the Circle is come to claim his own, and the circles must now all be joined. The white horse must go to the Hunter, and the river take the valley; there must be fire on the mountain, fire under the stone, fire over the sea. Fire to burn away the Dark, for the Dark, the Dark is rising!'

He stood there tall as a tree in the shadowed room, his deep voice ringing out in an echo, and Will could not take his eyes from him. *The Dark is rising.* That was exactly what he had felt last night. That was what he was beginning to feel again now, a shadowy awareness of evil pricking at his finger-tips and the top of his spine, but for the life of him he could not utter a word. Merriman said, in a singsong tone that came strangely from his awesome figure, as if he were a child reciting:

When the Dark comes rising, six shall turn it back;
Three from the circle, three from the track;
Wood, bronze, iron; water, fire, stone;
Five will return, and one go alone.

Then he swept forward out of the shadow, past the old lady, still and bright-eyed in her high-backed chair; with one hand he raised one of the thick white candles out of the burning ring, and with the other swung Will towards the towering side wall.

'Look well, for each moment, Will,' he said. 'The Old Ones will show something of themselves, and remind the deepest part of you. For one moment, look at each.' And with Will beside him he strode long-legged round the hall, holding the candle aloft again and again beside each of the hanging tapestries on the walls. Each time, as if he had commanded it, one bright image shone for an instant out of each glowing embroidered square, as bright and deep as a sunlit picture seen through a window-frame. And Will saw.

He saw a may tree white with blossom, growing from the thatched roof of a house. He saw four great grey standing stones on a green headland over the sea. He saw the empty-eyed grinning white skull of a horse, with a single stubby broken horn in the bony forehead and red ribbons wreathing the long jaws. He saw lightning striking a huge beech tree and, out of the flash, a great fire burning on a bare hillside against a black sky.

He saw the face of a boy not much older than himself, staring curiously into his own: a dark face beneath light-streaked dark hair, with strange cat-like eyes, the pupils light-bordered but almost yellow within. He saw a broad river in flood and beside it a wizened old man perched on an enormous horse. As

Merriman whirled him inexorably from one picture to the next, he saw suddenly with a flash of terror the brightest image of all: a masked man with a human face, the head of a stag, the eyes of an owl, the ears of a wolf, and the body of a horse. The figure leapt, tugging at some lost memory deep within his mind.

'Remember them,' Merriman said. 'They will be a strength.'

Will nodded, then stiffened. All at once he heard noises growing outside the hall, and knew with a dreadful shock of certainty why it was that he had felt such uneasiness a short time before. While the old lady sat motionless in her chair, and he and Merriman stood again beside the hearth, the great hall was filled suddenly with a hideous mixture of moaning and mumbling and strident wailing, like the caged voices of an evil zoo. It was a sound more purely nasty than any he had ever heard.

The hair prickled at the back of Will's neck, and then suddenly there was silence. A log fell, rustling, in the fire. Will heard the blood beating in his veins. And into the silence a new sound came from some-where outside, beyond the far wall: the heart-broken, beseeching whine of a forsaken dog, calling in panic for help and friendliness. It sounded exactly as Raq and Ci, their own dogs, had sounded when they were puppies crying for comfort in the dark; Will felt himself dissolve into sympathy, and he turned instinctively towards the sound.

'Oh, where is it? Poor thing—'

As he looked at the blank stone of the far wall, he saw a door take shape in it. It was not a door like the huge vanished pair by which he had entered, but far smaller; an odd, pinched little door looking totally out of place. But he knew he could open it to help the imploring dog. The animal whined again in more acute misery than before; louder, more pleading, in a desperate half-howl. Will swung impulsively forward to run to the door; then was frozen in mid-step by Merriman's voice. It was soft, but cold as winter stone.

'Wait. If you saw the shape of the poor sad dog, you would be greatly surprised. And it would be the last thing you would ever see.'

Incredulous, Will stood and waited. The whining died away, in a last long howl. There was silence for a moment. Then all at once he heard his mother's voice from behind the door.

'Will? Wiii-iill . . . Come and help me, Will!' It was unmistakably her voice, but filled with an unfamiliar emotion: there was in it a note of half-controlled panic that horrified him. It came again.

'Will? I need you . . . where are you, Will? Oh, please, Will, come and help me—' And then an unhappy break at the end, like a sob.

Will could not bear it. He lurched forward and ran towards the door. Merriman's voice came after him like a whiplash. 'Stop!'

'But I must go, can't you hear her!' Will shouted angrily. 'They've got my mother; I've got to help—'

'*Don't open that door!*' There was a hint of desperation in the deep voice that told Will, through instinct, that in the last resort Merriman was powerless to stop him.

'That is not your mother, Will,' the old lady said clearly.

'Please, Will!' his mother's voice begged.

'I'm coming!' Will reached out to the door's heavy latch, but in his haste he stumbled, and knocked against the great head-high candlestick so that his arm was jarred against his side. There was a sudden searing pain in his forearm, and he cried out and dropped to the floor, staring at the inside of his wrist where the sign of the quartered circle was burned agonizingly red into his skin. Once more the iron symbol on his belt had caught him with its ferocious bite of cold; it burned this time with a cold like white heat, in a furious flaring warning against the presence of evil – the presence that Will had felt but forgotten. Merriman and the old lady still had not moved. Will stumbled to his feet and listened, while outside the door his mother's voice wept, then grew angry, and threatened; then softened again and coaxed and cajoled; then finally ceased, dying away in a sob that tore at him even though his mind and senses told him it was not real.

And the door faded with it, melting like mist, until the grey stone wall was solid and unbroken as before. Outside, the dreadful inhuman chorus of moaning and wailing began again.

The old lady rose to her feet then and came across the hall, her long green dress rustling gently at every step. She took Will's hurt forearm in both her hands and put her cool right palm over it. Then she released him. The pain in Will's arm was gone, and where the red burn had been he saw now the shiny, hairless skin that grows in when a burn has been long healed. But the shape of the scar was clear, and he knew he would bear it to the end of his life; it was like a brand.

The nightmare sounds beyond the wall rose and fell in uneven waves.

'I'm sorry,' Will said miserably.

'We are besieged, as you see,' Merriman said,

coming forward to join them. 'They hope to gain a hold over you while you are not yet grown into your full power. And this is only the beginning of the peril, Will. Through all this midwinter season their power will be waxing very strong, with the Old Magic able to keep it at a distance only on Christmas Eve. And even past Christmas it will grow, not losing its high force until the Twelfth Day, the Twelfth Night – which once was Christmas Day, and once before that, long ago, was the high winter festival of our old year.'

'What will happen?' Will said.

'We must think only of the things that we must do,' the old lady said. 'And the first is to free you from the circle of dark power that is drawn now round this room.'

Merriman said, listening intently, 'Be on your guard. Against anything. They have failed with one emotion; they will try to trap you through another next.'

'But it must not be fear,' she said. 'Remember that, Will. You will be frightened, often, but never fear them. The powers of the Dark can do many things, but they cannot destroy. They cannot kill those of the Light. Not unless they gain a final dominion over the whole earth. And it is the task of the Old Ones – your task and ours – to prevent that. So do not let them put you into fear or despair.'

She went on, saying more, but her voice was drowned like a rock submerged in a high-tide wave, as the horrible chorus that whined and keened outside the walls rose louder, louder, faster and angrier, into a cacophony of screeches and unearthly laughter, shrieks of terror and cackles of mirth, howlings and roars. As Will listened, his skin crept and grew damp.

As if in a dream he heard Merriman's deep voice ring out through the dreadful noise, calling him. He could not have moved if the old lady had not taken his hand, drawing him across the room, back towards the table and the hearth, the only cave of light in the dark hall. Merriman spoke close to his ear, swift and urgent, 'Stand by the circle, the circle of light. Stand with your back to the table, and take our hands. It is a joining they cannot break.'

Will stood there, his arms spread wide, as out of sight beside him each of them took one of his hands. The light of the fire in the hearth died, and he became aware that behind him the flames of the candle-circle on the table had grown tall, gigantic, so high that when he tilted back his head he could see them rising far over him in a white pillar of light.

There was no heat from this great tree of flame, and though it glowed with great brilliance it cast no light beyond the table. Will could not see the rest of the hall, not the walls nor the pictures nor any door. He could see nothing but blackness, the vast black emptiness of the awful looming night.

This was the Dark, rising, rising to swallow Will Stanton before he could grow strong enough to do it harm. In the light from the strange candle, Will held fast to the old lady's frail fingers, and Merriman's wood hard fist. The shrieking of the Dark grew to an intolerable peak, a high triumphant whinnying, and Will knew without sight that before him in the darkness the great black stallion was rearing up as it had done outside the hut in the woods, with the Rider there to strike him down if the new-shod hooves did not do their work. And no white mare this time could spring from the sky to his rescue.

He heard Merriman shout, 'The tree of flame, Will! Strike out with the flame! As you spoke to the fire, speak to the flame, and strike!'

In desperate obedience Will filled his whole mind with the picture of the great circle of tall, tall candle-flames behind him, growing like a white tree; and as he did so, he felt the minds of his two supporters doing the same, knew that the three of them together could accomplish more than he ever imagined. He felt a quick pressure in each hand from the hand holding it, and he struck forward in his mind with the column of light, lashing it out as if it were a giant whip. Over his head there came a vast crashing flash of white light, as the tall flames reared forward and down in a bolt of lightning, and a tremendous shriek from the darkness beyond as something – the Rider, the black stallion, both – fell away, out, down, endlessly down.

And in the gap cleft in the darkness there before them, while he still blinked dazzled eyes, stood the two great carved wooden doors through which he had first come into the hall.

In the sudden silence Will heard himself shout triumphantly, and he leapt forward, tugging free of the hands that held his own, to run to the doors. Both Merriman and the old lady cried out in warning, but it was too late. Will had broken the circle, he was standing alone. No sooner did he realize it than he felt giddy, and staggered, clutching his head, a strange ringing sound beginning to thrum in his ears. Forcing his legs to move, he lurched to the doors, leaned against them, and beat feebly on them with his fists. They did not move. The eerie ringing in his head grew. He saw Merriman moving up before him, walking with great effort, leaning far forward as though he were straining against a high wind.

'Foolish,' Merriman gasped. 'Foolish, Will.' He seized the doors and shook them, thrusting forward with the strength of both his arms so that the twisted veins beside his brows stood up from the skin like thick wire; and as he did so, he lifted his head and shouted a long commanding phrase that Will did not understand. But the doors did not move, and Will felt weakness drawing him down, as if he were a snowman melting in the sun.

The thing that brought him back to wakefulness, just as he was beginning to drift into a kind of trance, was something he was never able to describe – or even to remember very well. It was like the ending of pain, like discord changing to harmony; like the lightening of the spirits that you may feel suddenly in the middle of a grey dull day, unaccountable until you realize that the sun has begun to shine. This silent music that entered Will's mind and took hold of his spirit came, he knew instantly, from the old lady. Without speech, she was speaking to him. She was speaking to both of them – and to the Dark. He looked back, dazzled; she seemed taller, bigger, more erect than before, a figure on an altogether larger scale. And there was a golden haze about her figure, a glow that did not come from the candlelight.

Will blinked, but he could not see clearly; it was as if he were separated from her by a veil. He heard Merriman's deep voice, gentler than he had yet heard it, but wrung with some strong sudden unhappiness. 'Madam,' Merriman said wretchedly. 'Take care, take care.'

No voice replied, but Will had a feeling of benison. Then it was gone, and the tall, glowing form that was and yet was not the old lady moved slowly forward in the darkness towards the doors, and for an instant Will heard again the haunting phrase of music that he could never capture in his memory, and the doors slowly opened. Outside there was a grey light and silence, and the air was cold.

Behind him, the light of the candle-ring was gone, and there was only darkness. It was an uneasy, empty darkness, so that he knew the hall was no longer there. And suddenly he realized that the luminous golden figure before him was fading too, vanishing away, like smoke that grows thinner, thinner, until it cannot be seen at all. For an instant there was a flash of rose-coloured brilliance from the huge ring that had been on the old lady's hand, and then that too dimmed, and her bright presence faded into nothing. Will felt a desperate ache of loss, as if his whole world had been swallowed up by the Dark, and he cried out.

A hand touched his shoulder. Merriman was at his side. They were through the doors. Slowly the great wooden carved portals swung back behind them, long enough for Will to see clearly that they were indeed the same strange gates that had opened for him before on the white untrodden slope of a Chiltern hill. Then, at the moment that they closed, the doors too were no longer there. He saw nothing: only the grey light of snow that reflects a grey sky. He was back in the snow-drowned woodland world into which he had walked early that morning.

Anxiously he swung round to Merriman. 'Where is she? What happened?'

'It was too much for her. The strain was too great, even for her. Never before – I have never seen this before.' His voice was thick and bitter; he stared angrily at nothing.

'Have they – taken her?' Will did not know what words to use for the fear.

'No!' Merriman said. The word was so quick with scorn it might have been a laugh. 'The Lady is beyond their power. Beyond any power. You will not ask a question like that when you have learned a little. She has gone away for a time, that is all. It was the opening of the doors, in the face of all that was willing them shut. Though the Dark could not destroy her, it has drained her, left her like a shell. She must recover herself, away alone, and that is bad for us if we should need her. As we shall. As the world always will.' He glanced down at Will without warmth; suddenly he seemed distant, almost threatening, like an enemy; he waved one hand impatiently. 'Close your coat, boy, before you freeze.'

Will fumbled with the buttons of his heavy jacket; Merriman, he saw, was wrapped in a long battered blue cloak, high-collared.

'It was my fault, wasn't it?' he said miserably. 'If I hadn't run forward, when I saw the doors – if I'd kept hold of your hands, and not broken the circle—'

Merriman said curtly: 'Yes.' Then he relented a little. 'But it was their doing, Will, not yours. They seized you, through your impatience and your hope. They love to twist good emotion to accomplish ill.'

Will stood hunched with his hands in his pockets, staring at the ground. Behind his mind a chant went sneering through his head: *you have lost the Lady, you have lost the Lady*. Unhappiness was thick in his throat; he swallowed; he could not speak.

A breeze blew through the trees, and sprayed snow-crystals into his face.

'Will,' Merriman said. 'I was angry. Forgive me. Whether you had broken the Three or not, things would have been the same. The doors are our great gateway into Time, and you will know more about the uses of them before long. But this time you could not have opened them, nor I, nor perhaps any of the circle. For the force that was pushing against them was the full midwinter power of the Dark, which none but the Lady can overcome alone – and even she, only at great cost. Take heart; at the proper time, she will return.'

He pulled at the high collar of his cloak, and it became a hood that he drew over his head. With the white hair hidden he was a dark figure suddenly, tall and inscrutable. 'Come,' he said, and led Will through the deep snow, among great beeches and oaks bare of leaves. At length they paused, in a clearing.

'Do you know where you are?' Merriman said.

Will stared round at the smooth snowbanks, the rearing trees. 'Of course I don't,' he said. 'How could I?'

'Yet before the winter is three-quarters done,' Merriman said, 'You will be creeping into this dell to look at the snowdrops that grow everywhere between the trees. And then in the spring you will be back to stare at the daffodils. Every day for a week, to judge from last year.'

Will gaped at him. 'You mean the Manor?' he said. 'The Manor grounds?'

In his own century, Huntercombe Manor was the great house of the village. The house itself could not be seen from the road, but its grounds lay along the side of Huntercombe Lane opposite the Stantons' house, and stretched a long way in each direction, edged alternately by tall wrought-iron railings and ancient brick walls. A Miss Greythorne owned it, as her family had for centuries, but Will did not know her well; he seldom saw her or her Manor, which he remembered vaguely as a mass of tall brick gables and Tudor chimneys. The flowers that Merriman had spoken of were private landmarks in his year. For as long as he could remember, he had slipped through the Manor railings at the end of winter to stand in this one magical clearing and gaze at the gentle winter-banishing snowdrops, and later the golden daffodil-glow of spring. He did not know who had planted the flowers; he had never seen anyone visiting them. He was not even sure whether anyone else knew they were there. The image of them glowed now in his mind.

But rearing questions very soon chased it out. 'Merriman? Do you mean this clearing is here hundreds of years before I first saw it? And the great hall, is it a Manor before the Manor, out of centuries ago? And the forest all round us, that I came through when I saw the smith and the Rider – it stretches everywhere, does it all belong to—'

Merriman looked down at him and laughed, a gay laugh, suddenly without the heaviness that had been over them both.

'Let me show you something else,' he said, and he drew Will further through the trees, away from the clearing, until there was an end to the sequence of trunks and mounds of snow. And before him Will saw not the morning's narrow track that he had been expecting, winding its way through an endless forest of ancient crowding trees – but the familiar twentieth-century line of Huntercombe Lane, and beyond it, a little way up the road, a glimpse of his own house. The Manor railings were before them, somewhat shortened by the deep snow; Merriman stepped stiff-legged over, Will crept through his usual gap, and they were standing on the snow-banked road.

Merriman put back his hood again, and lifted his white-maned head as if to sniff the air of this newer

century. 'You see, Will,' he said, 'we of the Circle are
planted only loosely within Time. The doors are a
way through it, in any direction we may choose. For
all times co-exist, and the future can sometimes
affect the past, even though the past is a road that
leads to the future . . . But men cannot understand
this. Nor will you for a while yet. We can travel
through the years in other ways too – one of them
was used this morning to bring you back through
five centuries or so. That is where you were – in the
time of the Royal Forests, that stretched over all
the southern part of this land from Southampton
Water up to the valley of the Thames here.'

He pointed across the road to the flat horizon,
and Will remembered how he had seen the Thames
twice that morning: once among its familiar fields,
once buried instead among trees. He stared at the
intensity of remembering on Merriman's face.

'Five hundred years ago,' Merriman said, 'the
kings of England chose deliberately to preserve those
forests, swallowing up whole villages and hamlets
inside them, so that the wild things, the deer and the
boars and even the wolves, might breed there for
the hunt. But forests are not biddable places, and the
kings were without knowing it establishing a haven
too for the powers of the Dark, which might

otherwise have been driven back then to the mountains and remotenesses of the North . . . So that is where you were until now, Will. In the forest of Anderida, as they used to call it. In the long-gone past. You were there in the beginning of the day, walking through the forest in the snow; there on the empty hillside of the Chilterns; still there when you had first walked through the doors – that was a symbol, your first walking, for your birthday as one of the Old Ones. And there, in that past, is where we left the Lady. I wish that I knew where and when we shall see her again. But come she will, when she can.' He shrugged, as if to shake away the heaviness again. 'And now you can go home, for you are in your own world.'

'And you are in it too,' said Will.

Merriman smiled. 'Back again. With mixed feelings.'

'Where will you go?'

'About and roundabout. I have a place in this present time, just as you do. Go home now, Will. The next stage in the quest depends on the Walker, and he will find you. And when his circle is on your belt beside the first, I shall come.'

'But—' Will suddenly wanted to clutch at him, to beg him not to go away. His home no longer seemed quite the unassailable fortress it had always been.

'You will be all right,' Merriman said gently. 'Take things as they come. Remember that the power protects you. Do nothing rash to draw trouble towards you, and all will be well. And we shall meet soon, I promise you.'

'All right,' Will said uncertainly.

An odd gust of wind eddied round them, in the still morning, and gobbets of snow spattered down from the roadside trees. Merriman drew his cloak around him, its bottom edge swirling a pattern in the snow; he gave Will one sharp look, of warning and encouragement mixed, pulled his hood forward over his face, and strode off down the road without a word. He disappeared round the bend beside Rooks' Wood, on the way to Dawsons' Farm.

Will took a deep breath, and ran home. The lane was silent in the deep snow and the grey morning; no birds moved or chirped; nothing stirred anywhere. The house too was utterly quiet. He shed his outdoor clothes, went up the silent stairs. On the landing he stood looking out at the white roofs and fields. No great forest mantled the earth now. The snow was as deep, but it was smooth over the flat fields of the valley, all the way to the curving Thames.

'All right, all right,' said James sleepily from inside his room.

From behind the next door, Robin gave a kind of formless growl and mumbled, 'In a minute. Coming.'

Gwen and Margaret came stumbling together out of the bedroom they shared, wearing night-dresses, rubbing their eyes. 'There's no need to bellow,' Margaret said reproachfully to Will.

'Bellow?' He stared at her.

'*Wake up, everyone!*' she said in a mock shout. 'I mean, it's a holiday, for goodness' sake.'

Will said, 'But I—'

'Never mind,' Gwen said. 'You can forgive him for wanting to wake us up today. After all, he has a good reason.' And she came forward and dropped a quick kiss on the top of his head.

'Happy birthday, Will,' she said.

The Walker on the Old Way

'More snow to come, they say,' said the fat lady with the string bag to the bus conductor.

The bus conductor, who was West Indian, shook his head and gave a great glum sigh. 'Crazy weather,' he said. 'One more winter like this, and I going back to Port of Spain.'

'Cheer up, love,' said the fat lady. 'You won't see no more like this. Sixty-six years I've lived in the Thames Valley, and I never saw it snow like this, not before Christmas. Never.'

'Nineteen forty-seven,' said the man sitting next to her, a thin man with a long pointed nose. 'That was a year for snow. My word it was. Drifts higher than your head, all down Huntercombe Lane and Marsh Lane and right across the Common. You couldn't even cross the Common for two weeks. They had to get snow ploughs. Oh, that was a year for snow.'

'But not before Christmas,' said the fat lady.

'No, it was January.' The man nodded mournfully. 'Not before Christmas, no—'

They might have gone on like this all the way to Maidenhead, and perhaps they did, but Will suddenly noticed that his bus-stop was approaching in the featureless white world outside. He jumped to his feet, clutching at bags and boxes. The conductor punched the bell for him.

'Christmas shopping,' he observed.

'Uh-huh . . . four . . . five . . .' Will squashed the packages against his chest, and hung on to the rail of the lurching bus. 'I've finished it all now,' he said. 'About time.'

'Wish I had,' said the conductor. 'Christmas Eve tomorrow too. Frozen blood, that's my problem – need some warm weather to wake me up.'

The bus stopped, and he steadied Will as he stepped off. 'Merry Christmas, man,' he said. They knew one another from Will's bus rides to and from school.

'Merry Christmas,' Will said. On an impulse he called after him, as the bus moved away. 'You'll have some warm weather on Christmas Day!'

The conductor grinned a broad white grin. 'You gonna fix it?' he called back.

Perhaps I could, Will thought, as he tramped along the main road towards Huntercombe Lane. *Perhaps I could.* The snow was deep even on the pavements; few people had been out to tread it down in the last two days. For Will they had been peaceful days, in spite of the memory of what had gone before. He had spent a cheerful birthday, with a family party so boisterous that he had fallen into bed and asleep with scarcely a thought of the Dark. After that, there had been a day of snowball fights and improvised toboggans with his brothers, in the sloping field behind the house. Grey days, with more snow hanging overhead but inexplicably not falling yet. Silent days; hardly a car came down the lane, except the vans of the milkman and the baker. And the rooks were quiet, only one or two of them drifting slowly to and fro sometimes over their wood.

The animals, Will found, were no longer frightened of him. If anything, they seemed more affectionate than before. Only Raq, the elder of the two collies, who liked to sit with his chin resting on Will's knee, would jerk away from him sometimes for no apparent reason, as if propelled by an electric shock. Then he would prowl the room restlessly for a few moments, before coming back to gaze inquiringly up into Will's face, and make himself comfortable again as before. Will did not know what to make of it. He knew that Merriman would know; but Merriman was out of his reach.

The crossed circle at his belt had remained warm to the touch since he had arrived home two mornings before. He slipped his hand under his coat now as he walked, to check it, and the circle was cold; but he thought that must simply be because he was outdoors, where everything was cold. He had spent most of the afternoon shopping for Christmas presents in Slough, their nearest large town; it was an annual ritual, the day before Christmas Eve being the day when he was certain of having birthday present money from assorted aunts and uncles to spend. This, however, was the first year he had gone alone. He was enjoying it; you could think things out better on your own. The all-important present for Stephen – a book about the Thames – had been bought long before, and posted off to Kingston, Jamaica, where his ship was on what was called the Caribbean Station. Will thought it sounded like a train. He decided he must ask his bus conductor friend what Kingston was like; though since the bus conductor came from Trinidad perhaps he might have stern feelings about other islands.

He felt again the small drooping of the spirits

that had come in the last two days, because this year for the first time that he could remember there had been no birthday present from Stephen. And he pushed the disappointment away for the hundredth time, with the argument that the posts had gone wrong, or the ship had suddenly sailed on some urgent mission among the green islands. Stephen always remembered; Stephen would have remembered this time, if something had not got in the way. Stephen couldn't possibly forget.

Ahead of him, the sun was going down, visible for the first time since his birthday morning. It blazed out fat and gold-orange through a gap in the clouds, and all around the snow-silver world glittered with small gold flashes of light. After the grey slushy streets of the town, everything was beautiful again. Will plodded along, passing garden walls, trees, and then the top of a small unpaved track, scarcely a road, known as Tramps' Alley, that wandered off from the main road and eventually curled round to join Huntercombe Lane close to the Stantons' house. The children used it as a short cut sometimes. Will glanced down it now, and saw that nobody had been along the path since the snow began; down there it lay untrodden, smooth and white and inviting, marked only by the picture-writing of birds' footprints. Unexplored territory. Will found it irresistible.

So he turned down into Tramps' Alley, crunching with relish through the clear, slightly crusted snow, so that fragments of it clung in a fringe to the trousers tucked into his boots. He lost sight of the sun almost at once, cut off by the block of woodland that lay between the little track and the few houses edging the top of Huntercombe Lane. As he stomped through the snow, he clutched his parcels to his chest, counting them again: the knife for Robin, the chamois-leather for Paul, to clean his flute; the diary for Mary, the bathsalts for Gwennie; the super-special felt-tipped pens for Max. All his other presents were already bought and wrapped. Christmas was a complicated festival when you were one of nine children.

The walk down the Alley began quite soon to be less fun than he had expected. Will's ankles ached from the strain of kicking a way through the snow. The parcels were awkward to carry. The red-golden glow from the sun died away into a dull greyness. He was hungry, and he was cold.

Trees loomed high on his right: mostly elms, with an occasional beech. At the other side of the track was a stretch of wasteland, transformed by the snow from a messy array of rank weeds and scrub into a moon-landscape of white sweeping slopes and shaded hollows. All around him on the snow-covered track twigs and small branches lay scattered, brought down from the trees by the weight of snow; just ahead, Will saw a huge branch lying right across his path. He glanced apprehensively upward, wondering how many other dead arms of the great elms were waiting for wind or snow-weight to bring them crashing down. A good time for collecting firewood, he thought, and had a sudden tantalizing image of the leaping fire that had blazed in the fireplace of the great hall: the fire that had changed his world, by vanishing at the word of his command and then obediently blazing into life again.

As he stumbled along in the cold snow, a sudden wild cheerful idea sprang up in his mind out of the thought of that fire, and he paused, grinning to himself. *You gonna fix it?* Well, no, friend, I probably can't get you a warm Christmas Day really, but I could warm things up a bit here, now. He looked confidently at the dead branch lying before him, and with easy command now of the gift he knew was in him, he said to it softly, mischievously, 'Burn!'

And there on the snow, the fallen arm of the tree burst into flame. Every inch of it, from the thick rotted base to the smallest twig, blazed with licking yellow fire. There was a hissing sound, and a tall shaft of brilliance rose from the fire like a pillar. No smoke came from the burning, and the flames were steady; twigs that should have blazed and crackled briefly and then fallen into ash burned continuously, as if fed by other fuel within. Standing there alone, Will felt suddenly small and alarmed; this was no ordinary fire, and not to be controlled by ordinary means. It was not behaving at all in the same way as the fire in the hearth had done. He did not know what to do with it. In panic, he focused his mind on it again and told it to go out, but it burned on, steady as before. He knew that he had done something foolish, improper, dangerous perhaps. Looking up through the pillar of quivering light, he saw high in the grey sky four rooks flapping slowly in a circle.

Oh Merriman, he thought unhappily, where are you?

Then he gasped, as someone grabbed him from behind, blocked his kicking feet in a scuffle of snow, and twisted his arms by the wrists behind his back. The parcels scattered in the snow. Will yelled with the pain in his arms. The grip on his wrists slackened at once, as if his attacker were reluctant to do him any real harm; but he was still firmly held.

'Put out the fire!' said a hoarse voice in his ear, urgently.

'I can't!' Will said. 'Honestly. I've tried, but I can't.'

The man cursed and mumbled strangely, and instantly Will knew who it was. His terror fell away, like a released weight. 'Walker,' he said, 'let me go. You don't have to hold me like that.'

The grip tightened again at once. 'Oh no you don't, boy. I know your tricks. You're the one all right, I know now, you're an Old One, but I don't trust your kind any more than I trust the Dark. You're new awake, you are, and let me tell you something you don't know – while you're new awake, you can't do nothing to anyone unless you can see him with your eyes. So you aren't going to see me, that I know.'

Will said: 'I don't want to do anything to you. There really are some people who can be trusted, you know.'

'Precious few,' the Walker said bitterly.

'I could shut my eyes, if you'd let me go.'

'Pah!' the old man said.

Will said, 'You carry the second Sign. Give it to me.'

There was a silence. He felt the man's hands fall

away from his own arms, but he stood where he was and did not turn round. 'I have the first Sign already, Walker,' he said. 'You know I do. Look, I'm undoing my jacket, and I'll pull it back, and you can see the first circle on my belt.'

He pulled aside his coat, still without moving his head, and was aware of the Walker's hunched form slipping round at his side. The man's breath hissed out through his teeth in a long sigh as he looked, and he turned his head up to Will without caution. In the yellow light from the steadily-burning branch Will saw a face contorted with hauling emotions: hope and fear and relief wound tightly together by anguished uncertainty.

When the man spoke, his voice was broken and simple as that of a small sad child.

'It's so heavy,' he said plaintively. 'And I've been carrying it for so long. I don't even remember why. Always frightened, always having to run away. If only I could get rid of it, if only I could rest. Oh, if only it was gone. But I daren't risk giving it to the wrong one, I daren't. The things that would happen to me if I did, they're too terrible, they can't be put into words. The Old Ones can be cruel, cruel . . . I think you're the right one, boy, I've been looking for you a long time, a long time, to give the Sign to you.

But how can I be really sure? How can I be sure you aren't a trick of the Dark?'

He's been frightened so long, Will thought, that he's forgotten how to stop. How awful, to be so absolutely lonely. He doesn't know how to trust me; it's so long since he trusted anyone, he's forgotten how . . . 'Look,' he said gently. 'You must know I'm not part of the Dark. Think. You saw the Rider try to strike me down.'

But the old man shook his head miserably, and Will remembered how he had fled shrieking from the clearing the moment the Rider had appeared.

'Well, if that doesn't help,' he said, 'doesn't the fire tell you?'

'The fire almost,' the Walker said. He looked at it hopefully; then his face twisted in recalled alarm. 'But the fire, it'll bring them, boy, you know that. The rooks will already be guiding them. And how do I know whether you lit the fire because you're a new-awake Old One playing games, or as a signal to bring them after me?' He moaned to himself in anguish, and clutched his arms round his shoulders. He was a wretched thing, Will thought pityingly. But somehow he had to be made to understand.

Will looked up. There were more rooks circling lazily overhead now, and he could hear them calling harshly to one another. Was the old man right, were the dark birds messengers of the Dark? 'Walker, for goodness' sake,' he said impatiently. 'You must trust me – if you don't trust someone just once, for long enough to give him the Sign, you'll be carrying it for ever. Is that what you want?'

The old tramp wailed and muttered, staring at him from mad little eyes; he seemed caught in his centuries of suspicion like a fly in a web. But the fly still has wings that can break the web; give him the strength to flap them, just once . . . Driven by some unfamiliar part of his mind, without quite knowing what he was doing, Will gripped the iron circle on his belt, and he stood up as straight and tall as he could and pointed at the Walker, and called out, 'The last of the Old Ones has come, Walker, and it is time. The moment for giving the Sign is now, now or never. Think only of that – no other chance will come. Now, Walker. Unless you would carry it for ever, obey the Old Ones now. *Now!*'

It was as if the word released a spring. In an instant, all the fear and suspicion in the twisted old face relaxed into childish obedience. With a smile of almost foolish eagerness the Walker fumbled with a broad leather strap that he wore diagonally across his chest, and he pulled from it a quartered circle identical with the one that Will wore on his belt, but gleaming with the dull brown-gold sheen of bronze. He put it into Will's hands, and gave a high cackling little laugh of astonished glee.

The yellow-flaming branch on the snow before them blazed suddenly brighter, and went out.

The branch lay just as it had when Will first came down the Alley: grey, uncharred, cold, as if no part of it had ever been touched by spark or flame. Clutching the bronze circle, Will stared down at the rough-barked wood, lying there on unmarked snow. Now that its light was gone, the day seemed suddenly much more murky, full of shadows, and he realized with a shock how little of the afternoon was left. It was late. He must go. And then a clear voice said, out of the shadows ahead, 'Hello, Will Stanton.'

The Walker squealed in terror, a thin, ugly sound. Will slipped the bronze circle quickly into his pocket, and stepped stiffly forward. Then he almost sat down on the snow in relief, as he saw that the newcomer was only Maggie Barnes, the dairy-girl from Dawsons' Farm. Nothing sinister about Maggie, Max's apple-cheeked admirer. Her dumpling form was all muffled up in coat and boots and scarf; she was carrying a covered basket, and heading down towards the main road. She beamed at Will, then peered accusingly at the Walker.

'Why,' she said, in her round Buckinghamshire voice, "tis that old tramp that's been hanging around this past fortnight. Farmer said he wanted to see the back of you, old man. He been bothering you, young Will? I bet he has, now.' She glared at the Walker, who shrank sullenly into his dirty cape-like coat.

'Oh, no,' Will said. 'I was just running down from the bus from Slough, and I – bumped into him. Really bumped. Dropped all my Christmas shopping,' he added hastily, and bent to collect his parcels and packages that still lay scattered on the snow.

The Walker sniffed, hunched himself deeper inside his coat, and made to shuffle off past Maggie up the track. But as he drew level with her, he stopped abruptly, jerking back as if he had struck some invisible barrier. He opened his mouth, but no sound came. Will straightened up slowly, watching, his arms full of bundles. A dreadful sense of misgiving began to creep over him, like the chill of a cold breeze.

Maggie Barnes said amiably: 'Long time since the last bus from Slough, young Will. Fact, I'm just off to catch the next one. You always take half an hour to do that five-minute walk from the bus-stop, Will Stanton?'

'I don't see that it's any business of yours how long I take about anything,' Will said. He was watching the frozen Walker, and some very confused images were turning about in his head.

'Manners, manners,' said Maggie. 'Such a nicely brought-up little boy as you, too.' Her eyes were very bright, peering at Will from the scarf-wrapped head.

'Well, good-bye, Maggie,' said Will. 'I've got to get home. Tea's past ready.'

'The trouble with nasty dirty tramps, like this one you just bumped into but who isn't bothering you,' Maggie Barnes said softly, without moving, 'the trouble with them is, they steal things. And this one stole something the other day from the farm, young Will, something belonging to me. An ornament. A big goldeny-brown coloured kind of ornament, circle-shaped, that I wore on a chain round my neck. And I want it back. *Now!*' The last word flicked out viciously, and then she was all soft sweetness again, as if her gentle voice had never changed. 'I want it back, I do. And I do think he might just have slipped it in your pocket when you weren't looking, when you bumped into him. If he saw me coming, that is, as he might well have done in the light of that funny little bonfire I saw burning up here just now. What do you think of all that, young Will Stanton, hey?'

Will swallowed. The hair was prickling upright on the back of his neck as he listened to her. There she stood, looking just the same as ever, the rosy-cheeked, uncomplicated farm girl who ran Dawsons' milking-machine and reared the smallest calves; and yet the mind out of which these words were coming could be nothing but the mind of the Dark. Had they stolen Maggie? Or had Maggie always been one of them? If she had, what else could she do?

He stood facing her, one hand clutching his parcels, one hand sliding cautiously into his pocket. The bronze Sign was cold, cold to his touch. He summoned up all the power of thought that he could find to drive her away, and still she stood there, smiling coldly at him. He conjured her to leave by all the names of power that he could remember Merriman using: by the Lady, by the Circle, by the Signs. But he knew he did not have the right things to say. And Maggie laughed aloud and moved deliberately forward, looking into his face, and Will found that he could not move a muscle.

He was caught, frozen just like the Walker; fixed immobile in a position he could not alter by so much as an inch. He glared furiously at Maggie Barnes, in her smooth red scarf and demure black coat, as she calmly slipped her hand past his into his coat pocket and drew out the bronze Sign. She held it in front of his face, and then rapidly unbuttoned his coat, flicked his belt away from him, and threaded the bronze circle on it to stand next to the iron.

'Hold up your trousers, Will Stanton,' she said mockingly. 'Oh, dear now, you can't, can you . . . But then you don't really wear that belt to keep up your trousers, do you? You wear it to keep this little . . . decoration . . . safe . . .' Will noticed that she held the two Signs as lightly as possible, and winced when she had to touch them with any firmness; the cold that was beating out of them must surely be burning her to the bone.

He watched in utter despair. There was nothing he could do. All his effort and questing was coming to an end before it had even properly begun, and there was nothing he could do. He wanted both to shout with rage and to weep. And then, deep down, something stirred in his mind. Some detail of memory flickered, but he could not catch it. He remembered it only at the moment when fresh-faced Maggie Barnes held up his belt before him with the first and second circle threaded there together, dull iron and gleaming bronze side by side. Staring greedily at the two circles, Maggie broke into a low gurgle of sneering laughter that sounded the more evil for the rosy openness of the face from which it came. And Will remembered.

. . . *when his circle is on your belt beside the first, I shall come . . .*

At that same moment, fire leaped up out of the fallen elm tree branch that Will had briefly lighted before, and flames cracked down from nowhere in a circle of searing white light all around Maggie Barnes, a circle of light higher than her head. She crouched down suddenly on the snow, cringing, her mouth slack with fear. The belt with the two linked Signs dropped out of her limp hand.

And Merriman was there. Tall in the long dark cloak, his face hidden in shadow by the enveloping hood, he was there at the side of the road, just beyond the flaring circle and the cowering girl.

'Take her from this road,' he said in a clear loud voice, and the blazing circle of light moved slowly to one side, forcing the girl Maggie to stumble with it, until it hovered on the rough ground next to the road. Then with an abrupt crackling sound it was gone, and Will saw instead a great barrier of light spring up on either side of the road, edging it on both sides with leaping fire, stretching far into the distance in both directions – a great deal further than the length of the track that Will knew as Tramps' Alley. He stared at it, a little frightened. Out in the dimness he could see Maggie Barnes grovelling wretchedly in the snow, her arms shielding her eyes from the light. But he and Merriman and the Walker stood in a great endless tunnel of cold white flame.

Will bent and picked up his belt, and in a kind of relieved greeting he grasped the two Signs in his hands, iron in his left hand, bronze in his right. Merriman came to his side, raised his right arm so that the cloak swept down from it like the wing of some great bird, and pointed one long finger at the girl. He called out a long strange name, that Will had never heard before and could not keep in his mind, and the girl Maggie wailed aloud.

Merriman said, with scorn death-cold in his voice, 'Go back, and tell them that the Signs are beyond their touching. And if you would remain unharmed, do not try again to work your will while you stand on one of our Ways. For the old roads are wakened, and their power is alive again. And this time, they will have no pity and no remorse.' He called out the strange name again, and the flames edging the road leaped higher, and the girl screamed high and shrill as if she were in great pain. Then she scuffled away across the snowy field like a small hunched animal.

Merriman looked down at Will. 'Remember the two things that saved you,' he said, the light glinting now on his beaked nose and deep-set eyes under the shadowing hood. 'First, I knew her real name. The only way to disarm one of the creatures of the Dark is to call him or her by his real name: names that they keep very secret. Then, as well as the name, there was the road. Do you know the name of this track?'

'Tramps' Alley,' Will said automatically.

'That is not a real name,' Merriman said with distaste.

'Well, no. Mum won't ever use it, and we're not supposed to. It's ugly, she says. But nobody else I know ever calls it anything else. I'd feel silly if I called it Oldway—' Will stopped suddenly, hearing and tasting the name properly for the first time in his life. He said slowly, 'If I called it by its real name, Oldway Lane.'

'You would feel silly,' said Merriman grimly. 'But the name that would make you feel silly has helped to save your life. Oldway Lane. Yes. And it was not named for some distant Mr Oldway. The name simply tells you what the road is, as the names of roads and places in old lands very often do, if only men would pay them more attention. It was lucky for you that you were standing on one of the Old Ways, trodden by the Old Ones for some three thousand years, when you played your little game with fire, Will Stanton. If you had been anywhere else, in your state of untrained power, you would have made yourself so vulnerable that all the things of the Dark that are in this land would have been drawn towards you. As the witch-girl was drawn by the birds. Look hard at this road now, boy, and do not call it by vulgar names again.'

Will swallowed and stared at the flame-edged Way stretching into the distance like some noble road of the sun, and on a sudden wild impulse he made it a clumsy little bow, bending from the waist as well as his armful of packages would let him. The flames leapt again, and curved inward, almost as if they were bowing in return. Then they went out.

'Well done,' said Merriman, with surprise and a touch of amusement.

Will said, 'I will never, never again do anything with the – the power, unless there is a reason. I promise. By the Lady and the old world. But' – he could not resist it – 'Merriman, it was my fire that brought the Walker to me, wasn't it, and the Walker had the Sign.'

'The Walker was waiting for you, stupid boy,' said Merriman irritably. 'I told you that he would find you, and you did not remember. Remember now. In this our magic, every smallest word has a weight and a meaning. Every word that I say to you – or that any other Old One may say. The Walker? He has been waiting for you to be born, and to stand alone with him and command the Sign from him, for time past your imagining. You did that well, I will say – it was a problem to bring him to the point of giving up the Sign when the time came. Poor soul. He betrayed the Old Ones once, long ago, and this was his doom.' His voice softened a little. 'It has been a hard age for him, the carrying of the second Sign. He has one more part in our work, before he may have rest, if he chooses. But that is not yet.'

They both looked at the motionless figure of the Walker, still standing caught in frozen movement at the side of the road as Maggie Barnes had left him.

'That's an awfully uncomfortable position,' Will said.

'He feels nothing,' said Merriman 'Not a muscle will even grow stiff. Some small powers the Old Ones and the people of the Dark have in common, and one of them is this catching a man out of Time, for as long as is necessary. Or in the case of the Dark, for as long as they find it amusing.'

He pointed a finger at the immobile, shapeless form, and spoke some soft rapid words that Will did not hear, and the Walker relaxed into life like a figure in a moving film that has been stopped and then started again. Staring wide-eyed, he looked at Merriman and opened his mouth, and made a curious dry, speechless sound.

'Go,' Merriman said. The old man cringed away, clasping his flapping garments around him, and shambled off at a half-run up the narrow path. Watching him as he went, Will blinked, then peered hard, then rubbed his eyes; for the Walker seemed to be fading, growing strangely thinner, so that you could see the trees through his body. Then all at once he was gone, like a star blotted out by a cloud.

Merriman said, 'My doing, not his own. He deserves peace for a while, I think, in another place than this. That is the power of the Old Ways, Will. You would have used the trick to escape from the witch-girl, very easily, if you had known how. You will learn that, and the proper names and much else very soon now.'

Will said curiously, 'What is your proper name?'

The dark eyes glinted at him from inside the

hood. 'Merriman Lyon. I told you when we met.'

'But I think that if that had really been your proper name, as an Old One, you would not have told me it,' Will said. 'At any rate, not out loud.'

'You are learning already,' Merriman said cheerfully. 'Come, it grows dark.' They set off together down the lane. Will trotted beside the striding, cloaked figure, clutching his bags and boxes. They spoke little, but Merriman's hand was always there to catch him if he stumbled at any hollow or drift. As they came out at the far curve of the track into the greater breadth of Huntercombe Lane, Will saw his brother Max walking briskly towards them.

'Look, there's Max!'

'Yes,' Merriman said.

Max called, gaily waving, and then he was close. 'I was just coming to meet you off this bus,' he said. 'Mum was getting in a bit of a tizz because her baby boy was late.'

'Oh, for goodness' sake,' Will said.

'Why were you coming that way?' Max waved in the direction of Tramps' Alley.

'We were just—' Will began, and as he turned his head to include Merriman in the remark he stopped, so abruptly that he bit his tongue.

Merriman was gone. In the snow where he had

been standing a moment before, no mark of any kind was left. And as Will looked back the way they had walked across Huntercombe Lane, and down the top curve of the smaller track, he could see only one line of footprints – his own. He thought he heard a faint silvery music, somewhere in the air, but even as he raised his head to listen, it too was gone.

Part Two: *The Learning*

Christmas Eve

Christmas Eve. It was the day when the delight
of Christmas really took fire in the Stanton
family. Hints and glimmerings and promises of
special things, which had flashed in and out of life
for weeks before, now suddenly blossomed into a
constant glad expectancy. The house was full of
wonderful baking smells from the kitchen, in a
corner of which Gwen could be found putting the
final touches to the icing of the Christmas cake. Her
mother had made the cake three weeks before; the
Christmas pudding, three months before that.
Ageless, familiar Christmas music permeated the
house whenever anyone turned on the radio.
The television set was never turned on at all; it
had become, for this season, an irrelevance. For
Will, the day brought itself into natural focus very
early. Straight after breakfast – an even more
haphazard affair than usual – there was the double

ritual of the Yule log and the Christmas tree.

Mr Stanton was finishing the last piece of toast. Will and James stood on either side of him at the breakfast table, fidgeting. Their father held a crust forgotten in one hand as he pored over the sports page of the newspaper. Will too was passionately interested in the fortunes of Chelsea Football Club, but not on Christmas Eve morning.

'Would you like some more toast, Dad?' he said loudly.

'Mmm,' said Mr Stanton. 'Aaah.'

James said, 'Have you had enough tea, Dad?'

Mr Stanton looked up, turned his round, mild-eyed head from one to the other of them, and laughed. He put down the paper, drained his teacup, and crammed the piece of toast into his mouth. 'C'mon, then,' he said indistinctly, taking each of them by an ear. They howled happily, and ran for boots and jackets and scarves.

Down the road with the handcart they went, Will, James, Mr Stanton, and tall Max, bigger than his father, bigger than anyone, with his long dark hair jutting in a comical fringe out of a disreputable old cap. What would Maggie Barnes think of that, Will wondered cheerfully, when she peeped roguishly as usual round the kitchen curtain to catch

Max's eye; and then in the same instant he remembered about Maggie Barnes, and he thought in a rush of alarm: *Farmer Dawson is one of the old Ones, he must be warned about her* – and he was distraught that he had not thought of it before.

They stopped in Dawsons' yard, old George Smith coming out to meet them with his gaping grin. The going had been easier along the road that morning, since a plough had been through; but everywhere the snow still lay unmoving in a constant, grey, windless cold.

'Got you a tree to beat all!' Old George called joyfully. 'Straight as a mast, like Farmer's. Both Royal trees again, I reckon.'

'Royal as they come,' said Mr Dawson, pulling his coat tight round him as he came out. He meant it literally, Will knew; every year, a number of Christmas trees were sold from the Crown plantations round Windsor Castle, and several came back in the Dawson farm lorry to the village.

'Morning, Frank,' said Mr Stanton.

'Morning, Roger,' said Farmer Dawson, and beamed at the boys. 'Hey lads. Round the back with that cart.' His eyes slid impersonally over Will, without so much as a flicker of notice, but Will had deliberately left his jacket swinging open in such a way that it was plain there were now two crossed-circle Signs on his belt, not one.

'Good to see you looking so lively,' said Mr Dawson breezily to them all, as they heaved the handcart round behind the barn; and his hand rested briefly on Will's shoulder with a faint pressure that told him Farmer Dawson had a good idea of what had been happening in the last few days. He thought of Maggie Barnes and searched hastily for words to frame a warning.

'Where's your girl friend, Max?' he said, carefully loud and clear.

'Girl friend?' said Max indignantly. Being deeply involved with a blonde-tressed student at his London art school, from whom enormous blue-enveloped letters arrived in the post every day, he was totally uninterested in all local girls.

'Ho, ho, ho,' said Will, trying hard. 'You know.'

Fortunately James was fond of this kind of thing, and joined in with enthusiasm. 'Maggie-maggie-maggie,' he chanted gaily. 'Oh, Maggie the dairymaid's sweet on Maxie the great artist, oooh – oooh . . .' Max punched him in the ribs, and he lapsed into snorting giggles.

'Young Maggie's had to leave us,' Mr Dawson said coolly. 'Illness in the family. Needed at home.

She packed up and went early this morning. Sorry to disappoint you, Max.'

'I'm not disappointed,' said Max, turning scarlet. 'It's just these stupid little—'

'Oooooh – oooooh,' sang James, dancing about out of arm's length. 'Oooh poor Maxie, lost his Maggie—'

Will said nothing. He was satisfied.

The tall fir tree, its branches tied down with bands of hairy white string, was loaded on to the handcart, and with it the gnarled old root of a beech tree that Farmer Dawson had cut down earlier that year, split in half, and put aside to make Yule logs for himself and the Stantons. It had to be the root of a tree, not a branch, Will knew, though nobody had ever explained why. At home, they would put the log on the fire tonight in the big brick fireplace in the living-room, and it would burn slowly all the evening until they went to bed. Somewhere stored away was a piece of last year's Yule log, saved to be used as kindling for its successor.

'Here,' Old George said, appearing suddenly at Will's side as they all pushed the cart out of the gate. 'You should have some of this.' He thrust forward a great bunch of holly, heavy with berries.

'Very good of you, George,' said Mr Stanton.

'But we do have that big holly tree by the front door, you know. If you know anyone who hasn't—'

'No, no, you take it.' The old man wagged his finger. 'Not half so many berries on that bush o' yours. Partic'lar holly, this is.' He laid it carefully in the cart; then quickly broke off a sprig and slipped it into the top buttonhole of Will's coat. 'And a good protection against the Dark,' the old voice said low in Will's ear, 'if pinned over the window, and over the door.' Then the pink-gummed grin split his creased brown face in a squawk of ancient laughter, and the Old One was Old George again, waving them away. 'Happy Christmas!'

'Happy Christmas, George!'

When they carried the tree ceremonially through the front door, the twins seized it with cross-boards and screwdrivers, to give it a base. At the other end of the room Mary and Barbara sat in a rustling sea of coloured paper, cutting it into strips, red, yellow, blue, green, and gluing them into interlocked circles for paper-chains.

'You should have done those yesterday,' Will said. 'They'll need time to dry.'

'*You* should have done them yesterday,' Mary said resentfully, tossing back her long hair. 'It's supposed to be the youngest's job.'

'I cut up lots of strips the other day,' Will said.

'We used those up hours ago.'

'I did cut them, all the same.'

'Besides,' Barbara said peaceably, 'he was Christmas shopping yesterday. So you'd better shut up, Mary, or he might decide to take your present back.'

Mary muttered, but subsided, and Will half-heartedly stuck a few paper-chains together. But he kept an eye on the doorway, and when he saw his father and James appear with their arms full of old cardboard boxes, he slipped quietly away after them. Nothing could keep him from the decorating of the Christmas tree.

Out of the boxes came all the familiar decorations that would turn the life of the family into a festival for twelve nights and days: the golden-haired figure for the top of the tree; the strings of jewel-coloured lights. Then there were the fragile glass Christmas-tree balls, lovingly preserved for years. Half-spheres whorled like red and gold-green seashells, slender glass spears, spider-webs of silvery glass threads and beads; on the dark limbs of the tree they hung and gently turned, shimmering.

There were other treasures, then. Little gold stars and circles of plaited straw; light, swinging silver-paper bells. Next, a medley of decorations made by assorted Stanton children, ranging from Will's infant pipe-cleaner reindeer to a beautiful filigree cross that Max had fashioned out of copper wire in his first year at art school. Then there were strings of tinsel to be draped across any space, and then the box was empty.

But not quite empty. Rifling his fingers gingerly through the crumpled handfuls of packing-paper, in an old cardboard container nearly as tall as himself, Will found a small flat box not much larger than his hand. It rattled.

'What's this?' he said curiously, trying to open the lid.

'Good heavens,' said Mrs Stanton from her central armchair. 'Let me see that a moment, love. Is it . . . yes it is! Was it in the big box? I thought we'd lost it years ago. Just look at this, Roger. See what your youngest son's found. It's Frank Dawson's box of letters.'

She pressed a catch on the lid of the box, so that it flicked up, and Will saw inside a number of ornate little carvings done in some light wood that he could not name. Mrs Stanton held one up: a curved letter S, with the beautifully detailed head and scaly body of a snake, twirling on an almost invisible thread.

Then another: an arched M, with peaks like the twin spires of a faery cathedral. The carvings were so delicate that it was quite impossible to see where they joined the threads from which they hung.

Mr Stanton came down from the step-ladder, and poked one gentle finger into the box. 'Well, well,' he said. 'Clever old Will.'

'I've never seen them before,' said Will.

'Well, you have really,' his mother said. 'But so long ago that you wouldn't remember. They disappeared years and years ago. Fancy them being at the bottom of that old box all the time.'

'But what are they?'

'Christmas-tree ornaments, of course,' Mary said, peering over her mother's shoulder.

'Farmer Dawson made them for us,' Mrs Stanton said. 'They're beautifully carved, as you see. And exactly as old as the family – on our first Christmas Day in this house Frank made an R for Roger' – she fished it out – 'and an A for me.'

Mr Stanton pulled out two letters which both hung together from the same thread. 'Robin and Paul. This pair came a bit later than usual. We hadn't been expecting twins . . . Really, Frank was awfully good. I wonder if he has time for anything like this now?'

Mrs Stanton was still turning the small wooden curlicues in her thin, strong fingers. 'M for Max, and M for Mary . . . Frank was very cross with us for having a repeat, I remember . . . Oh, Roger,' she said, her voice suddenly softening. 'Look at this one.'

Will stood beside his father to look. It was a letter T, carved like an exquisite little tree spreading two branches wide. 'T?' he said. 'But none of us begins with T.'

'That was Tom,' his mother said. 'I don't really know why I've never spoken to you younger ones about Tom. It was just so long ago . . . Tom was your little brother who died. He had something wrong with his lungs, a disease some new babies get, and he only lived for three days after he was born. Frank had the initial already carved for him, because it was our first baby and we had two names chosen; Tom if it was a boy, Tess if it was a girl . . .'

Her voice sounded slightly muffled, and Will suddenly regretted finding the letters. He patted her shoulder awkwardly. 'Never mind, Mum,' he said.

'Oh, gracious,' said Mrs Stanton briskly. 'I'm not sad, love. It was a very long while ago. Tom would have been a grown-up man by now, older than Stephen. And after all' – she gave a comical look round the room, cluttered with people and boxes – 'a brood of nine should be enough for any woman.'

'You can say that again,' said Mr Stanton.

'It comes of having farming forebears, Mum,' said Paul. 'They believed in large families. Lots of free labour.'

'Speaking of free labour,' said his father, 'where have James and Max gone?'

'Fetching the other boxes.'

'Good Lord. Such initiative!'

'Christmas spirit,' said Robin from the step-ladder. 'Good Christian men rejoice, and all that. Why doesn't someone turn some music on?'

Barbara, sitting on the floor beside her mother, took the little carved wooden T from her hand and added it to a row she had made on the carpet of every initial in order. 'Tom, Steve, Max, Gwen, Robin and Paul, me, Mary, James,' she said. 'But where's the W for Will?'

'Will's was there with all the rest. In the box.'

'It wasn't a W actually, if you remember,' said Mr Stanton. 'It was a kind of pattern. I dare say Frank had got tired of doing initials by then.' He grinned at Will.

'But it's not here,' Barbara said. She held the box upside down, then shook it. Then she looked at her youngest brother solemnly. 'Will,' she said, 'you don't exist.'

But Will was feeling a growing uneasiness that seemed to come from some very deep faraway part of his mind. 'You said it was a pattern, not a W,' he said casually. 'What sort of pattern, Dad?'

'A mandala, as I recall,' said Mr Stanton.

'A what?'

His father chuckled. 'Pay no attention, I was only showing off. I don't imagine Frank would have called it that. A mandala is a very ancient kind of symbol dating back to sun-worship and that kind of thing – any pattern made of a circle with lines radiating outward or inward. Your little Christmas ornament was just a simple one – a circle with a star inside, or a cross. A cross, I think it was.'

'I can't think why it isn't there with the rest,' said Mrs Stanton.

But Will could. If there was power in knowing the proper names of the people of the Dark, perhaps the Dark could in its turn work magic over others by using some sign that was a symbol of a name, like a carved initial . . . Perhaps someone had taken his own sign in order to try to get power over him that way. And perhaps, indeed, this was why Farmer Dawson had carved him not an initial, but a symbol that nobody of the Dark could use. They had stolen it anyway, to try . . .

A little while later, Will slipped away from the tree-decorating and went upstairs and pinned a sprig of holly over the door and each of the windows of his room. He tucked a piece into the newly-mended catch of the skylight as well. Then he did the same for the windows of James's room, which he would share for Christmas Eve, and came downstairs and fixed a small bunch neatly over the front and back doors of the house. He would have done the same to all the windows, too, if Gwen hadn't crossed the hall and noticed what he was doing.

'Oh, Will,' she said. 'Not *everywhere*. Put it all along the mantelpiece or somewhere, so it's controllable. I mean, otherwise we shall have holly berries underfoot every time anyone draws the curtains.'

A typical female attitude, Will thought in disgust; but he was not inclined to draw attention to his holly by making any great protest. In any case, he reflected as he tried to arrange the holly artistically over the mantel, up here it would be a protection against the only entry into the house that he had forgotten about. Having left his Father Christmas days behind, he had not thought about the chimney.

The house was glowing now with light and

colour and excitement. Christmas Eve was almost accomplished. But last of all there came the carol-singing.

After tea that day, when the Christmas lights had been turned on, and when the last rustling scuttlings of present-wrappings were ending, Mr Stanton stretched back in his battered leather armchair, took out his pipe, and beamed pontifically at them all.

'Well,' he said, 'who's going on the trek this year?'

'Me,' said James.

'Me,' said Will.

'Barbara and I,' said Mary.

'Paul, of course,' said Will. His brother's flute-case was all ready on the kitchen table.

'I don't know whether I shall,' Robin said.

'Yes, you will,' said Paul. 'No good without a baritone.'

'Oh, all right,' said his twin begrudgingly. This brief exchange had been repeated annually now for three years. Being large, mechanically-minded and an excellent footballer, Robin felt it was not quite proper for him to show eagerness for any activity as lady-like as carol-singing. In fact he was genuinely devoted to music, like the rest of them, and had a pleasant dark-brown voice.

'Too busy,' Gwen said. 'Sorry.'

'What she means is,' said Mary from a safe distance, 'that she has to wash her hair in case Johnnie Penn might come round.'

'What do you mean, *might*?' said Max from the armchair next to his father's.

Gwen made a terrible face at him. 'Well,' she demanded, 'and what about you going carolling?'

'Even busier than you,' Max said lazily. 'Sorry.'

'And what *he* means is,' said Mary, now hovering beside the door, 'that he has to sit up in his room and write another enormous long letter to his blonde bird in Southampton.'

Max pulled off one of his slippers to hurl, but she was gone.

'Bird?' said his father. 'Whatever will the word be next?'

'Good grief, Dad!' James looked at him in horror. 'You really do live in the Stone Age. Girls have been birds since the year one. Just about as much brains as birds too, if you ask me.'

'Some real birds have quite a lot of brains,' Will said reflectively. 'Don't you think?' But the episode of the rooks had been so effectively removed from James's mind that he took no notice; the words bounced off.

'Off you all go,' said Mrs Stanton. 'Boots, thick coats, and back by eight-thirty.'

'Eight-thirty?' Robin said. 'If we give Miss Bell three carols, and Miss Greythorne asks us all in for punch?'

'Well, nine-thirty at the very outside,' she said.

It was very dark by the time they left; the sky had not cleared, and no moon nor even a single star glimmered through the black night. The lantern that Robin carried on a pole cast a glittering circle of light on the snow, but each of them had a candle in one coat pocket just the same. When they reached the Manor, old Miss Greythorne would insist on their coming in and standing in her great stone-floored entrance hall with all the lights turned out, each holding up a lighted candle while they sang.

The air was freezing, and their breath clouded out thick and white. Now and then a stray snowflake drifted down from the sky, and Will thought of the fat lady in the bus and her predictions. Barbara and Mary were chattering away as cosily as if they were sitting at home, but behind the chatter the footsteps of all the group rang out cold and hard on the snow-caked road. Will was happy, snug in the thought of Christmas and the pleasure of carol-singing; he walked along in a contented dreamy state, clutching the big collecting box they carried in aid of Huntercombe's small, ancient, famous and rapidly crumbling Saxon church. Then, there ahead of them was Dawsons' Farm with a large bunch of the many-berried holly nailed above the back door, and the carol-singing had begun.

On through the village they sang: 'Nowell' for the rector; 'God Rest Ye Merry Gentlemen' for jolly Mr Hutton, the enormous businessman in the new mock-Tudor house at the end of the village, who always looked as though he were resting very merry indeed; 'Once in Royal David's City' for Mrs Pettigrew, the widowed postmistress, who dyed her hair with tea-leaves and kept a small limp dog which looked like a skein of grey wool. They sang 'Adeste Fideles' in Latin and 'Les Anges dans nos Campagnes' in French for tiny Miss Bell, the retired village schoolmistress, who had taught every one of them how to read and write, add and subtract, talk and think, before they went on to other schools else-where. And little Miss Bell said huskily, 'Beautiful, beautiful,' put some coins that they knew she could not afford into the collecting box, gave each of them a hug, and – 'Merry Christmas! Merry Christmas!' – they were off to the next house on the list.

There were four or five more, one of them the home of lugubrious Mrs Horniman, who 'did' for their mother once a week and had been born and bred in the East End of London until a bomb had blown her house to bits thirty years before. She had always given them a silver sixpence each, and so she still did, coolly disregarding changes in the currency. 'Wouldn't be Christmas without sixpences,' Mrs Horniman said. 'I laid a good stock in before we got landed with all them decimals, so I did. So I can go on every Christmas just the way I used to, me ducks, and I reckon my stock'll see me out, until I'm deep in me grave and you're singing to someone else at this here door. Merry Christmas!'

And then it was the Manor, the last stop before home.

Here we come a-wassailing among the leaves so green,
Here we come a-wandering, so fair to be seen . . .

They always began with the old Wassail Song for Miss Greythorne, and this year the bit about the green leaves, Will reflected, was even more inappropriate than usual. The carol bounded its way along, and for the last verse Will and James soared up into the high pealing descant that they did not always use for an ending because it took so much breath.

> Good master and good mistress while you're sitting
>   by the fire,
> Pray think of us poor children who are wandering in
>   the mire . . .

Robin tugged the big metal bell-pull, whose deep clanging always filled Will with an obscure alarm, and as they spiralled up in the last verse the great door opened, and there stood Miss Greythorne's butler, in the tail-coat he wore always on Christmas Eve night. He was not a very grand butler; his name was Bates, a tall, lean, morose man who could often be seen helping the one aged gardener in the vegetable garden near the Manor's back gate, or discussing his arthritis with Mrs Pettigrew at the Post Office.

> Love and joy come to you
> And to you your wassail too . . .

The butler smiled and nodded politely at them and held the door wide, and Will all but swallowed his last high note, for it was not Bates; it was Merriman.

The carol ended, and they all relaxed, shuffling in the snow. 'Enchanting,' Merriman said gravely, surveying them impersonally, and Miss Greythorne's high imperious tones came ringing past him. 'Bring them in! Bring them in! Don't keep them waiting on the doorstep!'

She sat there in the long entrance hall, in the same high-backed chair that they saw every Christmas Eve. She had not been able to walk for years after an accident when she was a young woman – her horse had fallen and rolled on her, the village said – but she flatly refused ever to be seen in a wheelchair. Thin-faced and bright-eyed, her grey hair always swept up on top of her head in a kind of knot, she was a figure of total mystery in Huntercombe.

'How's y'mother?' Miss Greythorne demanded of Paul. 'And y'father?'

'Very well, thank you, Miss Greythorne.'

'Havin' a good Christmas?'

'Splendid, thanks. I hope you are.' Paul, who was sorry for Miss Greythorne, always went to some trouble to be warmly polite; he made sure now that his eyes did not flicker round the high-roofed hall as he spoke. For although the cook-housekeeper and the maid were standing beaming at the back of the hall, and though of course there was the butler who had opened the front door, otherwise in all this great house there was no trace of any visitor, tree, decoration, or any other sign of Christmas festivity, save for one gigantic branch of many-berried holly hanging over the mantel.

'An odd season, this,' Miss Greythorne said, looking at Paul pensively. 'So full of a number of things, as that odious little girl in the poem said.' She turned suddenly to Will. 'And are you having a busy time this year, eh, young man?'

'I certainly am,' said Will frankly, caught off balance.

'A light for your candles,' said Merriman in low respectful tones, coming forward with a box of enormous matches. Hastily they all tugged the candles from their pockets, and he struck a match and moved carefully among them, the light turning his eyebrows into fantastic bristling hedges and the lines from nose to mouth into deep-shadowed ravines. Will looked thoughtfully at his tail-coat, which was cut away at the waist, and which he wore with a kind of jabot at the neck instead of a white tie. He was having some difficulty in thinking of Merriman as a butler.

Someone at the back of the hall turned out the

lights, leaving the long room lit only by the group of flickering flames in their hands. There was the soft tap of a foot; then they began with the sweet, soft lullaby carol, 'Lullay lullay, thou little tiny child . . .' ending it with a last wordless verse played only by Paul. The clear, husky sound of the flute fell through the air like bars of light and filled Will with a strange aching longing, a sense of something waiting far off, that he could not understand. Then for contrast they sang 'God Rest Ye Merry Gentlemen'; then 'The Holly and the Ivy'. And then they were back at 'Good King Wenceslas', always a grand finale for Miss Greythorne, and always making Will sorry for Paul, who had once observed that this carol was so totally unsuited to his kind of music that it must have been written by someone who despised the flute.

But it was fun being the page, trying to make his voice so exactly match James's that the two of them together sounded like one boy.

Sire, he lives a good league hence . . .

. . . and Will thought: we're really doing well this time, I'd swear James wasn't singing at all if . . .

Underneath the mountain . . .

. . . if it weren't for the fact that his mouth's moving . . .

Right against the forest fence . . .

. . . and he glanced through the gloom as he sang, and saw, with a shock as brutal as if someone had thumped him in the stomach, that in fact James's mouth was not moving, nor was any other part of James, nor of Robin or Mary or any of the Stantons. They stood there immobile, all of them, caught out of Time, as the Walker had stood in Oldway Lane when the girl of the Dark enchanted him. And the flames of their candles flickered no longer, but each burned with the same strange, unconsuming pillar of white luminous air that had risen from Will's burning branch that other day. Paul's fingers no longer moved on his flute; he too stood motionless, holding it to his mouth. Yet the music, very much like but even sweeter than the music of a flute, went on, and so did Will, singing in spite of himself, finishing the verse . . .

By Saint Agnes' fou . . . oun . . . tain . . .

. . . And just as he began to wonder, through the strange sweet accompanying music that seemed to come out of the air, quite how the next verse could be done, unless a boy soprano were expected to sound like good King Wenceslas as well as his page, a great beautiful deep voice rolled out through the room with the familiar words, a great deep voice that Will had never heard employed in song before and yet at once recognized.

> . . . Bring me flesh and bring me wine
> Bring me pine-logs hither;
> Thou and I will see him dine
> When we bear them thither . . .

Will's head swam a little, the room seemed to grow and then shrink again; but the music went on, and the pillars of light stood still above the candle-flames, and as the next verse began Merriman reached casually out and took his hand, and they walked forward singing together:

> Page and monarch forth they went,
> Forth they went together,
> Through the rude wind's wild lament
> And the bitter weather.

They walked down the long entrance hall, away from the motionless Stantons, past Miss Greythorne in her chair, and the cook-housekeeper, and the maid, all unmoving, alive and yet suspended out of life. Will felt as though he were walking in the air, not touching the ground at all, down the dark hall; no light ahead of them now, but only a glow from behind. Into the dark . . .

> Sire, the night is darker now,
> And the wind blows stronger;
> Fails my heart I know not how,
> I can go no longer . . .

Will heard his voice shake, for the words were right words for what was in his mind.

> Mark my footsteps, good my page;
> Tread thou in them boldly . . .

Merriman sang; and suddenly more was ahead of Will than the dark.

There before him rose the great doors, the great carved doors that he had first seen on a snow-mounded Chiltern hillside, and Merriman raised his left arm and pointed at them with his five fingers spread wide and straight. Slowly the doors opened, and the elusive silvery music of the Old Ones came swelling up briefly to join the accompaniment of the carol, and then was lost again. And he walked forward with Merriman into the light, into a different time and a different Christmas, singing as if he could pour all the music in the world into these present notes – and singing so confidently that the school choirmaster, who was very strict about raised heads and well-moving jaws, would have fallen mute in astonished pride.

The Book of Gramarye

They were in a bright room again, a room unlike anything Will had ever seen. The ceilings were high, painted with pictures of trees and woods and mountains; the walls were panelled in shiny gold wood, lit here and there by strange glowing white globes. And the room was full of music, their own carol taken up by many voices, in a gathering of people dressed like a brilliant scene from a history book. The women, bare-shouldered, wore long full dresses with elaborately looped and ruffled skirts; the men wore suits not unlike Merriman's, with squared-off tail-coats, long straight trousers, white ruffles or black silk cravats at the neck. Indeed now that Will came to look again at Merriman, he realized that the clothes he wore had never really been those of a butler at all, but belonged totally to this other century, whichever it might be.

A lady in a white dress was sweeping forward to

meet them, people round her moving respectfully back to make way, and as the carol ended she cried: 'Beautiful! Beautiful! Come in, come in!' The voice was exactly the voice of Miss Greythorne greeting them at the Manor door a little while earlier, and when Will looked up at the face he saw that in a sense this was Miss Greythorne too. There were the same eyes and rather bony face, the same friendly but imperious manner – only this Miss Greythorne was much younger and prettier, like a flower that has unfolded from the bud but not yet been battered by the sun and wind and days.

'Come, Will,' she said, and took his hand, smiling down at him, and he went easily to her; it was so clear that she knew him and that those around her, men and women, young and old, all smiling and gay, knew him too. Most of the bright crowd was leaving the room now, couples and chattering groups, in the direction of a delicious cooking smell that clearly signalled supper some-where else in the house. But a group of a score or so remained.

'We were waiting for you,' said Miss Greythorne, and drew him towards the back of the room where a fire blazed warm and friendly in an ornate fireplace. She was looking at Merriman too, including him in the words. 'We are all ready, there are no – hindrances.'

'You are sure?' Merriman's voice came quick and deep like a hammer-stroke, and Will glanced up curiously. But the hawk-nosed face was as secret as ever.

'Quite sure,' said the lady. Suddenly she knelt down beside Will, her skirt billowing round her like a great white rose; she was at his eye-level now, and she held both his hands, gazing at him, and spoke softly and urgently. 'It is the third Sign, Will. The Sign of Wood. We call it sometimes the Sign of Learning. This is the time for remaking the Sign. In every century since the beginning, Will, every hundred years, the Sign of Wood must be renewed, for it is the only one of the six that cannot keep its nature unchanged. Every hundred years we have remade it, in the way that we were first taught. And now this will be the last time, because when your own century comes you will take it out for all time, for the joining, and there need be no more renewing then.'

She stood up, and said clearly, 'We are glad to see you, Will Stanton, Sign-seeker. Very, very glad.' And there was a general rumble of voices, low and high, soft and deep, all approving and agreeing; it was like a wall, Will thought, you could lean against it and feel support. Very strongly he could feel the strength of friendship that came out of this small group of unfamiliar, handsomely dressed people; he wondered whether all of them were Old Ones. Looking up at Merriman beside him, he grinned in delight, and Merriman smiled down at him with a look of more open relaxed pleasure than Will had yet seen on the stern, rather grim face.

'It is almost time,' Miss Greythorne said.

'Some small refreshment for the newcomers first, perhaps,' a man beside them said: a small man, not much taller than Will. He held out a glass. Will took it, glandng up, and found himself staring into a thin, lively face, almost triangular, thickly lined yet not old, with a pair of startlingly bright eyes staring at and somehow into him. It was a disturbing face, with much behind it. But the man had swung away from him, presenting Will only with a neat, green-velvet-covered back, and was handing a glass to Merriman

'My lord,' he said deferentially as he did so, and bowed.

Merriman looked at him with a comical twist of the mouth, said nothing, but stared mockingly and waited. Before Will had a chance even to begin puzzling over the greeting, the small man blinked and seemed suddenly to collect his wits, like a dreamer abruptly woken. He burst out laughing.

'Ah, no,' he said spluttering. 'Stop it. I have had the habit for long years, after all.' Merriman chuckled affectionately, raised the glass to him, and drank; and since he could make no sense of this odd exchange Will drank too, and was filled with astonishment by an unrecognizable taste that was less a taste than a blaze of light, a burst of music, something fierce and wonderful sweeping over all his senses at once.

'What is it?'

The small man swung round and laughed, his creased face slanting all its lines upwards. 'Metheglyn used to be the nearest name,' he said, taking the empty glass. He blew into it, said unexpectedly, 'An Old One's eyes can see', and held it out; and staring into the clear base, Will suddenly felt he could see a group of figures in brown robes making whatever it was that he had just drunk. He glanced up to see the man in the green coat watching him closely, with a disturbing expression that was like a mixture of envy and satisfaction. Then the man chuckled and whisked the glass away, and Miss Greythorne was calling for them to come to her; the white globes of light in the room grew dim, and the voices quiet.

Somewhere in the house Will thought he could still hear music, but he was not sure.

Miss Greythorne stood by the fire. For a moment she looked down at Will, then up at Merriman. Then she turned away from them and looked at the wall. She stared and stared for a long time. The panelling and the fireplace and the over-mantel were all one, all carved from the same golden wood: very plain, with no curves or flourishes, but only a simple four-petalled rose set in a square here and there. She put up her hand to one of these small rose carvings on the top left-hand corner of the fireplace, and she pressed its centre. There was a click, and below the rose, at the level of her waist, a square dark hole in the panelling appeared. Will did not see any panel slide away; the hole was simply, suddenly, there. And Miss Greythorne put in her hand and drew out an object shaped like a small circle. It was the image of the two that he had himself, and he found that his hand, as once before, had already moved of its own accord and was clasping them protectively. There was total silence in the room. From outside the doors Will could certainly hear music now, but could not make out the nature of it.

The sign-circle was very thin and dark, and one of its inside cross-arms broke as he watched. Miss

Greythorne held it out to Merriman, and a little more fell away into dust. Will could see now that it was wood, roughened and worn, but with a grain running through.

'That's a hundred years old?' he said.

'Every hundred years, the renewing,' she said. 'Yes.'

Will said impulsively, into the silent room, 'But wood lasts much longer than that. I've seen some in the British Museum. Bits of old boats they dug up by the Thames. Prehistoric. *Thousands* of years old.'

'*Quercus Britannicus*,' Merriman said, severely and abruptly, sounding like a cross professor. 'Oak. The canoes you refer to were made of oak. And further south, the oaken piles on which the present cathedral of Winchester stands were sunk some nine hundred years ago, and are as tough today as they were then. Oh yes, oak lasts a very long time, Will Stanton, and there will come a day when the root of an oak tree will play a very important part in your young life. But oak is not the wood for the Sign. Our wood is one which the Dark does not love. Rowan, Will, that's our tree. Mountain ash. There are qualities in rowan, as in no other wood on the earth, that we need. But also there are strains on the Sign that rowan cannot survive as oak might, or as iron and bronze do. So the Sign must be reborn' – he held it up, between one long finger and a deeply back-curved thumb – 'every hundred years.'

Will nodded. He said nothing. He found himself very conscious of the people in the room. It was as if they were all concentrating very hard on one thing, and you could hear the concentration. And they seemed suddenly multiplied, endless, a vast crowd stretching out beyond the house and beyond this century or any other.

He did not fully understand what happened next. Merriman jerked his hand forward suddenly, broke the wooden Sign easily in half and tossed it in the fire, where a great single log like their own Yule log was half-way burned down. The flames leapt. Then Miss Greythorne reached out towards the small man in the green velvet coat, took from him the silver jug from which he had poured drinks, and threw the contents of the jug on the fire. There was a great hissing and smoking, and the fire was dead. And she leaned forward in her long white dress and put her arm into the smoke and the smouldering ashes, and brought out a part-burned piece of the big log. It was like a large irregular disc.

Holding the lump of wood high so that everyone could see, she began to take blackened pieces from it as though she were peeling an orange; her fingers moved quickly, and the burned edges fell away and the skeleton of the wooden piece was left: a clear, smooth circle, containing a cross.

There was no irregularity to it at all, as though it had never before had any other shape than this. And on Miss Greythorne's white hands there was not even a trace of soot or ash.

'Will Stanton,' she said, turning to him, 'here is your third Sign. I may not give it to you in this century. Your quest must all along be fulfilled within your own time. But the wood is the Sign of Learning, and when you have done with your own particular learning you will find it. And I can leave in your mind the movements that the finding will take.' She looked hard at Will, then reached up and slipped the strange wooden circle into the dark hole in the panelling. With her other hand, she pressed the carved rose in the wall above it, and with the same sight-defeating flash as before the hole was suddenly no longer there. The wood-panelled wall was smooth and unbroken as if there had been no change at all.

Will stared. Remember how it was done, remember . . . She had pressed the first carved rose at the top left-hand corner. But now there were three roses in a group at that corner; which one should it be? As he looked more closely, he saw in fearful astonishment that now the whole wall of panelling was covered in squares of carved wood, each containing a single four-petalled rose. Had they grown at this moment, beneath his eyes? Or had they been there all along, invisible because of a trick of the light? He shook his head in alarm and looked round for Merriman. But it was too late. Nobody was close by him. Solemnity had left the air; the lights were bright again, and everybody was cheerfully talking. Merriman was murmuring something to Miss Greythorne, bending almost double to speak close to her ear. Will felt a touch on his arm, and swung round.

It was the small man in the green coat, beckoning to him. Near the doors at the other end of the room, the group of musicians who had accompanied the carol began playing again: a gentle sound of recorders and violins and what he thought was a harpsichord. It was another carol they were playing now, an old one, much older than the century of the room. Will wanted to listen, but the man in green had hold of his arm and was drawing him insistently towards a side door.

Will stood firm, rebellious, and turned towards Merriman. The tall figure jerked upright instantly, swinging round to look for him; but when he saw what was happening Merriman relaxed, merely raising one hand in assent. Will felt the reassurance put into his mind: *go on, it's all right. I'll follow.*

The small man picked up a lamp, glanced casually about him, then quickly swung the side door open just far enough for Will and himself to slip through. 'Don't trust me, do you?' he said in his sharp, jerky voice. 'Good. Don't trust anyone unless you have to, boy. Then you'll survive to do what you're here for.'

'I seem to know about people now, mostly,' Will said. 'I mean, somehow I can tell which ones I can trust. Usually. But you—' he stopped.

'Well?' said the man.

Will said: 'You don't fit.'

The man shouted with laughter, his eyes disappearing in the creases of his face, then stopped abruptly and held up his lamp. In the circle of wavering light, Will saw what seemed to be a small room, wood-panelled, with no furniture except an armchair, a table, a small step-ladder, and a wall-height glass-fronted bookcase in the centre of each wall. He heard a deep measured ticking and saw, peering through the gloom, that a very large grandfather clock stood in the corner. If the room were dedicated only to reading, as it seemed to be, then it held a timepiece that would give a very loud warning against reading for too long.

The small man thrust the lamp into Will's hand. 'I think there's a light over here – ah.' There began an indefinable hissing sound that Will had noticed once or twice in the room next door; then there was the crack of a match lighting and a loud 'Pop!', and a light appeared on the wall, burning at first with a reddish flame and then expanding into one of the great white glowing globes.

'Mantles,' he said. 'Still very new in private houses, and most fashionable. Miss Greythorne is uncommonly fashionable, for this century.'

Will was not listening. 'Who are you?'

'My name is Hawkin,' said the man cheerfully. 'Nothing more. Just Hawkin.'

'Well look here, Hawkin,' Will said. He was trying to work something out, and it was making him most uneasy. 'You seem to know what's happening. Tell me something. Here I am brought into the past, a century that's already happened, that's part of the history books. But what happens if I do something to alter it? I might, I could. Any little thing. I'd be making something in history different, just as if I'd really been there.'

'But you were,' Hawkin said. He touched a spill to the flame in the lamp Will held.

Will said helplessly, '*What?*'

'You were – are – in this century when it happened. If anyone had written a history recording this party here tonight, you and my lord Merriman would be in it, described. Unlikely, though. An Old One hardly ever lets his name be recorded anywhere. Generally you people manage to affect history in ways that no man ever knows . . .'

He touched the burning spill to a three-candle holder on the table beside one of the armchairs; the leather back of the chair shone in the yellow light. Will said, 'But I couldn't – I don't see—'

'Come,' Hawkin said swiftly. 'Of course you do not. It is a mystery. The Old Ones can travel in Time as they choose; you are not bound by the laws of the Universe as we know them.'

'Aren't you one?' Will said. 'I thought you must be.'

Hawkin shook his head, smiling. 'Nay,' he said. 'An ordinary sinful man.' He looked down and smoothed his hand over the green sleeve of his coat. 'But a most privileged one. For like you, I do not belong to this century, Will Stanton. I was brought here only to do a certain thing, and then my

Lord Merriman will send me back to my own time.'

'Where,' said Merriman's deep voice to the soft click of the closing door, 'they do not have such stuff as velvet, which is why he is taking such particular pleasure in that pretty coat. Rather a foppish coat, by the present standard, I must tell you, Hawkin.'

The little man looked up with a quick grin, and Merriman put a hand affectionately on his shoulder. 'Hawkin is a child of the thirteenth century, Will,' he said. 'Seven hundred years before you were born. He belongs there. By my art, he has been brought forward out of it for this one day, and then he will go back again. As few ordinary men have ever done.'

Will ran one hand distractedly through his hair; he felt as though he were trying to work out a railway timetable. Hawkin chuckled softly. 'I told you, Old One. It is a mystery.'

'Merriman?' Will said. 'Where do you belong?'

Merriman's dark, beaked face gazed at him without expression, like some long-carved image. 'You will understand soon,' he said. 'We have another purpose here than the Sign of Wood, we three. I belong nowhere and everywhere, Will. I am the first of the Old Ones, and I have been in every age. I existed – exist – in Hawkin's century. There, Hawkin is my liege man. I am his lord, and more than his lord, for he has been with me all his life, reared as if he were a son, since I took him when his parents had died.'

'No son ever had better care,' Hawkin said, rather huskily; he looked at his feet, and tugged the jacket straight, and Will realized that for all the lines on his face Hawkin was not much older than his own brother Stephen.

Merriman said, 'He is my friend who serves me, and I have deep affection for him. And hold him in great trust. So great that I have given him a vital part to play in the quest we must all accomplish in this century – the quest for your learning, Will.'

'Oh,' Will said weakly.

Hawkin grinned at him; then jumped forward and swept him a low bow, deliberately snapping the grave mood. 'I must thank you for being born, Old One,' he said, 'and giving me the chance to scurry like a mouse into another time than my own.'

Merriman relaxed, smiling. 'Did you notice, Will, how he loves to light the gas-lamps? In his day, they use smoky, foul-smelling candles that are not candles at all, but reeds dipped in tallow.'

'Gas-lamps?' Will looked up at the white globe attached to the wall. 'Is that what they are?'

'Of course. No electricity yet.'

'Well,' Will said defensively. 'I don't even know what year this is, after all.'

'Anno Domini eighteen seventy-five,' Merriman said. 'Not a bad year. In London, Mr Disraeli is doing his best to buy the Suez Canal. More than half the British merchant ships that will pass through it are sailing ships. Queen Victoria has been on the British throne for thirty-eight years. In America, the President has the splendid name of Ulysses S. Grant and Nebraska is the newest of the thirty-four states of the Union. And in a remote manor house in Buckinghamshire, distinguished or notorious in the public eye only for its possession of the world's most valuable small collection of books on necromancy, a lady named Mary Greythorne is holding a Christmas Eve party, with carols and music, for her friends.'

Will moved to the nearest bookcase. The books were all bound in leather, mostly brown. There were shiny new volumes with spines glittering in gold leaf; there were fat little books so ancient that their leather was worn down to the roughness of thick cloth. He peered at some of the titles: *Demonolatry*, *Liber Poenitalis*, *Discoverie of Witchcraft*, *Malleus Maleficarum* – and so on through French, German, and other languages of which he could not even recognize the alphabet. Merriman waved a dismissive hand at them, and at the shelves all around.

'Worth a small fortune,' he said, 'but not to us. These are the tales of small people, some dreamers and some madmen. Tales of witchcraft and the appalling things that men once did to the poor simple souls they called witches. Most of whom were ordinary, harmless human beings, one or two of whom truly had dealings with the Dark . . . None of them, of course, had a thing to do with the Old Ones, for nearly every tale that men tell of magic and witches and such is born out of foolishness and ignorance and sickness of mind – or is a way of explaining things they do not understand. The one thing of which they know nothing, most of them, is what we are about. And that is contained, Will, in just one book in this room. The rest are useful now and then as a reminder of what the Dark can accomplish and the black methods it may sometimes use. But there is one book that is the reason why you have come back to this century. It is the book from which you will learn your place as an Old One, and there are no words to describe how precious it is. The book of hidden things, of the real magic. Long ago, when magic was the only written knowledge, our business was called simply Knowing. But there is far too much to know in your day, on all subjects under the sun. So we use a half-forgotten word, as we Old Ones ourselves are half-forgotten. We call it "gramarye".'

He moved across the room towards the clock, beckoning them after him. Will glanced at Hawkin, and saw his thin, confident face tight with apprehension. They followed. Merriman stood in front of the great old clock in the corner, which was a full two feet above even his head, took a key from his pocket, and opened the front panel. Will could see the pendulum in there swaying slowly, hypnotically to . . . and fro, to . . . and fro.

'Hawkin,' Merriman said. The word was very gentle, even loving, but it was a command. The man in green, without a word, knelt down at his left side and stayed there, very still. He said in a beseeching half-whisper: 'My lord—' But Merriman paid no attention. He laid his left hand on Hawkin's shoulder, and stretched his right hand into the clock. Very carefully, he slipped his long fingers back along one side, keeping them as flat as possible to avoid touching the pendulum, and then with a quick flip he pulled out a small black-covered book. Hawkin collapsed into a sitting heap, with a throaty gasp of such terrified relief that Will stared at him in astonishment. But Merriman was drawing him away. He made Will sit down in the room's one chair, and he put the book into his hands. There was no title on the cover.

'This is the oldest book in the world,' he said simply. 'And when you have read it, it will be destroyed. This is the Book of Gramarye, written in the Old Speech. It cannot be understood by any except the Old Ones, and even if a man or creature might understand any spell of power that it contains, he could not use their words of power unless he were an Old One himself. So there has been no great danger in the fact of its existence, these many years. Yet it is not good to keep a thing of this kind past the date of its destiny, for it has always been in danger from the Dark, and the endless ingenuity of the Dark would still find a way of using it if they had it in their hands. In this room now, therefore, the book will accomplish its final purpose, which is to bestow on you, the last of the Old Ones, the gift of gramarye – and after that it will be destroyed. When you have the knowledge, Will Stanton, there will no longer be any need of storing it, for with you the circle is complete.'

Will sat very still, watching the shadows move on the strong, stern face above him; then he gave his head a shake, as if to wake it, and opened the book. He said, 'But it's in English! You said—'

Merriman laughed. 'That is not English, Will. And when we speak to one another, you and I, we do not use English. We use the Old Speech. We were born with it in our tongues. You think you are speaking English now, because your common sense tells you it is the only language you understand, but if your family were to hear you they would hear only gibberish. The same with that book.'

Hawkin was back on his feet, though there was no colour in his face. Breathing unevenly, he leaned against the wall, and Will looked at him in concern.

But Merriman, ignoring him, went on, 'The moment you came into your power on your birthday, you could speak as an Old One. And did, not knowing that you were doing so. That was how the Rider knew you, when you met him on the road – you greeted John Smith in the Old Speech, and he therefore had to answer you in the same, and risk being marked as an Old One himself even though the craft of a smith is outside allegiance. But ordinary men can speak it too – like Hawkin here, and others in this house who are not of the Circle. And the Lords of the Dark can speak it too, though never without a certain betraying accent of their own.'

'I remember,' Will said slowly. 'The Rider did seem to have an accent, an accent I didn't know. Only of course I thought he was speaking English, and that he must just be someone from another part of the country. No wonder he came after me so soon.'

'As simple as that,' Merriman said. He looked at Hawkin for the first time, and laid a hand on his shoulder, but the small man did not stir. 'Listen now, Will. We shall leave you here until you have read the book. It will not be an experience quite like reading an ordinary book. When you have finished, I shall come back. Wherever I may be, I know always when the book is open or when it is closed. Read it now. You are of the Old Ones, and therefore you have only to read it once and it is in you for all Time. After that, we will make an end.'

Will said: 'Is Hawkin all right? He looks ill.'

Merriman looked down at the small drooping figure in green, and pain crossed his face. 'Too much to ask,' he said incomprehensibly, drawing Hawkin upright. 'But the book, Will. Read it. It has been waiting for you for a long time.'

He went out, supporting Hawkin, back to the music and voices of the next room, and Will was left with the Book of Gramarye.

Betrayal

Will was never able afterwards to tell how long he spent with the Book of Gramarye. So much went into him from its pages and changed him that the reading might have taken a year; yet so totally did it absorb his mind that when he came to an end he felt that he had only that moment begun. It was indeed not a book like other books. There were simple enough titles to each page: *Of Flying*, *Of Challenge*, *Of the Words of Power*, *Of Resistance*, *Of Time through the Doors*. But instead of presenting him with a story or instruction, the book would give simply a snatch of verse or a bright image, which somehow had him instantly in the midst of whatever experience was involved.

He might read no more than one line − *I have journeyed as an eagle* − and he was soaring suddenly aloft as if winged, learning through feeling, feeling the way of resting on the wind and tilting round the rising columns of air, of sweeping and soaring, of looking down at patchwork-green hills capped with dark trees, and a winding, glinting river between. And he knew as he flew that the eagle was one of the only five birds who could see the Dark, and instantly he knew the other four, and in turn he was each of them . . .

He read: . . . *you come to the place where is the oldest creature that is in this world, and he that has fared furthest afield, the Eagle of Gwernabwy* . . . and Will was up on a bare crag of rock above the world, resting without fear on a grey-black glittering shelf of granite, and his right side leaned against a soft, gold-feathered leg and a folded wing, and his hand rested beside a cruel steel-hard hooked claw, while in his ear a harsh voice whispered the words that would control wind and storm, sky and air, cloud and rain, and snow and hail – and everything in the sky save the sun and the moon, the planets and the stars.

Then he was flying again, at large in the blue-black sky, with the stars blazing timeless around his head, and the patterns of the stars made themselves known to him, both like and unlike the shapes and powers attributed to them by men long ago. The Herdsman passed, nodding, the bright star Arcturus at his knee; the Bull roared by, bearing the great sun

Aldebaran and the small group of the Pleiades singing in small melodic voices, like no voices he had ever heard. Up he flew, and outward, through black space, and saw the dead stars, the blazing stars, the thin scattering of life that peopled the infinite emptiness beyond. And when he was done, he knew every star in the heavens, both by name and as charted astronomical points and again as something much more than either; and he knew every spell of the sun and moon; he knew the mystery of Uranus and the despair of Mercury, and he had ridden on a comet's tail.

So, down out of the heavens the Book brought him, with one line.

. . . the wrinkled sea beneath him crawls . . .

And down he came plummeting, down towards the creeping wrinkled blue surface that changed, as he grew closer and closer, into a rearing sequence of great buffeting waves. Then he was in the sea, down out of the turmoil, through the green haze, into an astonishing, clear world of beauty and pitilessness and bleak cold survival. Each creature preyed on another, nothing was safe from all. And the Book taught Will here the patterns of survival against malevolence, and the spells of sea and river and stream, lake and beck and fjord, and showed him how water was the ore element that could in some measure defy all magic; for moving water would tolerate no magic whether for evil or good, but would wash it away as if it had never been made.

Through deadly sharp corals the Book sent him swimming, among strange waving fronds of green and red and purple, among rainbow-brilliant fish that swam up to him, stared, flicked a fin or tail and were gone. Past the black unkind spines of sea-urchins, past soft waving creatures that seemed neither plant nor fish; and then up on white sand, splashing through gold-flecked shallows – into trees. Dense bare trees like roots ran down into the sea-water all around him in a kind of leafless jungle, and in a flash Will was out of the tangle and blinking again at a page of the Book of Gramarye.

. . . I am fire-fretted and I flirt with wind . . .

He was among trees then, spring trees tender with the new matchless green of young leaves, and a clear sun dappling them; summer trees full of leaf, whispering, massive; dark winter firs that fear no master and let no light brighten their woods. He

learned the nature of all trees, the particular magics
that are in oak and beech and ash. Then, one verse
stood alone on a page of the Book:

> He that sees blowing the wild wood tree,
> And peewits circling their watery glass,
> Dreams about Strangers that yet may be
> Dark to our eyes, Alas!

And into Will's mind, whirling him up on a
wind blowing through and around the whole of
Time, came the story of the Old Ones. He saw them
from the beginning when magic was at large in the
world; magic that was the power of rocks and fire
and water and living things, so that the first men
lived in it and with it, as a fish lives in the water. He
saw the Old Ones, through the ages of men who
worked with stone, and with bronze, and with iron,
with one of the six great Signs born in each age. He
saw one race after another come attacking his island
country, bringing each time the malevolence of the
Dark with them, wave after wave of ships rushing
inexorably at the shores. Each wave of men in turn
grew peaceful as it grew to know and love the land,
so that the Light flourished again. But always the
Dark was there, swelling and waning, gaining a

new Lord of the Dark whenever a man deliberately chose to be changed into something more dread and powerful than his fellows. Such creatures were not born to their doom, like the Old Ones, but chose it. The Black Rider he saw in all times from the beginning.

He saw a time when the first great testing of the Light came, and the Old Ones spent themselves for three centuries on bringing their land out of the Dark, with the help in the end of their greatest leader, lost in the saving unless one day he might wake and return again.

A hillside rose up out of that time, grassy and sunlit before Will's eyes, with the sign of the circle and cross cut into its green turf, gleaming there huge and white in the Chiltern chalk. Round one arm of the white cross, scraping at it with curious tools like long-bladed axes, he saw a group of figures dressed in green: small men, made smaller still by the width of the great Sign. He saw one of these figures whirl dreamlike out of the group towards him: a man in a green tunic with a short dark-blue cloak, and a hood pulled over his head. The man flung wide his arms, with a short bronze-bladed sword in one hand and a glinting chalice-like cup in the other; spun round, and at once disappeared. Then, caught up by the next page, Will was walking along a path through a thick forest, with some fragrant dark-green herb under his feet; a path that broadened and hardened into stone, a well-worn, undulating stone-like limestone, and led him out of the forest until he was walking along a high, windy ridge under a grey sky, with a dark, mist-filled valley below. And all the while as he walked, though no one walked with him, firmly into his mind in procession came the secret words of power for the Old Ways, and the feelings and signs by which he would know, henceforth, anywhere in the world, where the nearest Old Way ran, either in substance or as the ghost of a road . . .

So it went, until Will found that he was almost at the end of the Book. A verse was written before him.

> I have plundered the fern
> Through all secrets I spie;
> Old Math ap Mathonwy
> Knew no more than I.

Facing the cover, on the very last page, was a drawing of the six circled-cross Signs, all joined into one circle. And that was all.

Will closed the Book, slowly, and sat staring at

nothing. He felt as though he had lived for a hundred years. To know so much, now, to be able to do so many things; it should have excited him, but he felt weighed down, melancholy, at the thought of all that had been and all that was to come.

Merriman came through the door alone, and stood looking down at him. 'Ah yes,' he said softly. 'As I told you, it is a responsibility, a heaviness. But there it is, Will. We are the Old Ones, born into the Circle, and there is no help for it.' He picked up the book, and touched Will's shoulder. 'Come.'

As he crossed the room to the towering grand-father clock, Will followed, and watched him take the key again from his pocket and unlock the front panel. There still was the pendulum, long and slow, swinging like the beat of a heart. But this time, Merriman took no care to avoid touching it. He reached in with the book in his hand, but he moved with an odd jerkiness, like an actor over-playing the part of a clumsy man; and as he pushed the book in, a corner of it brushed the long arm of the pendulum. Will had just the flash of a moment to see the slight break in the swing. Then he was staggering back-wards, his hands flying up to his eyes, and the room was filled with something he could never afterwards describe – a soundless explosion, a blinding flare of dark light, a great roar of energy that could not be seen or heard and yet made him feel for an instant that the whole world had blown up. When he took his hands from his face, blinking, he found that he was pressed against the side of the armchair, ten feet from where he had been before. Merriman was spreadeagled against the wall beside him. And where the grandfather clock had been, the corner of the room was empty. There was no damage, nor any sign of violence or explosion. There was simply nothing.

'That was it, you see,' Merriman said. 'That was one protection of the Book of Gramarye, since our time began. If the thing protecting it should be so much as touched, it and the book and the man touching it would become – nothing. Only the Old Ones were immune from destruction, and as you see' – he rubbed his arm ruefully – 'even we, in the event, can be bruised. The protection has taken many forms, of course – the clock was simply for this century. So now we have destroyed the Book, by the same means that through all these ages we used to preserve it. That is the only proper manner for using magic, as you have now learned.'

Will said shakily, 'Where's Hawkin?'

'He was not needed this time,' Merriman said.

'Is he all right? He looked—'

'Quite all right.' There was a strange tight note in Merriman's voice, like sadness, but none of his new art could tell Will the emotion that put it there.

They went back to the gathering in the next room, where the carol that had begun as they left was only now coming to an end, and where nobody behaved as though they had been away for more than a moment or two, or for any real time at all. But then, Will thought, we are not in real time; at least, we are in past time, and even that we seem to be able to stretch as we wish, to make it go fast, or slow . . .

The crowd had grown, and more people were still drifting back from the supper-room. Will realized now that most of these were ordinary folk, and that only the small group who had remained in the room earlier were Old Ones. Of course, he thought: only they would be able to witness the renewing of the Sign.

There were others, and he was turning to study them when suddenly astonishment and horror caught him up out of all reflection. His eye had caught a face in the very back of the room, a girl, not looking at him but busy in conversation with someone unseen. As he watched, she tossed her head with a bright self-conscious laugh. Then she was bent listening again, and then she was gone, as other guests blocked the group from view. But it had been long enough for Will to see that the laughing girl was Maggie Barnes, Maggie of Dawsons' Farm a century hence. She was not even a fore-shadowing, as this Victorian Miss Greythorne was a kind of early echo of the Miss Greythorne that he knew. This was the Maggie he had last seen in his own time.

He swung round in consternation, but as soon as he met Merriman's eyes he saw that he already knew. There was no surprise in the hawk-nosed face, but only the beginnings of a kind of pain. 'Yes,' he said wearily. 'The witch-girl is here. And I think you should stay beside me, Will Stanton, for this next while, and watch with me, for I do not greatly care to watch alone.'

Wondering, Will stood with him in the corner, unobserved. The girl Maggie was still concealed in the crowd somewhere. They waited; then saw Hawkin, in his dapper green coat, thread his way through the crowd to Miss Greythorne and stand deferentially beside her, in the way of a man accustomed to making himself available for help. Merriman stiffened slightly, and Will glanced up; the lines of pain had deepened on the strong face, as if Merriman were anticipating some great hurt about

to come. He looked across again at Hawkin and saw
his gay smile flash at something Miss Greythorne
had said; showing no sign now of whatever had
afflicted him in the library, the small man had a
brightness, like a precious stone, that would bring
delight to any gloom. Will could see why he was dear
to Merriman. But at the same time he had all at once
a dreadful, rushing conviction of hovering disaster.

He said huskily, 'Merriman! What is it?'

Merriman looked out over the heads at the lively
pointed face. He said, without expression, 'It is peril,
Will, that is to come to us through my doing. Great
peril, through all this quest. I have made the worst
mistake that an Old One may make, and the mistake
is about to come down on my head fullfold. To put
more trust in a mortal man than he has the strength
to take – it is something that all of us learned
never to do, centuries ago. Long before the Book of
Gramarye came into my charge. Yet in foolishness I
made that mistake. And now there is nothing that
we can do to put it right, but only watch and wait for
the result.'

'It's Hawkin, isn't it? Something to do with the
reason why you brought him here?'

'The spell of protection for the Book,' Merriman
said painfully, 'was in two parts, Will. You saw the

first, the protection against men – it was the pendulum, which would destroy them if they were to touch it, but would not destroy me or any Old One. But I wove another part into that spell that was a protection against the Dark. It set down that I could take the Book out past the pendulum *only if I were touching Hawkin with my other hand.* Whenever the Book was taken out for the last Old One, in whatever century, Hawkin would have to be brought out of his own time in order to be there.'

Will said: 'Wouldn't it have been safer to make an Old One part of the spell, not an ordinary man?'

'Ah no, the whole purpose was to have a man involved. This is a cold battle we are in, Will, and in it we must sometimes do cold things. This spell was woven around me, as keeper of the Book. The Dark cannot destroy me, for I am an Old One, but it could perhaps by magic have tricked me into taking out the Book. In case that happened, there had to be some way in which the other Old Ones could stop me before it was too late. They too could not destroy me, to stop me from doing the work of the Dark. But a man can be destroyed. If it had come to the worst, and the Dark had forced me by magic to take out the Book for them, then before I could begin, the Light would have killed Hawkin. That would have kept the

Book safe for ever, for in that case, I could not have worked the spell of release by touching him while taking out the Book. And so I should not have been able to reach the Book. Nor would the Dark, nor anyone else.'

'So he risked his life,' Will said slowly, watching Hawkin's sprightly walk as he crossed the floor to the musicians.

'Yes,' Merriman said. 'In our service he was safe from the Dark, but his life was in hazard all the same. He agreed because he was my liege man, and proud of it. I wish that I had made sure that he really knew the risk he ran. A double risk, for he might also have been destroyed today, by me, if I had accidentally touched the pendulum. You saw what happened when at the last I did that. You and I, as Old Ones, were merely shaken; but if Hawkin had been there, under my touch, he would have been killed in a flash, un-bodied like the Book itself.'

'He must not only be very brave, he must really love you as if he were your son,' said Will, 'to do things like this for you and the Light.'

'But still he is only a man,' said Merriman, and his voice was rough and the pain back deep in his face. 'And he loves as a man, requiring proof of love in return. My mistake was in ignoring the risk that this might be so. And as a result, in this room in the next few minutes, Hawkin will betray me and betray the Light and mould the whole course of your quest, young Will. The shock just now of actually risking his life, for me and the Book of Gramarye, was too much for his loyalty. Perhaps you saw his face, in the moment when I held his shoulder and took the Book from its perilous place. It was only in that moment that Hawkin fully understood that I was prepared to let him die. And now that he has understood it, he will never forgive me for not loving him as much – in his terms – as he has loved me, his lord. And he will turn on us.' Merriman pointed across the room. 'See where it begins.'

Music struck up brightly, and the guests began forming into couples to dance. One man whom Will had recognized as an Old One moved to Miss Greythorne, bowed, and offered his arm; all around them, couples joined into figures-of-eight for some dance he did not know. He saw Hawkin standing irresolute, moving his head a little to the beat of the music; and then he saw a girl in a red dress appear at his side. It was the witch-girl, Maggie Barnes.

She said something to Hawkin, laughing, and dropped him a small curtsey. Hawkin smiled politely, doubtfully, and shook his head. The girl's smile deepened, she shook her hair coquettishly and spoke to him again, her eyes fast on his.

'Oh,' Will said. 'If only we could hear!'

Merriman regarded him sombrely for a moment, his face absent and brooding.

'Oh,' Will said, feeling foolish. 'Of course.' It would take him some time, clearly, to grow accustomed to using his own gifts. He looked again at Hawkin and the girl, and wished to hear them, and could hear.

'Truly, Madam,' Hawkin said, 'I have no wish to seem churlish, but I do not dance.'

Maggie took his hand. 'Because you are out of your century? They dance here with their legs, just as you do beyond five hundred years. Come.'

Hawkin stared at her aghast as she led him into a set of couples. 'Who are you?' he whispered. 'Are you an Old One?'

'Not for all the world,' said Maggie Barnes in the Old Speech, and Hawkin turned quite white and stood still. She laughed softly and said in English, 'No more of that. Dance, or people will notice. It's easy enough. Watch the next man, as the music begins.'

Hawkin, pale and distressed, stumbled his way through the first part of the dance; gradually he picked up the steps. Merriman said in Will's ear, 'He was told that not one soul here would know of him, and that on pain of death he must not use the Old Speech to any but you.'

Then the speaking below began again.

'You look well, Hawkin, for a man escaped from death.'

'How do you know these things, girl? Who are you?'

'They would have let you die, Hawkin. How could you be so stupid?'

'My master loves me,' said Hawkin, but there was weakness in it.

'He used you, Hawkin. You are nothing to him. You should follow better masters, who would care for your life. And lengthen it through the centuries, not confine it to your own.'

'Like the life of an Old One?' Hawkin said, eagerness waking in his voice for the first time. Will remembered the tinge of envy when Hawkin had spoken to him of the Old Ones; now there was a hint of greed as well.

'The Dark and the Rider are kinder masters than the Light,' Maggie Barnes said softly in his ear, as the first part of the dance ended. Hawkin stood still again and stared at her, until she glanced round and said clearly: 'I need a cool drink, I believe.' And Hawkin jumped and led her away, so that now, with his attention caught and a chance to talk to him privately, the girl of the Dark would have a willing hearer. Will felt suddenly sickened by the approaching treachery, and listened no more. He found Merriman, beside him, still gazing black into space.

'So it will go,' Merriman said. 'He will have a sweet picture of the Dark to attract him, as men so often do, and beside it he will set all the demands of the Light, which are heavy and always will be. All the while he will be nursing his resentment of the way I might have had him give up his life without reward. You can be sure the Dark makes no sign of demanding any such thing – yet indeed, its lords never risk demanding death, but only offer a black life . . . Hawkin,' he said softly, bleakly, 'liege man, how can you do what you are going to do?'

Will felt fear suddenly, and Merriman sensed it. 'No more of this,' he said. 'It is clear already how it goes. Hawkin now will be a leak in the roof, a tunnel into the cellar. And just as the Dark could not touch him when he was my liege man, now that he is liege to the Dark, he cannot be destroyed by the Light. He will be the Dark's ear in our midst, in this house that has been our stronghold.' His voice was cold, accepting the inevitable; the pain was gone. 'Though the witch-girl managed to make her way in, she could have accomplished no scrap of magic without being destroyed by the Light. But now whenever Hawkin calls them, the Dark can attack us here as elsewhere. And the danger will grow with the years.'

He stood up, fingering his white ruffled cravat; there was a terrible sternness in his fierce-curved profile, and the look that for a moment flared out from the lowering brows made Will's blood run thick and slow. It was a judge's face, implacable, condemning.

'And the doom that Hawkin has brought upon himself, by this act,' Merriman said, without expression, 'is a dread matter, which will make him many times wish that he might die.'

Will stood dazed, caught in pity and alarm. He did not ask what would happen to small, bright-eyed Hawkin, who had laughed at him and helped him and been for so short a while his friend; he did not want to know. Out on the floor, the music of the second part of the dance jingled to a close, and the dancers made one another laughing courtesies. Will stood motionless and unhappy. Merriman's frozen look softened, and he reached out and turned him gently to face the centre of the room.

Will saw there only a gap in the crowd, with beyond it the group of musicians. As he stood there, they struck up once more 'Good King Wenceslas', the carol they had been playing when first he entered the room, through the Doors. Merrily the whole gathering joined in singing, and then the next verse came and Merriman's deep voice was ringing out across the room, and Will realized, blinking, that the verse to come was his.

He drew breath, and raised his head.

> Sire he lives a good league hence,
> Underneath the mountain . . .

And there was no moment of farewell, no moment in which he saw the nineteenth century vanish away, but suddenly with no awareness of change, as he sang he knew that Time had somehow blinked, and another young voice was singing with him, the two of them so nearly simultaneous that anyone who could not see the lips moving would have sworn that it was one boy's voice alone . . .

> Right against the forest fence,
> By St Agnes' fou-ou-ntain . . .

. . . and he knew that he was standing with James and Mary and the rest, and he and James were singing together, and that the music with their voices was Paul's lone flute. He stood there in the dark entrance-hall, with his hands raised before his chest holding the lighted candle, and he saw that the candle had not burned down one millimetre further than when he had last looked at it.

They finished the carol.

Miss Greythorne said, 'Very good, very good indeed. Nothing like Good King Wenceslas, it's always been my favourite.'

Will peered past his candle-flame to look at her motionless form in the big carved chair; her voice was older, harder, more toughened by the years, and so was her face, but otherwise she was just like – her grandmother, must that younger Miss Greythorne have been? Or her great-grandmother?

Miss Greythorne said, 'Huntercombe carol-singers have been singing "Good King Wenceslas" in this house for longer than you or even I can remember, you know. Well now, Paul and Robin and the rest of you, how about a little Christmas punch?' The question was traditional, and so was the answer.

'Well,' said Robin gravely, 'thank you, Miss Greythorne. Perhaps just a little.'

'Even young Will too, this year,' said Paul. 'He's eleven now, Miss Greythorne, did you know?'

The housekeeper was coming forward with a tray of glittering glasses and a great bowl of red-brown punch, and nearly every eye in the room was on Merriman, stepping up to fill the glasses. But Will's gaze was held by the strong, suddenly younger eyes of the figure in the high-backed chair. 'Yes,' said Miss Greythorne softly, almost absent-mindedly, 'I did remember. Will Stanton has had a birthday.' She turned to Merriman, who was already moving towards them, and took from him the two glasses in his hands. 'A happy birthday to you, Will Stanton, seventh son of a seventh son,' said Miss Greythorne. 'And success in your every quest.'

'Thank you, ma'm,' said Will, wondering. And they held up their glasses solemnly to one another, and drank, just as the Stanton children did for the Christmas toast on the one day of the year when they were all allowed wine at dinner.

Merriman was moving round, and now everyone had a glass of punch and was sipping contentedly. The Manor's Christmas punch was always delicious, though no one had ever quite worked out what went into it. As the senior members of the family, the twins strolled dutifully across to chat with Miss

Greythorne; Barbara, with Mary in tow, made a beeline for Miss Hampton the housekeeper and Annie the maid, both reluctant members of a village drama group she was trying to force into life. Merriman said to James, 'You and your little brother sing very well.'

James beamed. Though plumper, he was no taller than Will, and it was not often that a stranger gratified him by recognizing him as a superior older brother. 'We sing in the school choir,' he said. 'And solos at arts festivals. Even one in London last year. The music master's very keen on arts festivals.'

'I'm not,' said Will. 'All those mothers, glaring.'

'Well, you were top of your class in London,' James said, 'so of course they all hated you, beating their little darlings. I was only fifth in mine,' he said in matter-of-fact tones to Merriman. 'Will has a lot better voice than me.'

'Oh come off it,' said Will.

'Yes, you have.' James was a fair-minded boy; he genuinely preferred reality to daydreams. 'Till we both break, at any rate. Neither of us might be any good then.'

Merriman said absent-mindedly, 'In point of fact you will become a most accomplished tenor. Almost professional standard. Your brother's voice will be baritone — pleasant, but nothing special.'

'I suppose that might be possible,' said James, polite but disbelieving. 'Of course, there's no way at all for anyone to tell, yet.'

Will said belligerently, 'But he—' and caught Merriman's dark eye and stopped. 'Mmmm, aaah,' he said, and James looked at him with astonishment.

Miss Greythorne called across the room to Merriman, 'Paul would like to see the old recorders and flutes. Take him in, would you?'

Merriman inclined his head in a small bow. He said casually to Will and James, 'Care to come too?'

'No, thank you,' said James promptly. His eyes were on the far door, through which the housekeeper was advancing with another tray. 'I smell Miss Hampton's mince pies.'

Will said, understanding, 'I'd quite like to see.'

He moved with Merriman towards Miss Greythorne's chair, where Paul and Robin stood stiff and rather awkward, one at each side, like guardsmen. 'Off with you,' said Miss Greythorne briskly. 'Are you going too, Will? Of course, you're another musical one, I was forgetting. Quite a good little collection of instruments and stuff in there. Surprised you haven't seen them before.'

Lulled by the words, Will said thoughtlessly, 'In the library?'

Miss Greythorne's sharp eyes glittered at him. 'The library?' she said. 'You must be mixing us up with someone else, Will. There's no library here. Once there was a small one, with some most valuable books, I believe, but it burned down, almost a century ago. This part of the house was struck by lightning. Did a lot of damage, they say.'

'Oh, dear,' said Will in some confusion.

'Well, this is no talk for Christmas,' Miss Greythorne said, and waved them off. Glancing back at her, as she turned to Robin with a bright social smile, Will found himself wondering whether the two Miss Greythornes were not one after all.

Merriman led him, with Paul, to a side door, and they walked through a strange musty-smelling little passage into a high bright room that Will did not at once recognize. It was only when he caught sight of the fireplace that he realized where he was. There was the wide hearth, and the broad mantel with its square panels and carved Tudor rose-emblems. But round the rest of the room the panelling was gone; the walls were instead painted flat white, and brightened here and there by some large improbable-looking seascapes done in lurid blues and greens. In the place where Will had once gone into the little library, there was no longer any door.

Merriman was unlocking a tall, glass-fronted cabinet that stood against a side wall.

'Miss Greythorne's father was a very musical gentleman,' he said in his butler voice. 'And artistic too. He painted all those pictures on the walls over there. In the West Indies, I believe. These, though' – he lifted out a small beautiful instrument like a recorder, black inlaid with silver – 'he didn't actually play, they say. He just liked to look at them.'

Paul was absorbed at once, peering at, into, through the old flutes and recorders as Merriman handed them out of the cupboard. They were both most solemn in their handling; they would put each one carefully back before taking the next out. Will turned to study the panels round the fireplace; then jumped suddenly as he heard Merriman silently calling to him. At the same time he could hear Merriman's voice aloud speaking to Paul; it was an eerie combination.

'Quickly, now!' said the voice in his mind. 'You know where to look. Quick, while you have the chance. It is time to take the Sign!'

'But—' said Will's mind.

'Go on!' Merriman silently roared.

Will glanced back quickly over his shoulder. The door through which they had come was still half open, but his ears would surely warn him of anyone coming up the passage between this room and the next. He moved soft-footed to the fireplace, reached up, and put his hand on the panelling. Shutting his eyes for an instant, he appealed to all his new gifts, and the old world from which they came. Which square panel had it been? Which carved rose? He was confused by the loss of the panelled wall all around; the mantel seemed smaller than before. Was the sign lost, bricked up somewhere behind that flat white wall? He pressed every rose that he could see, round the top left-hand corner of the fireplace, but none moved even a fraction of an inch. Then at the last moment he noticed, at the very point of the corner, a rose part-buried in plaster, jutting out of the wall that clearly had been repaired as well as altered in the last hundred years – ten minutes, he thought wildly – since he had last seen it.

Hastily Will reached up high and pressed his thumb as hard as he could against the centre of the carved flower, as if it were a bell-push. And as he heard the soft click, he was staring into a black square hole in the wall, exactly on the level of his eyes. He reached in and touched the circle of the

Sign of Wood, and as he sighed in relief, his finger closing round the smooth wood, he heard Paul begin to play one of the old flutes.

It was very tentative playing: a slow arpeggio first, then a hesitant run; and then, very softly and gently, Paul began playing the melody 'Greensleeves'. And Will stood transfixed, not only by the lovely lilt of the old tune but by the sound of the instrument itself. For though the melody was different, this was his music, his enchantment, the same eerie, faraway tone that he heard always, and then always lost, at those moments in his life that mattered most. What was the nature of this flute that his brother was playing? Was it part of the Old Ones, belonging to their magic, or simply something very like, made by men? He drew his hand back from the gap in the wall, which closed instantly before he could press the rose again, and he was sliding the Sign of Wood into his pocket as he turned, lost in listening.

And then he froze.

Paul stood playing, across the room, beside the cabinet. Merriman had his back turned and his hands on the glass doors. But now the room held two other figures as well. In the doorway through which they had come stood Maggie Barnes, staring not at Will but at Paul, with a look of dreadful malevolence. And close beside Will, very close, in the spot where the door to the old library had once been, towered the Black Rider. He was within arm's length of Will, though he did not move, but stood transfixed, as if the music had arrested him in mid-stride. His eyes were closed, his lips silently moving; his hands were stretched out pointing ominously towards Paul, as the sweet, unearthly music went on.

Will did one thing well, from the instinct of his new learning. Instantly he flung up a wall of resistance round Merriman and Paul and himself, so that the two of the Dark swayed backward from the force of it. But at the same time he shrieked, '*Merriman!*' And as the music broke off, and both Paul and Merriman swung round in swift horror, he knew what he had done wrong. He had not called as the Old Ones should call one another, through the mind. He had made the very bad mistake of shouting aloud.

The Rider and Maggie Barnes vanished, instantly. Paul was striding across the room in concern. 'What on earth's up, Will? Did you hurt yourself?'

Merriman said swiftly, smoothly, from behind him, 'He stumbled, I think,' and Will had the wit to crease his face with pain, bend slowly over as if in anguish, and clutch hard at one arm.

There was the sound of running feet, and Robin burst into the room from the passage, with Barbara close behind. 'What's the matter? We heard the most awful yell—'

He looked at Will and slowed to a halt, puzzled. 'You all right, Will?'

'Uh,' said Will. 'I – uh – I just banged my funny-bone. Sorry. It hurt.'

'Sounded as if someone was murdering you,' Barbara said reproachfully.

Shamelessly Will took refuge in rudeness, his fingers curling in his pocket to make sure the third Sign was safe. 'Well, I'm sorry to disappoint you,' he said petulantly, 'but really I'm all right. I just banged myself and yelled, that's all. Sorry if you were frightened. I don't see what all the fuss is about.'

Robin glared at him. 'Catch me running any-where to rescue you, next time,' he said witheringly.

'Talk about the boy crying Wolf,' Barbara said.

'I think,' Merriman said gently, closing the cup-board and turning the key, 'that we should all go and give Miss Greythorne one more carol.' And quite for-getting that he was no more than the butler, they all filed dutifully out of the room in his wake. Will called after him, in proper silence this time: 'But I must speak to you! The Rider was here! And the girl!'

Merriman said into his mind, 'I know. Later. They have ways of hearing this kind of talk, remember.' And he moved on, leaving Will twitching with exasperation and alarm.

In the doorway, Paul paused, took Will firmly by the shoulder and turned him to look in his face. 'Are you really all right?'

'Honest. Sorry about the noise. That flute sounded super.'

'Fantastic thing.' Paul let him go, turning to gaze longingly at the cupboard. 'Really. I've never heard anything like it. And of course never played one. You've no idea, Will, I can't *describe* — it's tremendously old, and yet the condition it's in, it might be almost new. And the tone of it—' There was an ache in his voice and his face that something in Will responded to with a deep, ancient sympathy. An Old One, he suddenly knew, was doomed always to feel this same formless, nameless longing for something out of reach, as an endless part of life.

'I'd give anything,' Paul said, 'to have a flute like that one day.'

'Almost anything,' Will said gently. Paul stared at him in astonishment, and the Old One in Will suddenly realized belatedly that this was not perhaps the response of a small boy; so he grinned, stuck out his tongue impishly at Paul, and skipped through the passage, back to the normal relationships of the normal world.

They sang 'The First Nowell' as their last carol; they made their farewells; they were out again in the snow and the crisp air, with Merriman's impassive polite smile disappearing behind the Manor doors. Will stood on the broad stone steps and gazed up at the stars. The clouds had cleared at last, and now the stars blazed like pinpricks of white fire in the black hollow of the night sky, in all the strange patterns that had been a complicated mystery to him all his life, but were endlessly significant now. 'See how bright the Pleiades are tonight,' he said softly, and Mary stared at him in amazement and said, 'The *what*?'

So Will brought his attention down out of the fiery black heavens, and in their own small, yellow, torchlit world the Stanton carollers trooped home. He walked among them speechless, as if in a dream. They thought him tired, but he was floating in wonder. He had three of the Signs of Power now. He had, too, the knowledge to use the Gift of Gramarye: a long lifetime of discovery and wisdom, given to him in a moment of suspended time. He was not the same Will Stanton that he had been a very few days before. Now and for ever, he knew, he inhabited a different time-scale from that of everyone he had ever known or loved . . . But he managed to turn his thoughts away from all these things, even from the two invading, threatening figures of the Dark. For this was Christmas, which had always been a time of magic, to him and to all the world. This was a brightness, a shining festival, and while its enchantment was on the world the charmed circle of his family and home would be protected against any invasion from outside.

Indoors, the tree glowed and glittered, and the music of Christmas was in the air, and spicy smells came from the kitchen, and in the broad hearth of the living-room the great twisted Yule root flickered and flamed as it gently burned down. Will lay on his back on the hearth-rug staring into the smoke wreathing up the chimney, and was suddenly very sleepy indeed. James and Mary too were trying not to yawn, and even Robin looked heavy-lidded.

'Too much punch,' said James, as his tall brother stretched gaping in an armchair.

'Get lost,' said Robin amiably.

'Who'd like a mince pie?' said Mrs Stanton, coming in with a vast tray of cocoa mugs.

'James has had six already,' said Mary in prim disapproval. 'At the Manor.'

'Now it's eight,' said James, a mince pie in each hand. 'Yah.'

'You'll get fat,' Robin said.

'Better than being fat already,' James said, through a mouthful, and stared pointedly at Mary, whose plump form had recently become her most gloomy preoccupation. Mary's mouth drooped, then tightened, and she advanced on him, making a snarling sound.

'Ho-ho-ho,' said Will sepulchrally from the floor. 'Good little children never fight at Christmas.' And since Mary was irresistibly close to him, he grabbed her by the ankle. She collapsed on top of him, howling cheerfully.

'Mind the fire,' said Mrs Stanton, from years of habit.

'Ow,' said Will, as his sister thumped him in the stomach, and he rolled away out of reach. Mary stopped, and sat gazing at him curiously. 'Why on earth have you got so many buckles on your belt?' she demanded.

Will tugged his sweater hastily down over his belt, but it was too late; everyone had seen. Mary reached forward and yanked the sweater up again. 'What funny things. What are they?'

'Just decoration,' Will said gruffly. 'I made them in metalwork at school.'

'I never saw you,' said James.

'You never looked, then.'

Mary prodded a finger forward at the first circle on Will's belt and rolled back with a howl. 'It burned me!' she shrieked.

'Very probably,' said her mother. 'Will and his belt have both been lying next to the fire. And you'll both be on top of it if you go on rolling about like that. Come on, now. Christmas Eve drink, Christmas Eve mince pie – Christmas Eve bed.'

Will scrambled gratefully to his feet. 'I'll get my presents while the cocoa cools off.'

'So will I.' Mary followed him. On the stairs she said, 'Those buckle things are pretty. Will you make me one for a brooch next term?'

'I might,' Will said, and he grinned to himself. Mary's curiosity was never much to worry about; it always led to the same place.

They pounded up to their respective bedrooms, and came down laden with packages to be added to the growing pile beneath the tree. Will had been trying hard not to look at this magical heap ever since they came in from carol- singing, but it was sorely difficult, especially since he could see one gigantic box labelled with a name that clearly began with a W. Who else began with W, after all . . .? He forced himself to ignore it, and resolutely piled his own armful in a space at the side of the tree.

'You're watching, James!' Mary shrilled, behind him.

'I am not,' said James. Then he said, because it was Christmas Eve, 'Well, yes, I expect I was. Sorry.' And Mary was so taken aback that she deposited all her parcels in silence, unable to think of anything to say.

On Christmas night, Will always slept with James. Both twin beds were still in James's room from the time before Will had moved up to Stephen's attic. The only difference now was that James kept Will's old bed piled with op art cushions, and referred to it as 'my chaise longue'. There was something about Christmas Eve, they both felt, that demanded company; one needed somebody to whisper to, during the warm beautiful dream-taut moments between hanging the empty stocking at the end of the bed, and dropping into the cosy oblivion that would flower into the marvel of Christmas morning.

While James was splashing in the bathroom, Will slipped off his belt, buckled it again round the three Signs, and put them under his pillow. It seemed prudent, even though he still knew without question that no one and nothing would trouble him or his home during this night. Tonight, perhaps for the last time, he was an ordinary boy again.

Strands of music and the soft rumble of voices drifted up from below. In solemn ritual, Will and James looped their Christmas stockings over their bedposts: precious, unbeautiful brown stockings of a thick, soft stuff, worn by their mother in some unimaginably distant time and misshapen now by years of service as Christmas holdalls. When filled, they would become top-heavy, and could no longer hang; they would be discovered instead lying magnificent across the foot of the beds.

'Bet I know what Mum and Dad are giving you,' James said softly. 'Bet it's a—'

'Don't you dare,' Will hissed, and his brother giggled and dived under the blankets.

'G'night, Will.'

''Night. Happy Christmas.'

'Happy Christmas.'

And it was the same as it always was, as he lay curled up happily in his snug wrappings, promising himself that he would stay awake, until, until . . .

. . . until he woke, in the dim morning room with a glimmer of light creeping round the dark square of the curtained window, and saw and heard nothing for an enchanted expectant space, because all his senses were concentrated on the weighty feel, over and around his blanketed feet, of strange bumps and corners and shapes that had not been there when he fell asleep. And it was Christmas Day.

Christmas Day

When he knelt beside the Christmas tree and pulled off the gay paper wrapping from the giant box labelled 'Will', the first thing he discovered was that it was not a box at all, but a wooden crate. A Christmas choir warbled distant and joyful from the radio in the kitchen; it was the after-Christmas-stocking, before-breakfast gathering of the family, when each member opened just one of his 'tree presents'. The rest of the bright pile would lie there until after dinner, happily tantalizing.

Will, being the youngest, had the first turn. He had made a beeline for the box, partly because it was so impressively large and partly because he suspected it came from Stephen. He found that someone had taken the nails out of the wooden lid, so that he could open it easily.

'Robin pulled out the nails, and Bar and I put the paper on,' said Mary at his shoulder, all agog. 'But we didn't look inside. Come on, Will, come on.'

He took off the lid. 'It's full of dead leaves! Or reeds or something.'

'Palm leaves,' said his father, looking. 'For packing, I suppose. Mind your fingers, they can have sharp edges.'

Will tugged out handfuls of the rustling fronds, until the first hard shape of something began to show. It was a thin strange curving shape, brown, smooth, like a branch; it seemed to be made of a hard kind of papier-mâché. It was an antler, like and yet not like the antler of a deer. Will paused suddenly. A strong and totally unexpected feeling had leapt out at him when he touched the antler. It was not a feeling he had ever had in the presence of the family before; it was the mixture of excitement, security and delight that came over him whenever he was with one of the Old Ones.

He saw an envelope poking out of the packing beside the antler and opened it. That paper bore the neat letterhead of Stephen's ship.

Dear Will:

Happy birthday. Happy Christmas. I always swore never to combine the two, didn't I? And here I am doing it. Let me tell you why. I don't know whether you'll understand, specially after you see what the present is. But perhaps you will. You've always been a bit different from everybody else. I don't mean daft! Just different.

It was like this. I was in the oldest part of Kingston one day during carnival. Carnival in these islands is a very special time – great fun, with echoes going back a long, long way. Anyway I got mixed up in a procession, all laughing people and jingling steel bands and dancers in wild costumes, and I met an old man.

He was a very impressive old man, his skin very black and his hair very white, and he sort of appeared out of nowhere and took me by the arm and pulled me out of the dancing. I'd never seen him in my life before, anywhere, I'm sure of it. But he looked at me and he said, 'You are Stephen Stanton, of Her Majesty's Navy. I have something for you. Not for you yourself, but for your youngest brother, the seventh son. You will send it to him as a present, for his birthday this year and his Christmas, combined in one. It will be a gift from you his brother, and he will know what to do with it in due course, although you will not.'

It was all so unexpected it really knocked me off balance. All I could say was, 'But who are you? How do you know me?' And the old man just looked at me again with very dark, deep eyes that seemed to be looking through me into the day after tomorrow, and he said, 'I would know you anywhere. You are Will Stanton's brother. There is a look that we Old Ones have. Our families have something of it too.'

And that was about it, Will. He didn't say another word. That last bit makes no sense, I know, but that was what he said. Then he just moved into the carnival procession and out again, and when he came out he was carrying – wearing, actually – the thing you will find in this box.

So here I am sending it to you. Just as I was told. It seems mad, and I can think of lots of things you'd have liked better. But there it is. There was something extraordinary about that old man, and I just somehow had to do what he told me.

Hope you like your crazy present, mate. I'll be thinking of you, both days.

Love

Stephen

Slowly Will folded the letter and put it back in its envelope. 'A look that we Old Ones have . . .' So the circle stretched all the way round the world. But of course it did, there would be no point in it otherwise. He was glad to have Stephen part of the pattern; it was right, somehow.

'Oh, come *on*, Will!' Mary was hopping with

curiosity, her dressing-gown flapping. 'Open it, open it!'

Will suddenly realized that his tradition-minded family had been standing, patiently immobile, waiting for five minutes while he read his letter. Using the lid of the crate as a tray, he hastily began hauling out more and more palm-leaf packing until finally the object inside was clear. He pulled it out, staggering as he took the weight, and everybody gasped.

It was a giant carnival head, brilliant and grotesque. The colours were bright and crude, the features boldly made and easily recognizable, all done in the same smooth, light substance like papier-mâché or a kind of grainless wood. And it was not the head of a man. Will had never seen anything like it before. The head from which the branching antlers sprang was shaped like the head of a stag, but the ears beside the horns were those of a dog or a wolf. And the face beneath the horns was a human face – but with the round feather-edged eyes of a bird. There was a strong, straight human nose, a firm human mouth, set in a slight smile. There was not much else that was purely human about the thing at all. The chin was bearded, but the beard so shaped that it might as easily have been the chin of a goat or deer as of a man. The face could have been frightening; when everyone had gasped, the sound Mary made and hastily muffled had been more like a small scream. But Will felt that its effect would depend on who was looking at it. The appearance was nothing. It was neither ugly nor beautiful, frightening nor funny. It was a thing made to call out deep responses from the mind. It was very much a thing of the Old Ones.

'My word!' his father said.

'That's a funny sort of present,' said James.

His mother said nothing.

Mary said nothing, but edged away a little.

'Reminds me of someone I know,' Robin said, grinning.

Paul said nothing.

Gwen said nothing.

Max said softly, 'Look at those eyes!'

Barbara said, 'But what's it for?'

Will ran his fingers over the strange great face. It took him only a moment to find what he was looking for; it was almost invisible unless you were expecting it, engraved on the forehead, between the horns. The imprint of a circle, quartered by a cross.

He said, 'It's a West Indian carnival head. It's old. It's special. Stephen found it in Jamaica.'

James was beside him now, peering up inside the

head. 'There's a kind of wire framework that rests on your shoulders. And a slit where the mouth's just a bit open, I suppose you look out through that. Come on, Will, put it on.'

He heaved up the head from behind to slip it over Will's shoulders. But Will drew away, as some other part of his mind spoke silently to him, 'Not now,' he said. 'Somebody else open their present.'

And Mary forgot the head and her reaction to it, in the happy instant of finding that it was her turn for Christmas. She dived at the pile of presents by the tree, and the cheerful discoveries began again.

One present each; they had almost done, and it was almost time for breakfast, when the knocking came at the front door. Mrs Stanton had been about to reach for her own ritual parcel; her arm dropped to her side, and she looked up blankly.

'Who on earth can that be?'

They all stared at one another, and then at the door, as if it might speak. This was all wrong, like a phrase of music changing in mid-melody. Nobody ever came to the house at this hour on Christmas Day, it was not in the pattern.

'I wonder . . .' said Mr Stanton, with a faint surmise waking in his voice; and he pushed his feet more firmly into his slippers and got up to open the front door.

They heard the door open. His back filled the space and stopped them from seeing the visitor, but his voice rose in obvious pleasure. 'My dear chap, how very good of you . . . come in, do come in . . .' And as he turned back towards the living-room he was holding a small package in one hand that had not been there before, clearly a product of the tall figure that now loomed in the doorway, following him in, Mr Stanton was beaming and glowing, busy with introductions, 'Alice, love, this is Mr Mitothin . . . so kind, all this way on Christmas morning just to deliver . . . shouldn't have taken the . . . Mitothin, my son Max, my daughter Gwen . . . James, Barbara . . .'

Will listened without attention to the grown-up politenesses; it was only at the voice of the stranger that he glanced up. There was something familiar in the deep, slightly nasal voice with a trace of accent, carefully repeating the names: 'How do you do, Mrs Stanton . . . Compliments of the season to you, Max, Gwen . . .' And Will saw the outline of the face, and the longish red-brown hair, and he froze.

It was the Rider. This Mr Mitothin, his father's

friend from goodness-knows-where, was the Black Rider from somewhere outside Time.

Will seized the nearest thing to his hand, a sweep of bright cloth that was Stephen's present from Jamaica to his sister Barbara, and pulled it quickly over the carnival head to mask it from view. As he turned again, the Rider raised his head to look further back into the room, and saw him. He stared at Will in open triumphant challenge, a small smile on his lips. Mr Stanton beckoned, flapping a hand, 'Will, come here a minute – my youngest son, Mr—'

Will was instantly a furious Old One, so furious that he did not pause to think what he should do. He could feel every inch of himself, as if he had grown in his rage to three times his own height. He stretched out his right hand with its fingers spread stiff towards his family, and saw them instantly caught into a stop in time, frozen out of all movement. Like waxworks they stood stiff and motionless round the room.

'How dare you come in here!' he shouted at the Rider. The two of them stood facing one another across the room, the only living and moving objects there: no human moved, the hands of the clock on the mantelpiece did not move, and though the flames of the fire flickered, they did not consume the logs that they burned.

'How dare you! At Christmas, on Christmas morning! Get out!' It was the first time in his life he had ever felt such rage, and it was not pleasant, but he was outraged that the Dark should have dared to interrupt this his most precious family ritual.

The Rider said softly, 'Contain yourself.' In the Old Speech, his accent was suddenly much more marked. He smiled at Will without a flicker of change in his cold blue eyes. I can cross your threshold, my friend, and pass your berried holly, because I have been invited. Your father, in good faith, asked me to enter the door. And he is the master of this house, and there is nothing you can do about that.'

'Yes, there is,' Will said. Staring at the Rider's confident smile, he focused all his powers in an effort to see into his mind, find what he intended to do there. But he came up sharp against a black wall of hostility, unbreakable. Will felt this should not be possible, and he was shaken. He groped angrily in his memory for the words of destruction with which in the last resort – but only the very last resort – an Old One might break the power of the Dark. And the Black Rider laughed.

'Oh no, Will Stanton,' he said easily. 'That won't do. You cannot use weapons of that kind here, not unless you wish to blast your whole family out beyond Time.' He glanced pointedly at Mary, who stood unmoving next to him, her mouth half-open, caught out of life in the middle of saying something to her father.

'That would be a pity,' the Rider said. Then he looked back at Will, and the smile dropped from his face as if he had spat it away, and his eyes narrowed. 'You young fool, do you think that for all your Gift of Gramarye you can control *me*? Keep your place. You are not one of the masters yet. You may do things as best you can contrive, but the high powers are not for your mastering yet. *And nor am I.*'

'You are afraid of my masters,' Will said suddenly, not knowing quite what he meant, but knowing it was true.

The Rider's pale face flushed. He said softly, 'The Dark is rising, Old One, and this time we do not propose that anything shall hinder its way. This is the time for our rising, and these next twelve months shall see us established at last. Tell your masters that. Tell them that nothing shall stop us. Tell them, all the Things of Power that they hope to possess we shall take from them, the grail and the harp and the

Signs. We shall break your Circle before it can ever be joined. *And none shall stop the Dark from rising!*'

The last words keened out in a high shriek of triumph, and Will shivered. The Rider stared at him, his pale eyes glittering; then scornfully he spread out his hands towards the Stantons, and at once they started into life again and the bustle of Christmas was back, and there was nothing Will could do.

'—that box for?' Mary said.

'—Mitothin, this is our Will.' Mr Stanton put his hand on Will's shoulder.

Will said coldly, 'How do you do?'

'The compliments of the season to you, Will,' the Rider said.

'I wish you the same as you wish me,' Will said.

'Very logical,' said the Rider.

'Very pompous, if you ask me,' Mary said, tossing her head. 'He's like that sometimes. Daddy, *who* is that box for, that he brought?'

'Mr Mitothin, not "he",' said her father automatically.

'For your mother, a surprise,' the Rider said. 'Something that wasn't finished last night in time for your father to bring it home.'

'From you?'

'From Daddy, I think,' said Mrs Stanton, smiling

at her husband. She turned to the Rider. 'Will you have breakfast with us, Mr Mitothin?'

'He can't,' said Will.

'Will!'

'He sees I'm in a hurry,' the Rider said smoothly. 'No, I thank you, Mrs Stanton, but I am on the way to spend the day with friends, and I must be off.'

Mary said, 'Where are you going?'

'North of here . . . what long hair you have, Mary. Very pretty.'

'Thank you,' said Mary smugly, shaking her long, loose hair back from her shoulders. The Rider reached out and removed a stray hair delicately from her sleeve. 'Allow me,' he said politely.

'She's always showing it off,' James said calmly. Mary stuck out her tongue.

The Rider looked down the room again. 'That's a magnificent tree. A local one?'

'It's a Royal tree,' James said, 'From the Great Park.'

'Come and see!' Mary grabbed the Rider's hand and tugged him across. Will bit his lip, and deliberately blanked out all thought of the carnival head from his mind by concentrating very hard on what he was likely to have for breakfast. The Rider, he was fairly sure, could see into the top level of his mind but not perhaps the ones buried deeper than that.

But there was no danger. Though the great empty box and its pile of exotic packing stood right beside him, the Rider, surrounded by Stantons, simply peered obediently and admiringly at the ornaments on the tree. He seemed particularly taken with the tiny carved initials from Farmer Dawson's box. 'Beautiful,' he said, absently twirling Mary's left-twined M – which, Will noticed vaguely, was hanging upside-down.

Then he turned back to their parents. 'I really must go, and you must have your breakfasts. Will looks rather hungry, I think.' There was a flash of malice as they looked at one another, and Will knew that he had been right about the limits of the Dark's seeing.

'I'm really immensely grateful to you, Mitothin,' Mr Stanton said.

'No trouble at all, you were right on my way. Compliments of the season to you all—' With a flurry of farewells he was gone, striding down the path. Will rather regretted that his mother shut the door before they had a chance to hear a car's engine start up. He did not think the Rider had come by car.

'Well, my love,' said Mr Stanton, giving his wife

a kiss and handing her the box. 'There's your first tree-present. Happy Christmas!'

'Oh!' said their mother, when she had opened it. 'Oh, Roger!'

Will squeezed past his burbling sisters to have a look. Nestled on white velvet, in a box marked with the name of his father's shop, was his mother's old-fashioned ring: the ring he had watched Mr Stanton checking for loose stones some weeks before, the ring that Merriman had seen in the picture he took out of Will's mind. But encircling it was something else: a bracelet made as an enlargement of the ring, exactly matching it. A gold band, set with three diamonds in the centre, and three rubies on either side, and engraved with an odd pattern of circles and lines and curves round them all. Will stared at it, wondering why the Rider should have wanted to have it in his hands. For surely that must have been behind the visit this morning; no Lord of the Dark needed to enter any house merely to see what was inside.

'Did you make it, Dad?' said Max. 'Lovely bit of work.'

'Thank you,' said his father.

'Who was that man who brought it?' Gwen said curiously. 'Does he work with you? Such a funny name.'

'Oh, he's a dealer,' Mr Stanton said. 'In diamonds, mostly. Strange chap, but very pleasant. I've known him for a couple of years, I suppose. We get quite a lot of stones from his people – including these.' He poked one finger gently at the bracelet. I had to leave early yesterday while young Jeffrey was still tightening one setting – and Mitothin happened to be in the shop and offered to drop it off to save me coming back. As he said, he was coming past here this morning anyway. Still, it was good of him, he needn't have offered.'

'Very nice,' said his wife. 'But you're nicer. I think it's beautiful.'

'I'm hungry,' said James. 'When are we going to eat?'

It was only after the bacon and eggs, toast and tea, marmalade and honey were all gone, and the debris of the first present-opening cleared away, that Will realized his letter from Stephen was nowhere to be found. He searched the living-room, investigated everyone's belongings, crawled underneath the tree and around the waiting pile of still-unopened presents, but it was not there. It might, of course, have been inadvertently thrown away, in mistake for wrapping-paper; such things sometimes happened in their crowded Christmas Day.

But Will thought he knew what had happened to his letter. And he wondered whether, after all, it had been the chance of investigating his mother's ring that had brought the Black Rider to the house – or a quest for something else.

Before long they noticed that snow was falling again. Gently but inexorably the flakes came fluttering down, without once faltering. The footprints of Mr Mitothin, out on the path from door to drive, were soon covered over as if they had never been there. The dogs, Raq and Ci who had asked to go out before the snow began, came humbly scratching at the back door again.

'I'm all for a white Christmas now and then,' said Max, staring morosely out, 'but this is ridiculous.'

'Extraordinary,' said his father, looking out over his shoulder. 'I've never known it like this at Christmas, in my lifetime. If much more comes down today, there'll be real transport problems all over the South of England.'

'That's what I was thinking,' said Max. 'I'm supposed to be going to Southampton the day after tomorrow to stay with Deb.'

'Oh, woe, woe,' said James, clutching his chest.

Max looked at him.

'Happy Christmas, Max,' James said.

Paul came clomping into the living-room in boots, buttoning his overcoat. 'Snow or no snow, I'm off ringing. They ol' bells up in thiccy tower don' wait for no one. Any of you heathen mob coming to church this morning?'

'The nightingales will be along,' Max said, looking at Will and James, who between them constituted about one-third of the church choir. 'That should do you, don't you think?'

'If you were to perform your seasonal good deed,' said Gwen, passing, 'with some useful task like peeling the potatoes, then perhaps Mum could go. She does like to, when she can.'

The small muffled group which set out eventually into the thickening snow consisted of Paul, James, Will, Mrs Stanton and Mary, who was, James said unkindly but with truth, probably more interested in avoiding housework than in making her devotions. They plodded up the road, the snowflakes coming down harder now and beginning to sting their cheeks. Paul had gone ahead to join the other ringers, and soon the tumbling notes of the six sweet old bells that hung in the small square tower began chiming through the grey whirling world around them, brightening it back into Christmas. Will's spirits rose a little at the sound, but not much; the heavy persistence of the new snow troubled him. He could not shake off the creeping suspicion that it was being sent as a forerunner of something else, by the Dark. He thrust his hands deep into the pockets of his sheepskin jacket, and the fingertips of one hand found themselves curling round a rook's feather, forgotten since the dreadful night of Midwinter's Eve, before his birthday.

In the snowy road, four or five cars stood outside the church; there were more, usually, on Christmas morning, but few villagers outside walking range had chosen to brave this swirling white fog. Will watched the fat white flakes lie determined and unmelting on his jacket sleeve; it was very cold. Even inside the little church, the snowflakes obstinately remained, and took a long time to melt. He went with James and the handful of other choristers to struggle into surplices in the narrow vestry corridor, and then, as the bells merged into the beginning of the service, to make their procession down the aisle and up into the little gallery at the back of the small square nave. You could see everyone from there, and it was clear that the church of St James the Less was not Christmas-crammed this year, but half full.

The order of Morning Prayer, *as were in this*

Church of England, by the Authority of Parliament, in the Second Year of the Reign of King Edward the Sixth, made its noble way through the Christmas pattern led by the Rector's unashamedly theatrical bass-baritone.

'O ye Frost and Cold, bless ye the Lord, praise Him, and magnify Him for ever,' said Will, reflecting that Mr Beaumont had shown a certain wry humour in choosing the canticle.

'O ye Ice and Snow, bless ye the Lord, praise Him, and magnify Him for ever.'

Suddenly he found himself shivering, but not from the words, nor from any sense of cold. His head swam; he clutched for a moment at the edge of the gallery. The music seemed to become for a brief flash hideously discordant, jarring at his ears. Then it faded into itself again and was as before, leaving Will shaken and chilled.

'O ye Light and Darkness,' sang James, staring at him – '*are you all right? Sit down* – and magnify Him for ever.'

But Will shook his head impatiently, and for the rest of the service he sturdily stood, sang, sat, or knelt, and convinced himself that there had been nothing at all wrong except a vague feeling of faint-ness, brought on by what his elders liked to call 'over-excitement'. And then the strange sense of wrongness, of discordance, came again.

It was only once more, at the very end of the service. Mr Beaumont was booming out the prayer of St Chrysostom: '. . . who dost promise, that when two or three are gathered together in thy name thou wilt grant their requests . . .' Noise broke suddenly into Will's mind, a shrieking and dreadful howling in place of the familiar cadences. He had heard it before. It was the sound of the besieging Dark, which he had heard outside the Manor Hall where he had sat with Merriman and the Lady, in some century unknown. But in a church? said Will the Anglican choirboy, incredulous: surely you can't feel it inside a church? Ah, said Will the Old One unhappily, any church of any religion is vulnerable to their attack, for places like this are where men give thought to matters of the Light and the Dark. He hunched his head down between his shoulders as the noise beat at him – and then it vanished again, and the Rector's voice was ringing out alone, as before.

Will glanced quickly around him, but it was clear nobody else had noticed anything wrong. Through the folds of his white surplice he gripped the three Signs on his belt, but there was neither warmth nor cold under his fingers. To the warning power of the

Signs, he guessed, a church was a kind of no man's land; since no harm could actually enter its walls, no warning against harm should be necessary. Yet if the harm were hovering just outside . . .

The service was over now, everyone roaring out 'O Come, All Ye Faithful' in happy Christmas fervour, as the choir made their way down from the gallery and up to the altar. Then Mr Beaumont's blessing went rolling out over the heads of the congregation: '. . . the love of God, and the fellowship of the Holy Ghost . . .' But the words could not bring Will peace, for he knew that something was wrong, something looming out of the Dark, something waiting, out there, and that when it came to the point he must meet it alone, unstrengthened.

He watched everyone file beaming out of the church, smiling and nodding to each other as they gripped their umbrellas and turned up their collars against the swirling snow. He saw jolly Mr Hutton, the retired director, twirling his car keys, enveloping tiny Miss Bell, their old teacher, in the warm offer of a ride home; and behind him jolly Mrs Hutton, a galleon in full furry sail, doing the same with limp Mrs Pettigrew, the postmistress. Assorted village children scampered out of the door, escaping their best-hatted mothers, rushing to snowballs and

Christmas turkey. Lugubrious Mrs Horniman stumped out next to Mrs Stanton and Mary, busily foretelling doom. Will saw Mary, trying not to giggle, fall back to join Mrs Dawson and her married daughter, with the five-year-old grandson prancing gaily in gleaming new cowboy boots.

The choir, coated and muffled, began to leave too, with cries of 'Happy Christmas!' and 'See you on Sunday, Vicar!' to Mr Beaumont, who would be giving only this service here today and the rest in his other parishes. The rector, talking music with Paul, smiled and waved vaguely. The church began to empty, as Will waited for his brother. He could feel his neck prickling, as though with the electricity that hangs strongly oppressive in the air before a giant storm. He could feel it everywhere, the air inside the church was charged with it. The rector, still chatting, reached out an absentminded hand and turned off the lights inside the church, leaving it in a cold grey murk, brighter only beside the door where the whiteness of the snow reflected in. And Will, seeing some figures move towards the door out of the shadows, realized that the church was not empty after all. Down there by the little twelfth-century font, he saw Farmer Dawson, Old George, and Old George's son John, the smith, with his silent wife. The Old Ones of the Circle were waiting for him, to support him against whatever lurked outside. Will felt weak for a moment as relief washed over him in a great warm wave.

'All ready, Will?' said the rector genially, pulling on his overcoat. He went on, still preoccupied, to Paul, 'Of course, I do agree the double concerto is one of the best. I only wish he'd record the un-accompanied Bach suites. Heard him do them in a church in Edinburgh once, at the Festival – marvellous—'

Paul, sharper-eyed, said, 'Is anything wrong, Will?'

'No,' Will said. 'That is – no.' He was trying desperately to think of some way of getting the two of them outside the church before he came near the door himself. Before – before whatever might happen did happen. By the church door he could see the Old Ones move slowly into a tight group, supporting one another. He could feel the force now very strong, very close, all around, the air was thick with it, outside the church was destruction and chaos, the heart of the Dark, and he could think of nothing that he could do to turn it aside. Then as the rector and Paul turned to walk through the nave, he saw both of them pause in the same instant, and their heads go up like the heads of wild deer on the alert. It was too late now; the voice of the Dark was so loud that even humans could sense its power.

Paul staggered, as if someone had pushed him in the chest, and grabbed a pew for support. '*What is that?*' he said huskily. 'Rector? What on earth is it?'

Mr Beaumont had turned very white. There was a glistening of sweat on his forehead, though the church was very cold again now. 'Nothing on earth, I think, perhaps,' he said. 'God forgive me.' And he stumbled a few paces nearer the church door, like a man struggling through waves in the sea, and leaning forward slightly made a sweeping sign of the Cross. He stammered out, 'Defend us thy humble servants in all assaults of our enemies; that we, surely trusting in thy defence, may not fear the power of any adversaries . . .'

Farmer Dawson said very quietly but clearly from the group beside the door, 'No, Rector.'

The rector seemed not to hear him. His eyes were wide, staring out at the snow; he stood transfixed, he shook like a man with fever, the sweat came running down his cheeks. He managed to half-raise one arm and point behind him: '. . . vestry . . .' he gasped out. '. . . book, on table . . . exorcize . . .'

'Poor brave fellow,' said John Smith in the old

Speech. 'This battle is not for his fighting. He is bound to think so, of course, being in his church.'

'Be easy, Reverend,' said his wife in English; her voice was soft and gentle, strongly of the country. The rector stared at her like a frightened animal, but by now all his powers of speech and movement had been taken away.

Frank Dawson said: 'Come here, Will.'

Pushing against the Dark, Will came forward slowly; he touched Paul on the shoulder as he passed, looking into puzzled eyes in a face as twisted and helpless as the rector's, and said softly: 'Don't worry. It'll be all right soon.'

Each of the Old Ones touched him gently as he came into the group, as if joining him to them, and Farmer Dawson took him by the shoulder. He said, 'We must do something to protect those two, Will, or their minds will bend. They cannot stand the pressure, the Dark will send them mad. You have the power, and the rest of us do not.'

It was Will's first intimation that he could do anything another Old One could not, but there was no time for wonder; with the Gift of Gramarye, he closed off the minds of his brother and the rector behind a barrier that no power of any kind could break through. It was a perilous undertaking, since he the maker was the only one who could remove the barrier, and if anything were to happen to him the two protected ones would be left like vegetables, incapable of any communication, for ever. But the risk had to be taken; there was nothing else to be done. Their eyes closed gently as if they had gone quietly to sleep; they stood very still. After a moment their eyes opened again, but were tranquil and empty, unaware.

'All right,' said Farmer Dawson. 'Now.'

The Old Ones stood in the doorway of the church, their arms linked together. None spoke a word to another. Wild noise and turbulence rose outside; the light darkened, the wind howled and whined, the snow whirled in and whipped their faces with white chips of ice. And suddenly the rooks were in the snow, hundreds of them, black flurries of malevolence, cawing and croaking, diving down at the porch in shrieking attack and then swooping up, away. They could not come close enough to claw and tear; it was as if an invisible wall made them fall back within inches of their targets. But that would be only for as long as the Old Ones' strength could hold. In a wild storm of black and white the Dark attacked, beating at their minds as at their bodies, and above all driving hard at the Sign-seeker, Will. And Will knew that if he had been on his own his mind, for all its gifts of protection, would have collapsed. It was the strength of the Circle of the Old Ones that held him fast now.

But for the second time in his life, even the Circle could do no more than hold the power of the Dark at bay. Even together, the old Ones could not drive it back. And there was no Lady now to bring aid of a greater kind. Will realized once more, helplessly, that to be an Old One was to be very old before the proper time, for the fear he began to feel now was worse than the blind terror he had known in his attic bed, worse than the fear the Dark had put into him in the great hall. This time, his fear was adult, made of experience and imagination and care for others, and it was the worst of all. In the moment that he knew this, he knew too that he, Will, was the only means by which his own fear could be overcome, and thus the Circle fortified and the Dark driven away. Who are you? he asked himself – and answered: you are the Sign-seeker. You have three of the Signs, half the circle of Things of Power. *Use them.*

The sweat was standing on his own forehead now as it had done on the rector's – though now the rector and Paul stood in smiling peace, oblivious, outside everything that was going on. Will could see the strain on the faces of the others, Farmer Dawson most of all. Slowly he moved his hands inwards, bringing the hands each held closer to one another; John Smith's left hand nearer to Farmer Dawson's right. And when they were close enough, he joined his neighbours' hands, shutting himself out. For a panicking moment he clutched them again, as if he were tightening a knot. Then he let go, and stood alone.

Unprotected now by the Circle, though sheltered behind it, he swayed under the impact of the raging ill-will outside the church. Then moving very deliberately, he unclasped his belt with its three precious burdens and draped it over his arm; took from his pocket the rook's feather, and wove it into the centre Sign: the bronze quartered circle. Then he took the belt in both his hands, holding it up before him, and moved slowly round until he stood alone in the church porch, facing the howling, rook-screaming, icy dark beyond. He had never felt so lonely before. He did nothing, he thought nothing. He stood there, and let the Signs work for themselves.

And suddenly, there was silence.

The flapping birds were gone. No wind howled.

The dreadful, mad humming that had filled the air and the mind was vanished altogether. Every nerve and muscle in Will's body went limp as the tension disappeared. Outside, the snow still quietly fell, but the flakes were smaller now. The Old Ones looked at one another and laughed.

'The full circle will do the real job,' said Old George, 'but half a circle can do a lot, eh, young Will?'

Will looked down at the Signs in his hand, and shook his head in wonder.

Farmer Dawson said softly, 'In all my days since the grail disappeared, that's the first time I've seen anything but the mind of one of the great ones drive back the Dark. *Things*, this time. They did it alone, for all our willing. We have Things of Power again. It has been a long, long time.'

Will was still looking at the Signs, staring, as if they held his eyes for some purpose. 'Wait,' he said abstractedly. 'Don't move. Stay still for a moment.'

They paused, startled. The smith said, 'Is there trouble?'

'Look at the Signs,' Will said. 'Something's happening to them. They're – they're glowing.'

He turned slowly, still holding the belt with the three Signs as before, until his body was blocking the grey light from the door and his hands were in the gloom of the church; and the Signs grew brighter and brighter, each of them glowing with a strange, inward light.

The Old Ones stared.

'Is it the power of driving back the Dark?' said John Smith's wife in her soft lilt. 'Is it something in them that was sleeping, and begins to wake now?'

Will was trying vainly to sense what the Signs were telling him. 'I think it's a message, it means something. But I can't get through . . .'

The light poured out of the three Signs, filling their half of the dark little church with brilliance; it was a light like sunlight, warm and strong. Nervously, Will reached out a finger to touch the nearest circle, the Sign of Iron, but it was neither hot nor cold.

Farmer Dawson said suddenly, 'Look up there!'

His arm was out, pointing up the nave, towards the altar. In the instant they turned, they saw what he had seen: another light, blazing from the wall, just as beside them the light blazed from the Signs. It shone out like the beam from a great torch.

And Will understood. He said happily, 'So that's why.'

He walked up towards the second patch of

brilliance, carrying the belt and the Signs so that the shadows on the pews and on the beams of the roof moved with him as he went. As the two lights grew closer and closer together each seemed to grow brighter still. With Frank Dawson's tall, heavy form looming behind him, Will paused in the middle of the shaft of brilliance reaching out from the wall. It looked as if a slit window were letting light through from some unimaginably bright room beyond. He saw that the light was coming from something very small, as long as one of his fingers, lying on its side.

He said with certainty to Mr Dawson: 'I must take it quickly, you know, while the light still shines from it. If the light is not shining, it can't be found at all.' And putting the belt with the Sign of Iron and the Sign of Bronze and the Sign of Wood into Frank Dawson's hands, he went forward to the light-cleft wall and reached in to the small source of the enchanted beam.

The glowing thing came out of the wall easily from a break in the stucco where the Chiltern flints of the wall showed through. It lay on his palm: a circle, quartered by a cross. It had not been cut into that shape. Even through the light in it, Will could see the smooth roundness of the sides that told him this was a natural flint, grown in the Chiltern chalk fifteen million years ago.

'The Sign of Stone,' Farmer Dawson said. His voice was gentle and reverent, his dark eyes unreadable. 'We have the fourth Sign, Will.'

Together they walked back to join the others, carrying the bright Things of Power. The three Old Ones watched, in silence. Paul and the Rector now sat tranquil in a pew as if sleeping. Will stood with his fellows and took the belt, and threaded on the Sign of Stone to stand there next to the other three. He had to squint through half-closed eyes to keep the brightness from blinding him.

Then when the fourth Sign was in position next to the rest, all the light in them died. They were dark and quiet as they had been before, and the Sign of Stone showed itself as a smooth and beautiful thing with the grey-white surface of an undamaged flint.

The black rook's feather was still woven into the Sign of Bronze. Will took it out. He did not need it now.

When the light went out of the Signs, Paul and the rector stirred. They opened their eyes, startled to find themselves sitting in a pew when a moment ago – it seemed to them – they had been standing. Paul jumped up instinctively, his head turning, questing.

'It's gone!' he said. He looked at Will, and a peculiar expression of puzzlement and wonder and awe came over his face. His eyes travelled down to the belt in Will's hands. 'What happened?' he said.

The rector stood up, his smooth, plump face creased in an effort to make sense of the incomprehensible. 'Certainly it has gone,' he said, looking slowly round the church. 'Whatever – influence it was. The Lord be praised.' He too looked at the Signs on Will's belt, and he glanced up again, smiling suddenly, an almost childish smile of relief and delight. 'That did the work, didn't it? The cross. Not of the church, but a Christian cross, nonetheless.'

'Very old, them crosses are, Rector,' said Old George unexpectedly, firm and clear. 'Made a long time before Christianity. Long before Christ.'

The rector beamed at him. 'But not before God,' he said simply.

The Old Ones looked at him. There was no answer that would not have offended him, so no one tried to give one. Except, after a moment, Will.

'There's not really any before and after, is there?' he said. 'Everything that matters is outside Time. And comes from there and can go there.'

Mr Beaumont turned to him in surprise, 'You mean infinity, of course, my boy.'

'Not altogether,' said the Old One that was Will. 'I mean the part of all of us, and of all the things we think and believe, that has nothing to do with yesterday or today or tomorrow because it belongs at a different kind of level. Yesterday is still there, on that level. Tomorrow is there too. You can visit either of them. And all Gods are there, and all the things they have ever stood for. And,' he added sadly, 'the opposite, too.'

'Will,' said the rector, staring at him, 'I am not sure whether you should be exorcized or ordained. You and I must have some long talks, very soon.'

'Yes, we must,' Will said equably. He buckled on his belt, heavy with its precious burden. He was thinking hard and quickly as he did so, and the chief image before his mind was not Mr Beaumont's disturbed theological assumptions, but Paul's face. He had seen his brother looking at him with a kind of fearful remoteness that bit into him with the pain of a whiplash. It was more than he could stand. His two worlds must not meet so closely. He raised his head, gathering all his powers, spread staight the fingers of both hands and pointed one hand at each of them.

'You will forget,' he said softly in the Old Speech. 'Forget. Forget.'

'— in a church in Edinburgh once, marvellous,' the rector said to Paul, reaching to do up the top button of his overcoat. 'The Sarabande in the fifth suite literally had me in tears. He's the greatest cellist in the world, without a doubt.'

'Oh yes,' said Paul. 'Oh yes, he is.' He hunched his shoulders inside his own coat. 'Has Mum gone ahead, Will? Hey, Mr Dawson, hallo, happy Christmas!' And he beamed and nodded at the rest, as they all turned towards the church porch and the scattered flakes of drifting snow.

'Happy Christmas, Paul, Mr Beaumont,' said Farmer Dawson gravely. 'A nice service, sir, very nice.'

'Ah, seasonal warmth, Frank,' said the rector. 'A wonderful season too. Nothing can interfere with our Christmas services, not even all this snow.'

Laughing and chatting, they went out into the white world, where the snow lay mounded over the invisible tombstones and the white fields stretched down to the freezing Thames. There was no sound anywhere, no disturbance, only the occasional murmur of a car passing on the distant Bath Road. The rector turned aside to find his motor-bike. The rest of them went on, in a cheerful straggle, to take their respective paths home.

Two black rooks were perched on the lych-gate as Will and Paul drew close; they rose into the air slowly, half-hopping, dark incongruous shapes against the white snow. One of them passed close to Will's feet and dropped something there, giving a deprecatory croak as he passed. Will picked it up; it was a glossy horse-chestnut from the rooks' wood, as fresh as if it had ripened only yesterday. He and James always collected such nuts from the wood in early autumn for their school games of conkers, but he had never seen one as large and round as this.

'There, now,' said Paul, amused. 'You have a friend. Bringing you an extra Christmas present.'

'A peace offering, perhaps,' said Frank Dawson behind them, with no trace of expression in his deep Buckinghamshire voice. 'And then again, perhaps not. Happy Christmas, lads. Enjoy your dinner.' And the Old Ones were gone, up the road.

Will picked up the conker. 'Well I never,' he said.

They closed the church gate, knocking a shower of snow from its flat iron bars. Round the corner came the coughing roars of a motor-cycle as the rector tried to kick his steed into life. Then, a few feet ahead of them on the trampled snow, the rook flew down again. It walked backwards and forwards irresolutely and looked at Will.

'Caark,' it said, very gently, for a rook. 'Caaark, caark, caark.' Then it walked a few paces forward to the churchyard fence, jumped down again into the churchyard, and walked back a few paces as before. The invitation could hardly have been more obvious. 'Caark,' said the rook again, louder.

The ears of an Old One know that birds do not speak with the precision of words; instead they communicate emotion. There are many kinds and degrees of emotion, and there are many kinds of expression even in the language of a bird. But although Will could tell that the rook was obviously asking him to come and look at something, he could not tell whether or not the bird was being used by the Dark.

He paused, thinking of what the rooks had done; then he fingered the shiny brown chestnut in his hand. 'All right, bird,' he said. 'One quick look.'

He went back through the gate, and the rook, croaking like an old swinging door, walked clumsily ahead of him up the church path and round the corner. Paul watched, grinning. Then he saw Will suddenly stiffen as he reached the corner; vanish for a moment, and then reappear.

'Paul! Come quick! There's a man in the snow!'

Paul called the rector, who had just begun

pushing his cycle up the road to start it there, and together they came running. Will was bending over a hunched figure, lying in the angle between the church wall and the tower; there was no movement, and the snow had already covered the man's clothes half an inch thick with its cold, feathery flakes. Mr Beaumont moved Will gently aside and knelt, turning the man's head and feeling for a pulse.

'He's alive, thank God, but very cold. The pulse isn't very good. He must have been here long enough for most men to die of exposure – look at the snow! Let's get him inside.'

'In the church?'

'Well, of course.'

'Let's take him to our house,' Paul said impulsively. 'It's only just round the corner, after all. It's warm, and a lot better, at any rate until an ambulance or something can come.'

'A wonderful idea,' said Mr Beaumont warmly. 'Your good mother is a Samaritan, I know. Just until Dr Armstrong can be called . . . we certainly can't leave the poor fellow here. I don't think there's a broken bone. Heart trouble, probably.' He tucked his heavy cycle gloves under the man's head to keep it from the snow, and Will saw the face for the first time.

He said in alarm, 'It's the Walker!'

They turned to him. 'Who?'

'An old tramp who hangs around . . . Paul, we can't take him home. Can't we get him to Dr Armstrong's surgery?'

'In this?' Paul waved a hand at the darkening sky; the snow was whirling round them, thicker again, and the wind was higher.

'But we can't take him with us! Not the Walker! He'll bring back the—' He stopped suddenly, half-way through a yelp. 'Oh,' he said helplessly. 'Of course, you can't remember, can you?'

'Don't worry, Will, your mother won't mind – a poor man *in extremis*—' Mr Beaumont was bustling now. He and Paul carried the Walker to the gate, like a muffled heap of ancient clothes. He managed finally to start the motor-cycle, and they propped the inert shape on it somehow; then half riding, half pushing, the strange little group made its way to the Stantons' house.

Will glanced behind him once or twice, but the rook was nowhere to be seen.

'Well, well,' said Max fastidiously, as he came down into the dining-room. 'Now I've *really* met a dirty old man.'

'He smelled,' Barbara said.

'You're telling me. Dad and I gave him a bath. My Lord, you should have seen him. Well, no, you shouldn't. Put you off your Christmas dinner. Anyway, he's as clean as a new-born babe now. Dad even washed his hair and his beard. And Mum's burning his horrible old clothes, when she's made sure there's nothing valuable in them.'

'Not much danger of that, I should think,' said Gwen, on her way in from the kitchen. 'Here, move your arm, this dish is hot.'

'We should lock up all the silver,' said James.

'What silver?' said Mary witheringly.

'Well, Mum's jewellery then. And the Christmas presents. Tramps always steal things.'

'This one won't be stealing much for a time,' said Mr Stanton, coming to his place at the head of the table with a bottle of wine and a corkscrew. 'He's ill. And fast asleep now, snoring like a camel.'

'Have you ever heard a camel snore?' said Mary.

'Yes,' said her father. 'And ridden one. So there. When's the doctor coming, Max? Pity to interrupt his dinner, poor man.'

'We didn't,' said Max. 'He's out delivering a baby, and they don't know when he'll be back. The woman was expecting twins.'

'Oh, Lord.'

'Well, the old boy must be all right if he's asleep. Just needs rest, I expect. Though I must say he seemed a bit delirious, all that weird talk coming out.' Gwen and Barbara brought in more dishes of vegetables. In the kitchen their mother was making impressive clattering noises with the oven. 'What weird talk?' said Will.

'Goodness knows,' said Robin. 'It was when we first took him up. Sounded like a language unknown to human ear. Maybe he comes from Mars.'

'I only wish he did,' Will said. 'Then we could send him back.'

But a shout of approval had greeted his mother, beaming over the glossy brown turkey, and nobody heard him.

They turned on the radio in the kitchen while they were doing the washing-up.

'Heavy snow is falling again over the South and West of England,' said the impersonal voice. 'The blizzard which has been raging for twelve hours in the North Sea is still immobilizing all shipping on the South-east coasts. The London docks closed down this morning, due to power failures and transport difficulties caused by heavy snow and temperatures approaching zero. Snowdrifts blocking roads have isolated villages in many remote areas, and British Rail is fighting numerous electrical failures and minor derailments caused by the snow. A spokesman said this morning that the public is advised not to travel by rail except in cases of emergency.'

There was a sound of rustling paper. The voice went on: 'The freak storms which have intermittently raged over the South of England for the last few days are not expected to diminish until after the Christmas holiday, the Meteorological Office said this morning. Fuel shortages have worsened in the South-east, and householders have been asked not to use any form of electrical heating between the hours of nine a.m. and midday, or three and six p.m.'

'Poor old Max,' Gwen said. 'No trains. Perhaps he can hitch-hike.'

'Listen, listen!'

'A spokesman for the Automobile Association said today that road travel was at present extremely inadvisable on all roads except major motorways. He added that motorists stranded in heavy snowstorms should if possible remain with their vehicles until the snow stops. Unless a driver is quite certain of his location and knows he can reach help within ten minutes, the spokesman said, he should on no account leave his car.'

The voice went on, among exclamations and whistles, but Will turned away; he had heard enough. These storms could not be broken by the Old Ones without the power of the full circle of Signs – and by sending the storms, the Dark hoped to stop him from completing the circle. He was trapped; the Dark was spreading its shadow not only over his quest but over the ordinary world too. From the moment the Rider had invaded his cosy Christmas that morning, Will had watched the dangers grow; but he had not anticipated this wider threat. For days now, he had been too much caught up in his own perils to notice those of the outside world. But so many people were threatened now by the snow and cold: the very young, the very old, the weak, the ill . . . The Walker won't have a doctor tonight, that's certain, he thought. It's a good job he isn't dying . . .

The Walker. Why was he here? There had to be some meaning behind it. Perhaps he had simply been hovering for his own reasons, and been blasted by the attack of the Dark on the church. But if so, why had the rook, an agent of the Dark, brought Will to save him from freezing to death? Who was the Walker, anyway? Why could all the powers of Gramarye tell him nothing about the old man at all?

There were carols on the radio again. Will thought bitterly: Happy Christmas, world.

His father, passing, slapped him on the back. 'Cheer up, Will. It's bound to stop tonight, you'll be tobogganing tomorrow. Come on, time to open the rest of the presents. If we keep Mary waiting any longer she'll explode.'

Will went to join his cheerful, noisy family. Back in the cosy, brilliant cave of the long room with the fire and the glowing tree, it was untouched Christmas for a while, just as it had always been. And his mother and father and Max had joined to give him a new bicycle, with racing handlebars and eleven gear-speeds.

Will was never quite sure whether what happened that night was a dream.

In the darkest part of the night, the small chill hours that are the first of the next day, he woke, and Merriman was there. He stood towering beside the bed in a faint light that seemed to come from within his own form; his face was shadowed, inscrutable.

'Wake up, Will. Wake up. There is a ceremony we must attend.'

In an instant Will was standing; he found that he was fully dressed, with the Signs on their belt round his waist. He went with Merriman to the window. It was mounded to half its height with snow, and still the flakes were quietly falling. He said, suddenly desolate, 'Isn't there anything we can do to stop it? They're freezing half the country, Merriman, people will be dying.'

Merriman shook his white-maned head slowly, heavily. 'The Dark has its strongest power of all rising between now and the Twelfth Day. This is their preparing. Theirs is a cold strength, the winter feeds it. They mean to break the Circle for ever, before it is too late for them. We shall all face a hard test soon. But not all things go according to their will. Much magic still flows untapped, along the Old Ones' Ways. And we may find more hope in a moment. Come.'

The window ahead of them flew open, outwards, scattering all the snow. A faint luminous path like a broad ribbon lay ahead, stretching into the snow-flecked air; looking down, Will could see through it, see the snow-mounded outlines of roofs and fences and trees below. Yet the path was substantial too. In one stride Merriman had reached it through the window and was sweeping away at great speed with an eerie gliding movement, vanishing into the night. Will leapt after him, and the strange path swept him too off through the night, with no feeling either of speed or cold. The night around him was black and thick; nothing was to be seen except the glimmer of the Old Ones' airy way. And then all at once they were in some bubble of Time, hovering, tilted on the wind as Will had learned from his eagle of the Book of Gramarye.

'Watch,' Merriman said, and his cloak swirled round Will as if in protection.

Will saw in the dark sky, or in his own mind, a group of great trees, leafless, towering over a leafless hedge, wintry but without snow. He heard a strange, thin music, a high piping accompanied by the small constant thump of a drum, playing over and over again a single melancholy tune. And out of the deep dark and into the ghostly grove of trees a procession came.

It was a procession of boys, in clothes of some time long past, tunics and rough leggings; they had hair to their shoulders and bag-like caps of a shape he had never seen before. They were older than he: about fifteen, he guessed. They had the half-solemn expressions of players in a game of charades, mingling earnest purpose with a bubbling sense of fun. At the front came boys with sticks and bundles of birch twigs; at the back were the players of pipe and drum. Between these, six boys carried a kind of platform made of reeds and branches woven together, with a bunch of holly at each corner. It was like a stretcher, Will thought, except that they were holding it at shoulder height. He thought at first that it was no more than that, and empty; then he saw that it supported something. Something very small. On a cushion of ivy leaves in the centre of the woven bier lay the body of a minute bird: a dusty-brown bird, neat-billed. It was a wren.

Merriman's voice said softly over his head, out of the darkness: 'It is the Hunting of the Wren, performed every year since men can remember, at the solstice. But this is a particular year, and we may see more, if all is well. Hope in your heart, Will, that we may see more.'

And as the boys and their sad music moved on through the sky-trees and yet did not seem to pass, Will saw with a catch in his breath that instead of the little bird, there was growing the dim shape of a different form on the bier. Merriman's hand clutched at his shoulder like a steel clamp, though the big man made no sound. Lying on the bed of ivy between the four holly tufts now was no longer a tiny bird, but a small, fine-boned woman, very old, delicate as a bird, robed in blue. The hands were folded on the chest, and on one finger glimmered a ring with a huge rose-coloured stone. In the same instant Will saw the face, and knew that it was the Lady.

He cried out in pain, 'But you said she wasn't dead!'

'No more she is,' Merriman said.

The boys walked to their music, the bier with the silent form lying there came close, and then moved away, vanishing with the procession into the night, and the piping sad tune and the drumbeats dwindled after it. But on the very edge of disappearance, the three boys who had been playing paused, put down their instruments, and turned to stand gazing without expression at Will.

One of them said: 'Will Stanton, beware the snow!'

The second said: 'The Lady will return, but the Dark is rising.'

The third, in a quick sing-song tone, chanted something that Will recognized as soon as it began:

'When the Dark comes rising, six shall turn it back;
Three from the circle, three from the track.
Wood, bronze, iron; water, fire, stone;
Five will return, and one go alone.'

But the boy did not end there, as Merriman had done. He went on:

> 'Iron for the birthday, bronze carried long;
> Wood from the burning, stone out of song;
> Fire in the candle-ring, water from the thaw;
> Six signs the circle, and the grail gone before.'

Then a great wind came up out of nowhere, and in a flurry of snowflakes and darkness the boys were gone, whirled away, and Will too felt himself whirling backwards, back through Time, back along the shining way of the Old Ones. The snow lashed at his face. The night was in his eyes, stinging. Out of the darkness he heard Merriman calling to him, urgently, but with a new hope and resonance in his deep voice: 'Danger rises with the snow, Will – be wary of the snow. Follow the Signs, beware the snow . . .'

And Will was back in his room, back in his bed, falling into sleep with the one ominous word ringing in his head like the chiming of the deepest church bell over the mounting snow. 'Beware . . . beware . . .'

Part Three: *The Testing*

The Coming of the Cold

The next day the snow still fell, all day. And the next day too.

'I do wish it would stop,' said Mary unhappily, gazing at the blind white windows. 'It's horrible the way it just goes on and on – I hate it.'

'Don't be stupid,' said James. 'It's just a very long storm. No need to get hysterical.'

'This is different. It's creepy.'

'Rubbish. It's just a lot of snow.'

'Nobody's ever seen so much snow before. Look how high it is – you couldn't get out of the back door if we hadn't been clearing it since it started to fall. We're going to be buried, that's what. It's pushing at us – it's even broken a window in the kitchen, did you know that?'

Will said sharply, 'What?'

'The little window at the back, near the stove. Gwennie came down this morning and the kitchen was cold as ice, with snow and bits of glass all over that corner. The snow had pushed the window in, the weight of it.'

James sighed loudly. 'Weight isn't pushing. The snow gets blown into a drift at that side of the house, that's all.'

'I don't care what you say, it's horrible. As if the snow was trying to get in.' She sounded close to tears.

'Let's go and see if the Wa – the old tramp's woken up yet,' Will said. It was time to stop Mary before she came too near the truth. How many other people in the country were being made as frightened as this by the snow? He thought fiercely of the Dark, and longed to know what to do.

The Walker had slept through the previous day, hardly stirring except for occasional meaningless mutterings, and once or twice a small hoarse shout. Will and Mary went up to his room now carrying a tray, with cereal and toast and milk and marmalade. 'Good morning!' Will said loudly and brightly as they went in. 'Would you like some breakfast?'

The Walker opened a slit of an eye and peered at them through his shaggy grey hair, longer and wilder than ever now that it was clean. Will held out the tray towards him.

'Faugh!' the Walker croaked. It was a noise like spitting.

Mary said, '*Well!*'

'D'you want something else instead, then?' said Will. 'Or are you just not hungry?'

'Honey,' the Walker said.

'Honey?'

'Honey and bread. Honey and bread. Honey and—'

'All right,' Will said. They took the tray away.

'He doesn't even say please,' Mary said. 'He's a nasty old man. I'm not going near him any more.'

'Suit yourself,' Will said. Left alone, he found the tail-end of a jar of honey in the back of the larder, rather crystalline round the edges, and spread it lavishly on three hunks of bread. He took this with a glass of milk up to the Walker, who sat up greedily in bed and wolfed the lot. When eating, he was not a pretty sight.

'Good,' he said. He tried to wipe some honey off his beard and licked the back of his hand, peeping at Will. 'Still snowing? Still coming down, is it?'

'What were you doing out in the snow?'

'Nothing,' the Walker said sullenly. 'Don't remember.' His eyes narrowed craftily, and he gestured at his forehead and said in a plaintive whine, 'Hit my head.'

'D'you remember where we found you?'

'No.'

'Do you remember who I am?'

Very promptly he shook his head. 'No.'

Will said softly again, this time in the Old Speech, 'Do you remember who I am?'

The Walker's shaggy face was expressionless. Will began to think that perhaps he really had lost his memory. He leaned over the bed to pick up the tray with its empty plate and glass, and suddenly the Walker let out a shrill scream and flinched away from him, cowering down at the far side of the bed. 'No!' he screeched. 'No! Get away! Take them away!'

Eyes wide and terrified, he was staring at Will in loathing. For a moment Will was baffled; then he realized that his sweater had lifted as he reached out his arm, and the Walker had seen the four Signs on his belt.

'Take them away!' the old man howled. 'They burn! Get them out!'

So much for lost memory, Will thought. He heard concerned feet running up the stairs, and went out of the room. Why should the Walker be terrified by the Great Signs, when he had carried one of them himself for so long?

His parents were grave. The news on the radio grew worse and worse as the cold gripped the country and one restriction followed another. In all records of temperature Britain had never been so cold; rivers that had never frozen before stood as solid ice, and every port on the entire coast was iced in. People could do little more than wait for the snow to stop; but still the snow fell.

They led a restless, enclosed life – 'like cavemen in winter', said Mr Stanton – and went to bed early to save fires and fuel. New Year's Day came and went and was scarcely noticed. The Walker lay in bed fidgeting and muttering and refused to eat anything but bread and milk, which by now was tinned milk, watered down. Mrs Stanton said kindly that he was regaining his strength, poor man. Will kept away. He was growing increasingly desperate as the cold tightened and the snow floated down and down; he felt that if he did not get out of the house soon he would find the Dark had boxed him up for ever. His mother gave him an escape, in the end. She ran out of flour, sugar, and tinned milk.

'I know nobody's supposed to leave the house

except in dire emergency,' she said anxiously, 'but really this counts as one. We do need things to eat.'

It took the boys two hours to shovel a way through the snow in their own garden to the road, where a kind of roofless tunnel, the width of one snowplough, had been kept clear. Mr Stanton had announced that only he and Robin would go to the village, but throughout the two hours Will, panting and digging, begged to be allowed to go too, and by the end his father's resistance was so much lowered that he agreed.

They wore scarves over their ears, heavy gloves, and three sweaters each under their coats. They took a torch. It was mid-morning, but the snow was coming down as relentlessly as ever, and nobody knew when they might get home. From the steep-sided cutting in the one road of the village, tiny uneven paths had been trodden and shovelled to the few shops and most of the central houses; they could see from the footprints that someone had brought horses out from Dawsons' Farm to help carve a way to the cottages of people like Miss Bell and Mrs Horniman, who could never have managed it for themselves. In the village store, Mrs Pettigrew's tiny dog was curled up in a twitching grey heap in one comer, looking limper and unhappier than ever; Mrs

Pettigrew's fat son Fred, who helped run the store, had sprained his wrist by falling in the snow and had one arm in a sling, and Mrs Pettigrew was in a state. She twittered and dithered with nervousness, she dropped things, she hunted in quite the wrong places for sugar and flour and found neither of them, and in the end she sat down suddenly in a chair, like a puppet dropped from its strings, and burst into tears.

'Oh,' she sobbed, 'I'm so sorry, Mr Stanton, it's this terrible snow. I'm so frightened, I don't know . . . I have these dreams that we're cut off, and nobody knows where we are . . .'

'We already are cut off,' said her son lugubriously. 'Not a car's been through the village for a week. And no supplies, and everyone running out – there's no butter, and not even any tinned milk. And the flour won't last long; there's only five bags after this one.'

'And nobody with any fuel,' Mrs Pettigrew sniffed. 'And the little Randall baby sick with a fever and poor Mrs Randall without a piece of coal, and goodness knows how many more—'

The shop-bell twanged as the door opened, and in the automatic village habit, everyone turned to see who had come in. A very tall man in a voluminous black overcoat, almost a cloak, was taking off his broad-brimmed hat to show a mop of white hair;

deep-shadowed eyes looked down at them over a fierce hooked nose.

'Good afternoon,' Merriman said.

'Hallo,' said Will, beaming, his world suddenly bright.

'Afternoon,' said Mrs Pettigrew, and blew her nose hard. She said, muffled by the handkerchief, 'Mr Stanton, do you know Mr Lyon? He's at the Manor.'

'How d'you do?' said Will's father.

'Butler to Miss Greythorne,' Merriman said, inclining his head respectfully. 'Until Mr Bates comes back from holiday. That is to say, when the snow stops. At present, of course, I can't get out, and Bates can't get in.'

'It'll never stop,' Mrs Pettigrew wailed, and she burst into tears again.

'Oh, *Mum*,' said fat Fred in disgust.

'I have some news for you, Mrs Pettigrew,' said Merriman in loud soothing tones. 'We have heard an announcement over the local radio – our telephone being dead, of course, like yours. There's to be a fuel and food drop in the Manor grounds, as the place most easily visible from the air in this snow. And Miss Greythorne is asking if everyone in the village would not like to move into the Manor, for the emergency. It will be crowded, of course, but warm. And comforting, perhaps. And Dr Armstrong will be there – he is already on his way, I believe.'

'That's ambitious,' Mr Stanton said reflectively. 'Almost feudal, you might say.'

Merriman's eyes narrowed slightly. 'But with no such intention.'

'Oh, no, I do see that.'

Mrs Pettigrew's tears ceased. 'What a lovely idea, Mr Lyon! Oh dear, it would be such a relief to be with other people, especially at night.'

'I'm other people,' said Fred.

'Yes, dear, but—'

Fred said stolidly, 'I'll go and get some blankets. And pack some stuff from the shop.'

'That would be wise,' Merriman said. 'The radio says the storm will grow very much worse this evening. So the sooner everyone can gather, the better.'

'Would you like some help with telling people?' Robin began pulling up his collar again.

'Excellent. That would be excellent.'

'We'll all help,' said Mr Stanton.

Will had turned to look out of the window at the mention of the storm, but the snow floating down out of the solid grey sky seemed much as before. The

windows were so misted that it was difficult to see
out of them at all, but he caught a glimpse now of
something moving outside. There was someone
out there on the snow-road carved through
Huntercombe Lane. He saw clearly only for a
second, as the figure passed the end of the
Pettigrews' path, but a second was all he needed to
recognize the man sitting erect on the great black
horse.

'The Rider has passed!' he said quickly and
clearly in the old Speech.

Merriman's head jerked round; then he collected
himself and ostentatiously swept his hat on to his
head. 'I shall be very grateful to have assistance.'

'*What* did you say, Will?' Robin, distracted, was
staring at his brother.

'Oh, nothing,' Will went to the door, making a
great fuss over buttoning his coat. 'Just thought I saw
someone.'

'But you said something in some funny language.'

'Of course I didn't. I just said "Who's that out
there?" Only it wasn't anyone anyway.'

Robin was still staring at him. 'You sounded
just like that old tramp, when he was babbling
when we first put him to bed . . .' But he was not
given to wasting time on surmise; he shook his

practical head and dropped the subject. 'Oh well.'

Merriman managed to walk closely behind Will, as they were leaving the Pettigrews' to scatter and warn the rest of the villagers. He said softly in the Old Speech, 'Get the Walker to the Manor if you can. Quickly. Or he will stop you from getting out yourself. But you may have a little trouble with your father's pride.'

By the time the Stantons reached home, after their struggling tour of the village, Will had almost forgotten what Merriman had said about his father. He was too busy working out how they could get the Walker to the Manor without actually having to carry him. He remembered only when he heard Mr Stanton talking in the kitchen, as they pulled off their coats and delivered their supplies.

'. . . good of the old girl, having everyone in there. Of course they've got the space, and the fires, and those old walls are so thick they keep the cold out better than anyone's. Much the best thing for the people from the cottages – poor Miss Bell wouldn't have lasted long . . . Still, of course, we're all right here. Self-contained. No point in adding to the manorial load.'

'Oh, Dad,' Will said impulsively, 'don't you think we ought to go too?'

'I don't think so,' said his father, with the lazy assurance that Will should have known was harder to break than any fervour.

'But Mr Lyon said it would be much more dangerous later on, because of the storm getting worse.'

I think I can make my own judgement of the weather, Will, without help from Miss Greythorne's butler,' said Mr Stanton amiably.

'Oh, wow,' said Max with cheerful rudeness. 'You rotten old snob, hark at you.'

'Come on, that's not what I meant.' His father threw a wet scarf at him. 'Inverted snobbery, more like. I simply don't see any good reason for our trooping off to partake of the bounty of the Lady of the Manor. We're perfectly all right here.'

'Quite right,' Mrs Stanton said briskly. 'Now out of the kitchen, all of you. I want to make some bread.'

The only hope, Will decided, was the Walker himself.

He slipped away and went upstairs to the tiny spare room where the Walker lay in bed. 'I want to talk to you.'

The old man turned his head on the pillow. 'All right,' he said. He seemed muted and unhappy. Suddenly Will felt sorry for him.

'Are you better?' he said. 'I mean, are you actually ill now, or do you just feel weak?'

'I am not ill,' the Walker said listlessly. 'No more than usual.'

'Can you walk?'

'You want to throw me out in the snow, is that it?'

'Of course not,' Will said. 'Mum would never let you go off in this weather, and nor would I, not that I've got much say in it. I'm the very youngest in this family, you know that.'

'You are an Old One,' the Walker said, looking at him with dislike.

'Well, that's different.'

'It's not different at all. Just means there's no point talking about yourself to me as if you were just a little kid in a family. I know better.'

Will said, 'You were guardian of one of the Great Signs – I don't see why you should seem to hate us.'

'I did what I was made to do,' the old man said. 'You took me . . . you picked me out . . .' His brows creased, as though he were trying to remember something from a long time ago; then he grew vague again. 'I was made to.'

'Well, look, I don't want to make you do anything, but there's one thing we all have to do. The snow's getting so bad that everyone in the village is going to live at the Manor, like a kind of hostel, because it'll be safer and warmer.' He felt as he talked that the Walker might know what he was going to say already, but it was impossible to get inside the old man's mind; whenever he tried, he found himself floundering, as if he had broken into the stuffing of a cushion.

'The doctor will be there too,' he said. 'So if you were to let everyone feel you needed to be somewhere with a doctor, we could all go to the Manor.'

'You mean you aren't going otherwise?' The Walker squinted suspiciously at him.

'My father won't let us. But we have to, it's safer—'

'I won't go either,' the Walker said. He turned his head away. 'Go away. Leave me be.'

Will said softly, warningly, in the Old Speech, 'The Dark will come for you.'

There was a pause. Then very slowly the Walker turned his shaggy grey head back again, and Will flinched in horror as he saw the face. For just a moment, its history was naked upon it. There were bottomless depths of pain and terror in the eyes, the lines of black experience were carved clear and terrible; this man had known somewhere such a fearful dread and anguish that nothing could really ever touch him again. His eyes were wide for the first time, stretched open, with his knowledge of horror looking out.

The Walker said emptily, '*The Dark has already come for me.*'

Will took a deep breath. 'But now the circle of the Light comes,' he said. He pulled off the belt with the Signs and held it before the Walker. The old man flinched away, screwing up his face, whimpering like a frightened animal; Will felt sickened, but there was no help for it. He brought the Signs closer and closer to the twisted old face, until, like a piece of breaking wire, the Walker's self-control snapped. He shrieked and began to babble and thrash about, screaming for help. Will ran outside and called for his father, and half the family came running.

'I think he's having some sort of fit. Awful. Shouldn't we get him to Dr Armstrong at the Manor, Dad?'

Mr Stanton said doubtfully, 'We could get the doctor to come here, perhaps.'

'But he might very well be better off there,' said Mrs Stanton, staring at the Walker in concern. 'The old man, I mean. With the doctor able to watch him – and more comfort and food. Really, this is alarming, Roger. I don't know what to do for him here.'

Will's father gave in. They left the Walker still tossing and raving, with Max near by in case of accidents, and went to turn the big family toboggan into a mobile stretcher. Only one thing nagged in Will's mind. It had to be his imagining, but in the moment when the Walker had cracked at the sight of the Great Signs, and become a mad old man once more, he had thought he saw a flash of triumph in the flickering eyes.

The sky hung grey and heavy, waiting to snow, as they left for the Manor with the Walker. Mr Stanton took the twins with him, and Will. His wife watched them go with unfamiliar nervousness. 'I hope it really is over. D'you really think Will should go?'

'Comes in handy to have someone light sometimes, in this snow,' said his father, over Will's splutter, 'He'll be all right.'

'You aren't going to stay there, are you?'

'Of course not. The only point of the exercise is to deliver the old man to the doctor. Come on, Alice, this isn't like you. There's no danger, you know.'

'I suppose not,' Mrs Stanton said.

They set off, heaving the toboggan, with the Walker strapped to it so trussed in blankets that he was invisible, a thick human sausage. Will left last;

Gwen handed him the torches and a flask. 'I must say I'm not sorry to see your discovery go,' she said. 'He frightens me. More like an animal than an old man.'

It seemed a long while before they reached the Manor gates. The drive had been cleared, and trodden down by many feet, and two bright pressure-lamps hung by the great door, lighting the front of the house. Snow was falling again, and the wind beginning to blow chill round their faces. Before Robin's outstretched hand reached the door-bell, Merriman was opening the door. He looked first for Will, though no one else noticed the urgent flicker of his eyes. 'Welcome,' he said.

'Evening,' Roger Stanton said. 'Shan't stay. We're fine at the house. But there's an old chap here who's ill, and he needs a doctor. All things considered, it seemed better to bring him here, rather than have Dr Armstrong going to and fro. So we hopped out before the storm broke.'

'It is rising already,' Merriman said, gazing out. Then he stooped and helped the twins carry the Walker's motionless swaddled form into the house. At the threshold the bundle of blankets jerked convulsively, and the Walker could be heard muffled through his covers shouting, 'No! No! No!'

'The doctor, please,' said Merriman to a woman standing near by, and she scurried away. The great empty hall where they had sung their carols was filled with people now, warm and bustling, unrecognizable.

Dr Armstrong appeared, nodding briskly all round; he was a small bustling man with a monkish fringe of grey hair circling his bald head. The Stantons, like all Huntercombe, knew him well; he had cured every ailment in the family for more years than Will had been alive. He peered at the Walker, now twisting and moaning in protest. 'What's this, eh?'

'Shock, perhaps?' said Merriman.

'He really behaves very oddly,' Mr Stanton said. 'He was found unconscious in the snow some days ago, and we thought he was recovering, but now—'

The big front door slammed itself shut in the rising wind, and the Walker screamed. 'Hum,' said the doctor, and beckoned two large young helpers to carry him off to some inner room. 'Leave him to me,' he said cheerfully. 'So far, we've got one broken leg and two sprained ankles. He'll provide variety.'

He trotted off after his patient. Will's father turned to peer out of a darkening window. 'My wife will start worrying,' he said. 'We must go.'

Merriman said gently, 'If you go now, I think you will leave but not arrive. Probably in a little while—'

'The Dark is rising, you see,' Will said.

His father looked at him with a half-smile. 'You're very poetic all of a sudden. All right, we'll wait just a bit. I could do with a breather, to tell the truth. Better say hallo to Miss Greythorne in the meantime. Where is she, Lyon?'

Merriman, the deferential butler, led the way into the crowd. It was the oddest gathering Will had ever seen. Suddenly half the village was living in close intimacy, a tiny colony of beds and suitcases and blankets. People hailed them from small nests scattered all round the huge room: a bed or a mattress tucked into a corner or fenced in by a chair or two. Miss Bell waved gaily from a sofa. It was like an untidy hotel with everyone camping in the foyer. Miss Greythorne was sitting stiff and upright in her wheelchair beside the fire, reading *The Phoenix and the Carpet* to a speechless group of village children. Like everyone else in the room, she looked uncommonly bright and cheerful.

'Funny,' Will said, as they picked their way through. 'Things are absolutely awful and yet people look much happier than usual. Look at them all. Bubbling.'

'They are English,' Merriman said.

'Quite right,' said Will's father. 'Splendid in adversity, tedious when safe. Never content, in fact. We're an odd lot. You're not English, are you?' he said suddenly to Merriman, and Will was astonished to hear a slightly hostile note in his voice.

'A mongrel,' Merriman said blandly. 'It's a long story.' His deep-set eyes glittered down at Mr Stanton, and then Miss Greythorne caught sight of them all.

'Ah, there you are! Evenin', Mr Stanton, boys, how are you? What d'you think of this, eh? Isn't it a lark?' As she put down the book, the circle of children parted to admit the newcomers, and the twins and their father were absorbed into talk.

Merriman said softly to Will, in the Old Speech, 'Look into the fire, for the length of time that it takes you to trace the shape of each of the Great Signs with your right hand. Look into the fire. Make it your friend. Do not move your eyes for all that time.'

Wondering, Will moved forward as if to warm himself, and did as he was told. Staring at the leaping flames of the enormous log fire in the hearth, he ran his fingers gently over the Sign of Iron, the Sign of Bronze, the Sign of Wood, the Sign of Stone. He spoke to the fire, not as he had done long ago, when challenged to put it out, but as an Old One, out of Gramarye. He spoke to it of the red fire in the king's hall, of the blue fire dancing over the marshes, of the yellow fire lighted on the beacon hills for Beltane and Hallowe'en; of wild-fire and need-fire and the cold fire of the sea; of the sun and of the stars. The flames leaped. His fingers reached the end of their journey round the last Sign. He looked up. He looked, and he saw . . .

. . . he saw, not the genial muddle of collected villagers in a tall, panelled mdern room, lit by electric standard lamps, but the great candle-shadowed stone hall, with its tapestry hangings and high vaulted roof, that he had seen once before, a world ago. He looked up from the log fire that was the same fire, but blazing now in a different hearth, and he saw as before, out of the past, the two heavy carved chairs, one on either side of the fireplace. In the chair on the right sat Merriman, cloaked, and in the chair on the left sat a figure whom he had last seen, not a day before, lying on a bier as if dead. He bent quickly and knelt at the old lady's feet. 'Madam,' he said.

She touched his hair gently. 'Will.'

'I am sorry for breaking the circle, that first time,' he said. 'Are you – well – now?'

'Everything is well,' she said in her soft clear voice. 'And will be, if we can win the last battle for the Signs.'

'What must I do?'

'Break the power of the cold. Stop the snow and cold and frost. Release this country from the hold of the Dark. All with the next of the circle, the Sign of Fire.'

Will looked at her helplessly. 'But I haven't got it. I don't know how.'

'One sign of fire you have with you already. The other waits. In its winning, you will break the cold. But before that, our own circle of flame must be completed, that is an echo of the Sign, and to do that you must take power away from the Dark.' She pointed to the great wrought-iron ring of candle-sockets on the table, the circle quartered by a cross. As she raised her arm, the light glinted on the rose ring on her hand. The outer ring of candles was complete, twelve white columns burning exactly as they had when Will was last in the hall. But the cross-arms still stood empty-socketed; nine holes gaped.

Will stared at them unhappily. This part of his quest left him in despair. Nine great enchanted candles, to come out of nowhere. Power to be seized from the Dark. A Sign that he had already, without knowing it. Another that he must find without knowing where or how.

'Have courage,' the old lady said. Her voice was faint and tired; when Will looked at her, he saw that she herself seemed faint in outline, as if she were no more than a shadow. He reached out his hand in concern, but she drew back her arm. 'Not yet . . . There is another kind of work to be done yet, too . . . You see how the candles burn, Will.' Her voice dwindled, then rallied. 'They will show you.'

Will looked at the brilliant candle flames; the tall ring of light held his eyes. As he looked, he felt a strange jolting sensation, as if the whole world had shuddered. He looked up, and he saw . . .

. . . and he saw, when he raised his eyes, that he was back in the manor of Miss Greythorne's time, Will Stanton's time, with the panelled walls and the murmur of many voices, and one voice speaking in his ear. It was Dr Armstrong.

'. . . asking for you,' he was saying. Mr Stanton was standing beside him. The doctor paused and looked oddly at Will. 'Are you all right, young man?'

'Yes – yes, I'm fine. Sorry. What was it you said?'

'I was saying that your old tramp friend is asking

for you. "The seventh son", he lyrically puts it, though how he knew that I can't say.'

'I am though, aren't I?' Will said. 'I didn't know till the other day about the little brother who died. Tom.'

Dr Armstrong's eyes went a long way away for a moment. 'Tom,' he said. 'The first baby. I remember. That's a while ago.' His gaze came back. 'Yes, you are. So's your father, for that matter.'

Will's head jerked round, and he saw his father grin.

'You were a seventh son, Dad?'

'Certainly,' Roger Stanton said, his round pink face reminiscent. 'Half the family was killed in the last war, but there were twelve of us once. You knew that, didn't you? Proper tribe, it was. Your mother loved it, being an only child herself. I dare say that's why she had all you lot. Appalling, in this over-populated age. Yes, you're the seventh son of a seventh son – we used to joke about it when you were a baby. But not later on, in case you got ideas about having second sight, or whatever it is they say.'

'Ha, ha,' said Will with some effort. 'Did you find out what's wrong with the old tramp, Dr Armstrong?'

'To tell you the truth he has me rather confused,'

the doctor said. 'He should have a sedative in his disturbed state, but he's got the lowest pulse rate and blood pressure I've ever come across in my life, so I don't know ... There's nothing physically wrong with him, so far as I can tell. Probably he's just feeble-minded, like so many of these old wanderers – not that you see many of them nowadays. They've nearly disappeared. Anyway, he keeps shouting to see you, Will, so if you can put up with it I'll take you in for a moment. He's harmless enough.'

The Walker was making a lot of noise. He stopped when he saw Will, and his eyes narrowed. His mood had clearly changed; he was confident again, the lined, triangular face bright. He looked over Will's shoulder at Mr Stanton and the doctor. 'Go away,' he said.

'Hum,' said Dr Armstrong, but he drew Will's father with him nearer the door, within sight but out of earshot. In the small cloakroom that was serving as sick-bay, one other casualty – the broken leg – lay in bed, but he appeared to be asleep.

'You can't keep me here,' the Walker hissed. 'The Rider will come for me.'

'You were scared stiff of the Rider once,' Will said. 'I saw you. Have you forgotten that too?'

'I forget nothing,' the Walker said scornfully.

'That fear is gone. It went when the Sign left me. Let me go, let me get out to my people.' A curious stiff formality seemed to be coming into his speech.

'Your people didn't mind leaving you to die in the snow,' Will said. 'Anyway I'm not keeping you here. I just had you brought to the doctor. You can hardly expect him to let you go out in the middle of a storm.'

'Then the Rider will come,' the old man said. His eyes glittered, and he raised his voice so that he was shrieking to everyone in the room. 'The Rider will come! The Rider will come!'

Will left him, as his father and the doctor came rapidly towards the bed.

'What on earth was all that about?' said Mr Stanton.

The Walker, with the doctor bending over him, had fallen back and lapsed into angry mumbling again.

'Goodness knows,' said Will. 'He was just talking nonsense. I think Dr Armstrong's right, he's a bit cracked.' He looked all round the room, but saw no sign of Merriman.

'What's happened to Mr Lyon?'

'He's somewhere,' his father said vaguely. 'Find the twins, would you, Will? I'll go and see if the storm's dropped enough to let us out yet.'

Will stood in the bustling hall, as people came and went with blankets and pillows, cups of tea, sandwiches from the kitchen, empty plates going back again. He felt odd, detached, as though he were suspended in the middle of this preoccupied world and yet not part of it. He looked at the great hearth. Even the roar of the flames could not drown out the howling wind outside, and the lash of icy snow against the window-panes.

The flames leapt, holding Will's eyes. From somewhere outside Time, Merriman said into his mind: *'Take care. It is true. The Rider will come for him. That is why I had you bring him here, to a place strengthened by Time. The Rider would have come to your own house otherwise, and all that comes with the Rider too . . .'*

'Will!' Miss Greythorne's imperious contralto came ringing. 'Come over here!' And Will looked back into the present, and went to her. He saw Robin beside her chair, and Paul approaching with a long flat box of a familiar shape in his hands.

'We thought we'd have a kind of concert until the wind drops,' said Miss Greythorne briskly. 'Everyone doin' a little bit. Everyone who fancies the idea, that is. A cailey, or whatever the Scots call 'em.'

Will looked at the happy gleam in his brother's eye. 'And Paul's going to play that old flute of yours that he likes so much.'

'In due course,' Paul said. 'And you're going to sing.'

'All right.' Will looked at Robin.

'I,' said Robin, 'am going to lead the applause. There'll be a lot of that – we appear to be a madly talented village. Miss Bell will recite a poem, three boys from the Dorney end have a folk group – two of them even brought their guitars. Old Mr Dewhurst will do a monologue, just try and stop him. Somebody's little daughter wants to dance. There's no end to it.'

'I thought, Will,' said Miss Greythorne, 'that perhaps you would begin. If you were just to start singing, you know, anything you like, then gradually people would stop to listen until there'd be a complete hush – much better than me ringin' a bell or something and saying, "We will all now have a concert", don't you agree?'

'I suppose so, yes,' said Will, though nothing could have been further from his mind at that moment than the idea of making peaceful music. He thought briefly, and into his mind came a melancholy little song that the school music master had transposed for his voice just the term before, as an experiment. Feeling rather a show-off, Will opened his mouth where he stood, and began to sing.

'White in the moon the long road lies,
The moon stands blank above;
White in the moon the long road lies
That leads me from my love.

Still hangs the edge without a gust,
Still, still the shadows stay:
My feet upon the moonlit dust
Pursue the ceaseless way.'

The talking around him fell away into silence. He saw faces turned in his direction, and nearly dropped a note as he recognized some that he had hoped to see, but had not found before. There they were, keeping quietly in the background; Farmer Dawson, Old George, John Smith and his wife, the Old Ones ready again to make their circle if need be. Near by was the rest of the Dawson family, Will's father standing with them.

'The world is round, so travellers tell,
And straight though reach the track,

Trudge on, trudge on, 'twill all be well,
The way will guide one back.'

From the corner of one eye he saw, with a shock, the figure of the Walker; with a blanket wrapped round him like a cloak, the old man was standing in the doorway of the little sickroom, listening. For an instant Will saw his face, and was astonished. All guile and terror were gone from that lined triangle; there was only sadness on it, and hopeless longing. There was even a glint of tears in the eyes. It was the face of a man shown something immensely precious that he had lost.

For a second, Will felt that with his music he could draw the Walker into the Light. He gazed at him as he sang, making the plaintive notes an appeal, and the Walker stood limp and unhappy, looking back.

'But ere the circle homeward hies
Far, far must it remove;
White in the moon the long road lies
That leads me from my love.'

The room had stilled dramatically as he sang, and the boy's clear soprano that always seemed to belong to a stranger soared high and remote through the air. Now there was a small silence, the only part of performing that really meant anything to him, and afterwards quite a lot of clapping. Will heard it from a long way away. Miss Greythorne called to them all, 'We thought, to pass the time, that anyone who feels inclined might do a little entertainin'. To drown out the storm. Who'd like to join in?'

There was a cheerful buzz of voices, and Paul began to play the old Manor flute, very soft and low. Its gentle sweetness filled the room, and Will stood more confidently as he listened and thought of the Light. But in the next moment the music could no longer bring him strength. He could not hear it at all. His hair prickled, his bones ached; he knew that something, somebody was coming near, wishing ill to the Manor and all inside it, and most of all himself.

The wind rose. It whipped screeching at the window. There was a tremendous thump of a knock at the door. Across the room, the Walker jumped up, his face twisted again, tight with waiting. Paul played, unhearing. The crashing knock came again. None of them could hear, Will realized suddenly; though the wind was near to deafening him, it was not for their ears, nor would they know what was happening now. The crash came a third time, and he knew that he was bound to answer. He walked along through unheeding people to the door, took hold of the big iron circle that was the handle, muttered some words under his breath in the Old Speech, and flung open the door.

Snow spat in at him, sleet slashed his face, winds whistled through the hall. Out in the darkness, the great black horse reared up high over Will's head, hooves flailing, eyes rolling white, the foam flying from bared teeth. And above it gleamed the blue eyes of the Rider and the flaring red of his hair. In spite of himself Will cried out, and threw up one arm instinctively in self-defence.

And the black stallion screamed and fell back with the Rider into the Dark; and the door swung shut, and there was all at once nothing in Will's ears except the sweet lilt of the old flute as Paul played on. People sat and sprawled tranquilly about just as they had before. Slowly Will brought down his arm, still crooked defensively up over his head, and as he did so he noticed something that he had totally for-gotten. On the underside of the forearm, which had been facing the Black Rider when he threw up his arm, was the burned-in scar of the Sign of Iron. In that other great hall, the first time, he had burned himself on the Sign when the Dark was making its first attempt on him. The Lady had healed the burn. Will had forgotten it was there. '*One sign of fire you have with you already . . .*'

So that was what she had meant.

One sign of fire had kept the Dark at bay; driven it out of its strongest attack, perhaps. Will leaned limply against the wall, and tried to breathe more slowly. But as he looked across the tranquil crowd listening to their music, he saw again a figure that sent all his confidence crashing into nothing, and the quick instinct of Gramarye told him that he had been tricked. He had thought he was out-facing a challenge, and so he was. But in doing it, he had opened the door between the Dark and the Walker, and thus in some way so strengthened the Walker that the old man had gained a power he had been waiting for.

For the Walker was standing tall now, his eyes bright, his head flung up, and his back straight. He held one arm high, and called out in a strong clear voice: 'Come wolf, come hound, come cat, come rat, come Held, come Holda, I call you in! Come Ura, come Tann, come Coll, come Quert, come Morra, come Master, I bring you in!'

The summons went on, a long list of names, all

familiar to Will from the Book of Gramarye. In Miss Greythorne's hall, no one could see or hear; all went on as before, and through the ending of Paul's music, and the loud determined beginning of old Mr Dewhurst's monologue, no eyes that glanced in Will's direction seemed to see him. He wondered whether his father, still standing talking to the Dawsons, would shortly notice that his youngest son was not to be seen.

But very soon as the ringing summons from the Walker went on and on, he ceased to wonder, for under his senses the hall began subtly to change; the old hall of the Lady came back into his consciousness and absorbed more and more of the appearance of the present. Friends and family faded; only the Walker remained clear as before, standing now at the far end of the great hall away from the fire. And while Will still stared at the group in which his father stood, even while it faded he saw take place the doubling by which the Old Ones were able to move themselves in and out of Time. He saw one form of Frank Dawson step easily out of the first, leaving his other self to fade as part of the present; the second form grew clearer and clearer as it came towards him, and after it in the same way came Old George, Young John, and the blue-eyed woman, and

Will knew this had been the manner of his own arrival too.

Soon the four were grouped round him in the centre of the Lady's hall, each facing outward, four corners of a square. And as the Walker called his long summons of the Dark, the hall itself began again to change. Strange lights and flames flickered along the walls, obscuring the windows and hangings. Here and there at the sound of a particular name, blue fire would dart up into the air, hiss, and die down again. On each of the three walls facing the hearth, three great sinister flames shot up which did not afterwards die down, but remained dancing and curving in ominous brilliance, filling the hall with cold light.

Before the hearth, in the big carved chair he had occupied from the beginning, Merriman sat motionless. There was a terrible restrained strength in his sitting; Will looked at the broad shoulders with foreboding, as he would have looked at a gigantic spring that might at any moment snap loose.

The Walker chanted louder: 'Come Uath, come Truith, come Eriu, come Loth! Come Heurgo, come Celmis, I bring you in . . .'

Merriman stood up, a great black white-plumed pillar. His cloak was wrapped round him. Only his carved-stone face was clear, with the light blazing in his mass of white hair. The Walker looked at him and faltered. Thick round the hall, the fires and flames of the Dark hissed and danced, all white and blue and black, with no gold or red or warm yellow in any. The nine tallest flames stood up like menacing trees.

But the Walker seemed to have lost his voice again. He looked once more at Merriman and shrank back a little. And through the mixture of longing and fear in the bright eyes, suddenly Will knew him.

'Hawkin,' Merriman said softly, 'there is still time to come home.'

The Hawk in the Dark

T he Walker said in a whisper, 'No.'
'Hawkin,' Merriman said again, gently, 'every
man has a last choice after the first, a chance of for-
giveness. It is not too late. Turn. Come to the Light.'

The voice was scarcely audible, a mere husking
breath. 'No.'

The flames hung still and stately round the great
hall. No one moved.

'Hawkin,' Merriman said, and there was no
command in the tone but only warmth and entreaty.
'Hawkin, liege man, turn away from the Dark. Try to
remember. There was love and trust between us,
once.'

The Walker stared at him like a doomed man,
and now in the pointed, lined face Will could see
clearly the traces of the small, bright man Hawkin,
who had been brought forward out of his time for
the retrieving of the Book of Gramarye, and had

through the shock of facing death betrayed the Old Ones to the Dark. He remembered the pain that had been in Merriman's eyes as they watched that betrayal begin, and the terrible certainty with which he had contemplated Hawkin's doom.

The Walker still stared at Merriman, but his eyes did not see. They looked back through time, as the old man rediscovered all that he had forgotten, or pushed out of his mind. He said slowly, with mounting reproach, 'You made me risk my life for a book. For a book. Then because I looked at kinder masters, you sent me back to my own time, but not as I had been before. You gave me then the doom of bearing the Sign.' His voice grew stronger with pain and resentment as he remembered. 'The Sign of Bronze, through the centuries. You changed me from a man into a creature always running, always searching, always hunted. You stopped me from growing decently old in my own time, as all men after their lives grow old and tired and sink to sleep in death. You took away my right to death. You set me in my own century with the Sign, long, long ago, and you made me carry it through six hundred years until this age.'

His eyes flickered towards Will, and flashed with hatred. 'Until the last of the Old Ones should be born, to take the Sign from me. You, boy, it is all through you. This turning in time, that took away my good life as a man, it was all on your account. Before you were born, and after. For your damned gift of Gramarye, I lost everything I had ever loved.'

'I tell you,' Merriman cried out, 'you may come home, Hawkin! Now! It is the last chance, and you may turn to the Light and be as you were.' His proud, towering figure leaned forward, beseeching, and Will felt pain for him, knowing that he felt it was his own misjudgement that had brought his servant Hawkin into betrayal and the life of the wretched Walker, a whining shell committed to the Dark.

Merriman said huskily: 'I pray you, my son.'

'No,' the Walker said. 'I found better masters than you.' The nine flames of the Dark round the walls sprang cold and high and burned with a blue light, quivering. He clutched closer at the dark blanket wrapped round him, and stared wildly about the hall. Shrilly defiant, he shouted, 'Masters of the Dark, I bring you in!'

And the nine flames moved in closer from the walls to the centre of the room, approaching Will and the four outward-facing Old Ones. Will was blinded by their blue-white brilliance; he could no longer see the Walker. Somewhere beyond the great lights, the shrill voice shrieked on, high and mad with bitterness. 'You risked my life for the Book! You made me carry the Sign! You let the Dark hound me through the centuries, but never let me die! Now it is your turn!'

'Your turn! Your turn!' echoed the scream round the walls. The nine tall flames moved slowly closer, and the Old Ones stood in the centre of the floor and watched them approach. Beside the hearth Merriman turned slowly towards the centre of the room. Will saw that his face was impassive again, the deep eyes dark and empty and the lines drawn firm, and he knew that no one would see any strong self-revealing emotion on that face for a very long time. The Walker's chance to turn back to the mind and heart of Hawkin had come and been rejected, and now it was gone for ever.

Merriman raised both his arms, and the cloak fell from them like wings. His deep voice whipped into the crackling silence: 'Stop!'

The nine flames paused, and hung.

'In the name of the Circle of Signs,' Merriman said, clear and firm, 'I command you to leave this house.'

The cold light of the Dark that was all around

the hall behind the great standing flames flickered and crackled like laughter. And out of the blackness beyond, the voice of the Black Rider came.

'Your circle is not complete and has not that force,' he called mockingly. 'And your liege man has called us into this house, as he did before, and can again. *Our* liege man, my lord. The hawk is in the Dark . . . You can drive us from here no longer. Not with flame, nor force, nor conjoined power. We shall break your Sign of Fire before it can be released, and your Circle will never be joined. It will break in the cold, my lord, in the Dark and the cold . . .'

Will shivered. It was growing cold indeed in the hall, very cold. The air was like a current of chill water, coming at them from all sides. The fire in the great hearth gave out no warmth now, no warmth that was not sucked in by the cold blue flames of the Dark all around. The nine flames quivered again, and as he looked at them, he could have sworn that they were not flames but gigantic icicles, blue-white as before but solid, menacing, great pillars ready to topple inward and crush them all with weight and cold.

'. . . cold . . .' said the Black Rider softly from the shadows, '. . . cold . . .'

Will looked at Merriman in alarm. He knew that

each of them, every Old One in the room, had been thrusting against the Dark with every power he possessed since the Rider's voice began, and he knew that none of it had had any effect.

Merriman said softly, 'Hawkin lets them in, as he did in his first betrayal, and we cannot prevent that. He had my trust once, and it gives him still that power even though the trust is gone. Our only hope is what it was in the beginning: that Hawkin is no more than a man . . . When the spells of the deep cold are made, there is little that can be done against them.'

He stood frowning as the ring of blue-white fire flickered and danced; even he looked cold, with a dark pinched look round the bones of his face. 'They bring in the deep cold,' he said, half to himself. 'The cold of the void, of black space . . .'

And the cold grew more and more intense, cutting through the body to the mind. Yet the flames of the Dark seemed at the same time to grow dim, and Will realized that his own century was again fading in around them, and that they were back in Miss Greythorne's manor.

And the cold was there too.

Everything was changing now; the murmur of voices had dropped from a cheerful buzz to an anxious mutter, and the tall room was only dimly lit, by candles set in candlesticks and cups and plates, wherever there was space. All the bright electric lamps were dark, and the long metal radiators that warmed most of the room gave off no heat.

Merriman swooped bafflingly up near him with the speed of one returned from a brisk errand; his cloak was subtly different, changed to the sweeping overcoat he had worn earlier that day. He said to Miss Greythorne, 'There's not much we can do down there, ma'am. The furnace is out, of course. All the electric power lines are quite dead. So is the telephone. I have had all the house blankets and quilts brought out, and Miss Hampton is making quantities of soup and hot drinks.'

Miss Greythorne nodded in brisk approval. 'Good thing we kept the old gas stoves. They wanted me to change, y'know, Lyon, when we had the central heating done. I wouldn't, though. Electricity, bah – always knew the old house didn't approve.'

'I am having as much wood as possible brought in to keep the fire up,' Merriman said, but in the same instant, as if in mockery, a great hissing and steaming came from the broad fireplace, and those nearest it jerked away, choking and spluttering. Through the sudden inblown cloud of smoke Will could see Frank Dawson and Old George working to clear something out of the fire.

But the fire had gone out.

'Snow down the chimney!' Farmer Dawson called, coughing. 'We'll need buckets, Merry, quickly. There's a right mess here.'

'I'll go,' Will shouted, and bolted for the kitchen, glad of the chance to move. But before he could get to the door through the huddled groups of chilled, frightened people, a figure rose up before him to block his way, and two hands caught his arms in a grip so tight that he gasped in sudden pain. Bright eyes bored into his, glittering with wild triumph, and the Walker's high, thin voice was screeching in his ear.

'Old One, Old One, last of the Old Ones, you know what's going to happen to you? The cold is coming in, and the Dark will freeze you. Cold and stiff and all of you helpless. No one to protect the little Signs on your belt.'

'Let go!' Will twisted angrily, but the old man's hold on his wrist was the clasp of madness.

'And you know who will take the little Signs, Old One? I shall. The poor Walker, I shall wear them. They are promised to me in reward for my services – no lords of the Light ever offered me such reward.

Or any other . . . I shall be the Sign-seeker, I shall, and all that would have been yours at the last shall come to me . . .'

He grabbed for Will's belt, his face twisted with triumph, spittle ringing his mouth like foam, and Will yelled for help. In an instant John Smith was at his side with Dr Armstrong close behind, and the big smith had pinned the Walker's clutching hands behind his back. The old man cursed and shrieked, his eyes burning with hatred at Will, and both men had to struggle to hold him back. At length they had him trapped and harmless, and Dr Armstrong drew back with an exasperated sigh.

'This chap must be the only warm object in the country,' he said. 'Of all times to run berserk – pulse or no pulse I'm going to put him to sleep for a while. He's a danger to the community and to himself.'

Will thought rubbing his sore wrist: if you only knew quite what sort of danger he is . . . Then suddenly he began to see what Merriman had meant. *Our only hope is what it was in the beginning: that Hawkin is no more than a man . . .*

'Keep him there, John, while I get my bag.' The doctor disappeared. John Smith, one big fist grasping the Walker's shoulder and the other both his wrists, winked encouragingly at Will and jerked his head to the kitchen; Will suddenly remembered his original errand, and ran. When he came tearing back with two empty buckets swinging from each hand, there was a fresh commotion at the fireplace; a new hissing had begun, smoke spewed out, and Frank Dawson came staggering backwards.

'Hopeless!' he said furiously. 'Hopeless! You get the hearth clear for a moment and more snow comes pouring down. And the cold—' He looked despairingly about him. 'Look at them, Will.'

The room was misery and chaos: small babies wailing, parents huddling their bodies round their children to keep them warm enough to breathe. Will rubbed his chill hands together, and tried to feel his feet and his face through the numbness of cold. The room was becoming colder and colder, and from the freezing world outside there was no sound even of the wind. The sense of being within two levels of Time at once still hovered in his mind, though all that he could feel now of the ancient manor was the awareness, ominous and persistent, of the nine great ice-candles glimmering round three sides of the room. They had been ghost-like, scarcely visible, when first he found himself brought back by the new cold to his own time, but as the cold grew more intense, so they were growing clearer. Will stared at them. He knew that somehow they embodied the power of the Dark at its Midwinter peak; yet he knew too that they were part of an independent magic harnessed by the Dark, which like so much else in their long battle could be taken away by the Light if only the right thing were done at the right time. How? *How?*

Dr Armstrong was coming back towards the sickroom with his black bag. Perhaps there might after all be one way, just one, of stopping the Dark before the cold could reach the point of destruction. One man, unwitting, giving help to another: this might be the one small event to turn aside all the supernatural force of the Dark . . . Will waited, suddenly taut with excitement. The doctor moved towards the Walker, who still cursed incoherently in John Smith's grip, and he had slipped a needle deftly in and out of his arm before the old man knew what he was doing. 'There,' he said soothingly. 'That'll help you. Have a sleep.'

Instinctively Will moved forward in case there was need of help, and saw as he did so that Merriman and Farmer Dawson and Old George were drifting closer too. Doctor and patient were closed in by a ring of Old Ones, all round, protecting against interference.

The Walker caught sight of Will and snarled like a dog, showing broken, yellowing teeth. 'Freeze, you'll freeze,' he spat out at him, 'and the Signs will be mine, whatever . . . you try . . . whatever . . .' But he faltered and blinked, his voice dropping as the drug began to spread its drowsiness over him, and even as suspicion began to show in his eyes, the eyelids drooped. Each of the Old Ones took a step or two forward, tightening the circle. The old man blinked again, showing the whites of his eyes in a horrid flash, and then he was unconscious.

And with the mind of the Walker closed, the Dark's way into the house was closed too.

Instantly there was a difference in the room, a slackening of tension. The cold was less fierce, the unhappiness and alarm all round them like a fog began to lessen. Dr Armstrong straightened up, a questing, puzzled expression in his eyes; the eyes grew wider as he saw the circle of intent faces ringing him round. He began indignantly, 'What do—?'

But the rest of the words were lost to Will, for all at once Merriman was calling them out of the crowd, urgently, silently, in the speech of the mind that men could not hear. '*The candles! The candles of the winter! Take them, before they fade!*'

The four Old Ones scattered hastily into the hall,

where the strange blue-white cylinders still hung ghostly round the three walls, burning with their dead cold flames. Going swiftly to the candles, they grasped them, one in each hand; Will, smaller, leapt hastily on a chair to seize the last. It was cold and smooth and heavy to his touch, like ice that did not melt. In the moment that he touched it he was giddy; his head whirled . . .

. . . and he was back in the great hall of that earlier time with the other four, and beside the hearth the Lady was sitting in her high-backed chair again, with the smith's blue-eyed wife sitting at her feet.

It was clear what was to be done. Bearing the candles of the Dark, they advanced towards the great iron mandala-ring of holders on the massive table, and one by one fitted the candles into the nine sockets that still stood empty in the central cross-piece. Each candle changed subtly as it was put in place; its flame rose thinner and higher, taking on a golden-white tinge instead of the cold, threatening blue. Will, with his one candle, came last. He reached through to fit it into the last holder in the very centre of the pattern, and as he did so the flames of all the candles shot upwards in a triumphant circle of fire.

The old lady said, in her frail voice, 'There is the power seized from the Dark, Will Stanton. By cold magic they called up the candles of winter for destruction. But now that we have seized them for better purposes, the candles become stronger, able to bring you the Sign of Fire. See.'

They drew back, watching, and the last central candle that Will had put in place began to grow. When its flame stood high above the rest it took on colour, becoming yellow, orange, vermilion-red; as it still grew, it changed and became a strange flower on a strange stem. A curved, many-petalled blossom blazed there, each petal a different shade of the colours of flame; slowly and gracefully each petal opened and fell, floating away, melting into the air. And in the end, at the tip of the long curved stem of the flame-red plant, a glowing round seedpod was left, waving gently for a moment and then in a quick, silent burst breaking open, its five sides unfolding all at once like stiffer petals. Inside was a golden-red circle of a shape they all knew.

The Lady said: 'Take it, Will.'

Will took two wondering paces towards the table, and the great slender stalk bent over towards him; as he put out his hand, the golden circle fell into it. Instantly a surge of invisible power struck him, an echo of what he had felt at the destruction of the Book of Gramarye – and as he staggered and balanced himself again, he saw that the table was empty. In a flash of time, everything that was on it had vanished: the strange flower and the nine great blazing candles and the Sign-shaped iron holder that had contained them all. Gone. All gone: all except the Sign of Fire.

It was in his palm, warm to the touch, one of the most beautiful things he had ever seen. Gold of several different colours had been beaten together with great craftsmanship to make its crossed-circle shape, and on all sides it was set with tiny gems, rubies and emeralds and sapphires and diamonds, in strange runic patterns that looked oddly familiar to Will. It glittered and gleamed in his hand like all kinds of fire that ever were. Looking closer, he saw some words written very small around the outer edge:

LIHT MEC HEHT GEWYRCAN

Merriman said softly: 'The Light ordered that I should be made.'

They had all but one of the Signs now. Jubilantly Will flung up his arm into the air, holding the Sign high for the others to see; and from every light in the hall the circle of worked gold caught brilliance, flickering as if it were made of flame.

From somewhere outside the hall, there came a great crashing roar with a long wail of anger through it. The sound rumbled and growled and came crashing out again . . .

. . . and as it beat in his ears, suddenly Will was back again in Miss Greythorne's hall, with all around him the familiar village faces turned wondering to the roof, and to the grumbling roar beyond.

'Thunder?' someone said, puzzled.

Blue light flickered in all the windows, and the thunder slammed so earsplittingly close that everyone flinched. Again the light came, again the thudding roar, and somewhere a child began to weep, thin and high. But as all the crowded room waited for the next crash, there was nothing. No flash came, no thunder, not so much as a distant murmur. Instead, after a short breathless silence filled only by the hissing of the ashes in the herth, there came a soft pattering sound outside, growing gently, gradually louder into an unmistakable slurred staccato against windows and doors and roof.

The same anonymous voice cried out joyfully, 'Rain!'

Voices broke out all round in excitement, grim faces beamed; figures rushed to peer out of the dark windows, beckoning to others in delight. An old man Will never recalled seeing in his life before turned to him with a toothless grin. 'Rain'll melt thic snow!' he piped. 'Melt 'n in no time at all!'

Robin appeared out of the crowd. 'Ah, there you are. Am I going loopy, or does this perishing room suddenly feel warm?'

'It's warmer,' said Will, pulling down his sweater. Beneath it, the Sign of Fire was now looped on his belt secure with the rest.

'Funny. It was so hideously cold for a while. I suppose they've got the central heating going again . . .'

'Let's see the rain!' A pair of boys dashed past them to the main door. But while they still fumbled with the handle, a series of quick, loud knocks came from outside; and there on the step, when the door opened, his hair flattened to his head by the soft, pouring rain, stood Max.

He was out of breath; they could see him urgently gulp air to make the words. 'Miss Greythorne there? My father?'

Will felt a hand on his shoulder and saw Merriman beside him, and knew from the concern in his eyes that in some way this was the next attack of the Dark. Max caught sight of him and came forward, rain running down his face; he shook himself like a dog.

'Get Dad, Will,' he said. 'And the doctor if he can be spared. Mum's had an accident, she fell downstairs. She's still unconscious, and we think she's got a broken leg.'

Mr Stanton had already heard; he dashed for the doctor's room. Will stared unhappily at Max. He called silently to Merriman, frightened, 'Did they do that? Did they? The Lady said—'

'It's possible,' said the answering voice in his mind. 'They cannot harm you, true, and they cannot destroy men. But they can encourage men's own instincts to do them harm. Or bring an unexpected clap of thunder, when someone is standing at the top of a flight of stairs . . .'

Will heard no more than that. He was out of the door with his father and brothers and Dr Armstrong, following Max home.

The King of Fire and Water

James still looked pale and distressed, even when the doctor was safely arrived and examining Mrs Stanton in the living-room. He drew aside his nearest brothers, who happened to be Paul and Will, and moved them out of earshot of the rest. He said unhappily, 'Mary's disappeared.'

'Disappeared?'

'Honestly. I told her not to go. I didn't think she would, I thought she'd be too scared.' Worry had sent stoical James close to tears.

'Go where?' said Paul sharply.

'Out to the Manor. It was after Max went to get you. Gwennie and Bar were in the living-room with Mum. Mary and I were in the kitchen making some tea, and she got all upset and said Max had been gone far too long and we ought to go and check whether anything had happened to him. I told her not to be so daft, of course we shouldn't go, but just then Gwen called me to go and make up the fire in there, and when I came back, Mary was gone. And so were her coat and boots.' He sniffed. 'I couldn't see any sign of where she'd gone, outside – the rain had started, and there weren't any footprints. I was just going to go out after her without saying anything, because the girls had enough to worry about, but then you came, and I thought she'd be with you. Only she wasn't. Oh, dear,' said James woefully. 'She is a silly ass.'

'Never mind,' Paul said. 'She can't have gone far. Just go and wait for a good moment to explain to Dad, and tell him I've gone out to pick her up. I'll take Will, we're both still dressed for it.'

'Good,' said Will, who had hastily been trying to think of arguments for his going.

When they were out in the rain again, the snow already beginning to squelch grey-white underfoot, Paul said, 'Don't you think it's time you told me what all this is about?'

'What?' said Will, astounded.

'What are you mixed up in?' Paul said, his pale blue eyes peering severely through the heavy-spectacles.

'Nothing.'

'Look. If Mary's going off might have something

to do with it, you've absolutely got to explain.'

'Oh dear,' Will said. He looked at Paul's threatening determination, and wondered how you explained to an elder brother that an eleven-year-old was no longer quite an eleven-year-old, but a creature subtly different from the human race, fighting for its survival . . .

You didn't, of course.

He said, 'It's these, I think.' Glancing cautiously about him, he tugged his jacket and sweater clear of his belt and showed Paul the Signs. 'They're antiques. Just buckle things that Mr Dawson gave me for my birthday, but they must be really valuable because two or three weird people keep on turning up trying to get hold of them. One man chased me in Huntercombe Lane once . . . and that old tramp was mixed up with them somehow. That was why I didn't want to bring him home, that day we found him in the snow.'

He thought how very improbable it all sounded.

'Mmm,' Paul said. 'And that fellow at the Manor, the new butler? Lyon, isn't it? Is he mixed up with these clowns?'

'Oh, no,' Will said hastily. 'He's a friend of mine.'

Paul looked at him for a moment, expressionless. Will thought of his patient understanding that night in the attic, at the beginning, and of the way he played the old flute and knew that if there were any one of his brothers that he could confide in, it would be Paul. But that was out of the question.

Paul said, 'Obviously you haven't told me the half of it, but that'll have to do. I take it you think these antique-chasers might have nobbled Mary as some sort of hostage?'

They had reached the end of the driveway. The rain beat down on them, hard yet not vicious; it ran down the snow-banks, poured from the trees, turned the road into the beginning of a rapidly moving stream. They looked up and down in vain. Will said, 'They must have. I mean, she'd have gone straight towards the Manor, so why didn't we see her on our way home?'

'We'll go that way anyway, to check.' Paul tilted his head suddenly and glared at the sky. 'This rain! It's ridiculous! Just suddenly, out of all that snow – and it's so much warmer too. Makes no sense.' He splashed off up the running stream that was Huntercombe Lane and glanced at Will with a baffled half-grin. 'But then a lot of things aren't making much sense to me at the moment.'

'Ah,' Will said. 'Um. No.' He splashed away noisily to cover his remorse, and peered through the sheets of rain for some sign of his sister. The noise round them was astonishing now: an ocean noise of spattering foam and washing shingle and breaking waves, as the wind brought the rain sluicing rhythmically through the trees. A most ancient noise, as if they stood on the edge of some great ocean before men or their ancestors were ever born. Up the road they went, peering and doggedly calling, anxious now; everything they saw became strange all over again, as the rain carved the snow into new lanes and hillocks. But when they came to one corner, Will knew suddenly very well where they were.

He saw Paul duck defensively behind one raised arm; heard the harsh, raucous croaking abruptly loud and then gone; saw, even through the flying rain, the flurry of black feathers as the gaggle of rooks swooped low past their heads.

Paul straightened slowly, staring. 'What on earth—?'

'Get over the other side of the road,' Will said, pushing him firmly sideways. 'The rooks go sort of crazy sometimes. I've seen it before.'

Another shrieking swoop of birds came at Paul from behind, driving him forward, while the first dived again to force Will against the snowbank along the edge of the drift-buried wood. Again they came, and again. Will wondered, dodging, whether his brother had realized that they were being herded like sheep, driven where the rooks wanted them to go. But even as he wondered, he knew that he was too late. The grey sheet of rain had separated them entirely; he had no idea where Paul had gone.

He yelled in panic, 'Paul? Paul!'

But as the Old One in him took control, calming the fear, he cut off the shout. This was not a matter for ordinary human beings, even of his own family; he should be glad to be alone. He knew now that Mary must be caught, somewhere, held by the Dark. Only he had any chance of getting her back. He stood in the driving rain, staring about him. The light was dying rapidly. Will unbuckled his belt and strapped it round his right wrist; then he said a word in the Old Speech and held up his arm, and from the Signs a steady pathway of light beamed out as from a torch. It shone on ruffled brown water, where the road was becoming a river, deeper and flowing fast.

He remembered that Merriman had said, long before, that the most dangerous peak of the Dark's power would come at Twelfth Night. Was that time now come? He had lost his place in the days, they ran into one another in his mind. Water washed at the edge of his boot as he stood wondering; he jumped hastily backwards to the snowbank edging the wood, and a brown wave in the road-river took a large bite out of the snow-wall on which he had been standing. In the light from the Signs, Will saw that now other chunks of dirty snow and ice bobbed in the water; as it flowed past, it was gradually under-cutting the hard-packed banks left on either side by the snowplough, and carrying away broken pieces like miniature icebergs.

Other things were there in the water too. He saw a bucket bob past him, and a tufted object that looked like a sack of hay. The water must be rising high enough to carry things away from people's gardens – perhaps his own among them. How could it rise so fast? As if in answer, the rain hammered at his back, and more snow broke beneath his foot, and he remembered that the ground underneath him must still be frozen bone-hard by the great cold that had paralysed the land before the rain came. Nowhere would this rain be able to soak into the soil. The thawing of the land would take far longer than the melting of the snow – and in the meantime the snow-water had nowhere to go, no alternative but to run over the surface of the frozen countryside look-ing for a river to join. The floods will be dreadful,

Will thought: worse than they've ever been before. Worse even than the cold . . .

But a voice broke in on him, a shout through the rushing water and roaring rain. He stumbled up over the slush-edged mounds of snow to peer through the murk. The shout came again. 'Will! Over here!'

'Paul?' Will called hopefully, but he knew it was not Paul's voice.

'Here! Over here!'

The shout came from the river-road itself, out in the dark. Will held up the Signs; their light beamed out over the churning water and showed him what he took at first for clouds of steam. Then he saw that the curling steam was the puffing of breath: great deep breaths, from a gigantic horse standing four-square in the water, small wild waves foaming past its knees. Will saw the broad head, the long chestnut mane plastered wet to the neck, and he knew that this was either Castor or Pollux, one of the two great shire horses from Dawsons' Farm.

The light from the Signs flicked higher; he saw Old George, muffled in black oilskins, perched high on the back of the massive horse.

'Over here, Will. Through the water, before it rises too fast. We have work to do. Come on!'

He had never heard Old George sound

demanding before; this was the Old One, not the amiable old farm-hand. Leaning against the horse's neck, the old man urged it closer through the water. 'Come up, Polly, come by, Sir Pollux.' And big Pollux snorted puffs of steam through his broad nostrils and took a few solid paces forward so that Will was able to stumble out into the river-road and grasp at his tree-like leg. The water came almost to his thighs, but he was so wet from the rain already that it made little difference. There was no saddle on the great horse, only a sodden blanket; but with astonishing strength Old George leaned down and heaved at his hand, and with much struggling he was up. The light from the Signs strapped to his wrist did not waver through all the turning and twisting, but remained directed firmly forwards at the way they should go.

Will slipped and slithered on the broad back, too wide for his straddling. George tugged him to sit in front, astride the great curving neck. 'Polly's shoulders have taken greater weight than you,' he shouted in Will's ear. Then they were swaying forward as the stolid cart-horse lurched off again, splashing through the growing stream, away from the rooks' wood, away from the Stantons' house.

'Where are we going?' Will yelled, staring fearfully out at the darkness; he could see nothing anywhere, only the swirling water in the light of the Signs.

'We go to raise the Hunt,' the cracked old voice said close to his ear.

'The Hunt? What Hunt? George, I must find Mary, they've got Mary, somewhere. And I lost sight of Paul.'

'We go to raise the Hunt,' the voice at his back said steadily. 'I have seen Paul, he is safe on his way home by now. Mary you will find in due course. It is time for the Hunter, Will, the white horse must come to the Hunter, and you must take her there. This is the ordering of things, you have forgotten. The river is coming to the valley, and the white horse must come to the Hunter. And then we shall see what we shall see. We have work to do, Will.'

And the rain beat down on them harder, and somewhere distant thunder rumbled in the early night, as the huge shire horse Pollux splashed patiently on through the rising brown river that had once been Huntercombe Lane.

It was impossible to tell where they were. A wind was rising, and Will could hear the sounds of swaying trees above the steady churning of Pollux's feet. Scarcely a light showed in the village; he supposed that the electric power must still be cut off, either by accident or by agent of the Dark. In any case, most of the people of this part of the village were still at the Manor. 'Where's Merriman?' he called through the loud rain.

'At the Manor,' George shouted in his ear. 'With Farmer. Beset.'

'You mean they're trapped?' Will's voice turned shrill with alarm.

Old George said, hissing close, hard to hear, 'They hold attention, so we may work. And floods make them busy too. Look down, boy.'

In the churning water the light from the Signs showed a scatter of unlikely objects bobbing past: a wicker basket, several disintegrating cardboard boxes, a bright red candle, some tangled strands of ribbon. Suddenly Will recognized one piece of ribbon, a lurid purple and yellow check, as a wrapping he had seen Mary carefully pull off a parcel and roll up on Christmas Day. She was a great hoarder, like a squirrel; this had gone into her hoard.

'Those things are from our house, George!'

'Floods there too,' the old man said. 'Land's low. No danger though, be easy. Just water. And mud.'

Will knew he was right, but again he longed to see for himself. Rushing about, they would all be; moving furniture and rugs, clearing books and everything movable. These first floating objects must have escaped before anyone noticed the water was actually carrying things off . . .

Pollux stumbled for the first time, and Will clutched at the wet chestnut mane; for a moment he had almost slipped and been carried off himself. George made soothing noises, and the big horse sighed and snuffled through his nose. Will could see a few dim lights now that must come from the bigger houses on high ground at the end of the village; that meant they must be nearing the Common. If it was still the Common, and not a lake.

Something was changing. He blinked. The water seemed further away, harder to see. Then he realized that the light from the Signs linked on his wrist was growing dim, fading away to nothing; in a moment they were in darkness. As soon as all the light had died, Old George said softly: 'Whoa, Polly,' and the great shire horse splashed to a halt and stood there with the water rippling past his legs.

George said, 'This is where I have to leave you, Will.'

'Oh,' Will said, forlorn.

'There is the one instruction,' Old George said. 'That you are to take the white horse to the Hunter. That will happen, if you fall into no trouble.

And there are two bits of advice to keep you from trouble, just from me to you. The first is that you will find enough light to see by if you stand for a count of a hundred after I am gone. The second is to remember what you know already, that moving water is free of magic.' He patted Will comfortingly on the shoulder. 'Put the Signs round your waist again now,' he said, 'and get down.'

It was a wet business getting down, worse than getting up; Pollux was so high from the ground that Will splashed into the water like a falling brick. Yet he felt no cold; though the rain beat at him still, it was gentle, and in some curious way it seemed to keep him from being chilled.

Old George said again, 'I go to gather the Hunt,' and with no other word of farewell he set Pollux splashing off again towards the Common, and was gone.

Will clambered up the snowbank beside the river-road, found space to stand without toppling, and began counting up to one hundred. Before he had reached seventy, he began to see what Old George had meant. Gradually, the dark world was taking on a glimmer of light from within itself. The rushing water, the pitted snow, the gaunt trees; he could see them all, in a grey dead light like dawn.

And while he looked round, puzzling, something floating past him on the quick stream brought him such astonishment that he almost fell into the water again.

He saw the antlers first, turning lazily from side to side, as if the great head were nodding to itself. Then the colours showed, the bright blues and yellows and reds, just as he had first seen them on Christmas morning. He could not see the details of the strange face, the bird-like eyes, the pricked ears of the wolf. But it was his carnival head without a doubt, the inexplicable present that the old Jamaican had given Stephen to give to him, his most precious possession in the world.

Will let out a noise like a sob, and leapt forward desperately to seize it before the water carried it out of reach; but he slipped as he jumped, and by the time he had recovered his balance the bright grotesque head was bobbing out of sight. Will began to run along the bank; it was a thing of the Old Ones, and from Stephen, and he had lost it; he must at all costs get it back. But memory caught him in mid-stride, and he paused. 'The second thing,' Old George had said, 'is to remember that moving water is free of magic.' The head was in moving water, only too clearly. So long as it remained there, no one could harm it or use it for the wrong ends.

Reluctantly, Will put it out of his mind. The great open Common stretched before him, lit by a strange glimmer of its own. Nothing moved. Even the cattle that normally grazed there year round, looming up out of nowhere on misty days like solid ghosts, were away under cover now on the farms, driven off by the snow. Will moved on, carefully. Then the noise of the water that had been in his ears for so long began to change, growing louder, and before him the torrent filling Huntercombe Lane turned aside, joining a tiny local stream that had swollen now into a foaming river rushing over the Common and away. The road that had been the river-road wound on, unhindered, solid and gleaming; Old George, Will sensed, had gone that way. He would have liked to take the road too, but he felt that he was to stay with the river; through the extra sense of the Old Ones, he knew that it would show him how to take the white horse to the Hunter.

But who was the Hunter, and where was the white horse?

Will went gingerly forward, along the lumpy snowbank edging the new-swollen stream. Willows lined it, squat and pollarded. Then suddenly, out of the dark line of trees on the far side of the stream a white shape leapt. There was a glimmer of silver, in the darkness that was not quite dark, and in a spray of wet snow the great white mare of the Light was standing before Will, her breath clouding round the streaks of rain. She was tall as a tree, her mane blown wild by the wind.

Will touched her, gently. 'Will you carry me?' he said, in the Old Speech. 'As you did before?'

The wind spurted as he spoke, and bright lightning flashed jagged round the edge of the sky, closer than it had been. The white horse shuddered, her head jerking up. But she relaxed again almost at once, and Will too felt instinctively that this brewing thunderstorm was not a storm of the Dark. It was expected. It was part of what was to come. The Light was rising, before the Dark could rise.

He made sure the Signs were secure on his belt, and then as once before he reached up to wind his fingers in the long coarse hair of the white mane. Instantly his head spun in giddiness, and clear but far-off he heard his same music, bell-like and haunting, the same heart-catching phrase – till with a great jolt the world turned, the music vanished, and he was up on the back of the white mare, high among the willow trees.

Lightning was flickering all round the growling

sky now. Muscles bunched in the tremendous back beneath Will, and he gripped the long mane as the horse leapt out across the Common, out over the hillocks and ravines of snow, its hooves grazing the surface to leave a wake of icy spray. Through the rush of the wind he thought, as he clung close to the mare's arched neck, that he could hear a strange, high yelping in the wind, like the sound of migrating geese flying high. The sound seemed to curve around them, and then to go on ahead, dying out of range.

The white horse leapt high; Will clung tighter as they rose over hedges, roads, walls, all emerging from the melting snow. Then a new noise louder than the wind or the thunder was in his ears, and he saw glinting ruffled black glass ahead of them and knew that they had come to the Thames.

The river was far wider than he had ever seen it here. For more than a week it had been shut tight and narrow by icy walls of overhanging snow; now it had broken loose, foaming and roaring, with great chunks of snow and ice tossing like icebergs. This was not a river, it was a fury of water. It hissed and howled, it was not reasonable. As he looked, Will was frightened as he had never been by the Thames; it was as wild as a thing of the Dark could be, out of his knowledge or control. Yet he knew it was not of the Dark, but beyond either Light or Dark, one of the ancient things from the beginning of Time. The ancient things: fire, water, stone ... wood ... and then, after the beginning of men, bronze, and iron ... The river was loose, and would go according to its own will. '*The river will come to the valley ...*' Merriman had said.

The white mare paused irresolute on the edge of the wild cold water, then surged forward and leapt. It was only as they rose over the churning river that Will saw the island, an island where none had been before in this swollen torrent, divided by strange glinting channels. He thought, as the white horse jolted him to earth again among bare dark trees: it's a hill really, a piece of high ground cut off by the water. And suddenly he knew very clearly that he would meet great danger here. This was his place of testing, this island that was not an island. Once more he looked up into the sky and silently, desperately called for Merriman; but Merriman did not come, and no word or sign from him came into Will's mind.

The storm was not breaking yet, and the wind had dropped a little; the noise of the river was louder than all else. The white mare bent her long neck and Will scrambled awkwardly down.

Through the mounded snow, sometimes ice-hard and sometimes soft enough to drop him thigh-deep, he set out to explore his strange island. He had thought it a circle, but it was shaped like an egg, its highest point at the end where the white mare stood. Trees grew round the foot; above them was an open, snowy slope; above that a cap of rough scrub dominated by a single gnarled, ancient beech tree. Out of the snow at the foot of this great tree, most perplexingly, four streams ran down over the hill-island, dividing it into four quarters. The white horse stood motionless. Thunder rumbled out of the flickering sky. Will climbed to the old beech tree, and stood watching the nearest spring foam out from beneath a huge snow-mounded root. And the singing began.

It was wordless; it came in the wind; it was a thin, high, cold whine with no definable tune or pattern. It came from a long way off, and it was not pleasant to hear. But it held him transfixed, turning his thoughts away from their proper direction, turning them away from everything except contemplation of whatever happened to be closest at hand. Will felt he was growing roots, like the tree above him. As he listened to the singing, he saw a twig on a low branch of the beech close to his head that seemed for no reason so totally enthralling that he could do nothing but gaze at it, as if it contained the whole world. He stared for so long, his eyes moving very gradually along the tiny twig and back again, that he felt as if several months had passed, while the high, strange singing went on and on in the sky from its distant beginnings. And then suddenly it stopped, and he was left standing dazed with his nose almost touching a very ordinary beech twig.

He knew then that the Dark had its own way of putting even an Old One outside Time for a space, if they needed a space for their own magic. For before him, next to the trunk of the great beech, stood Hawkin.

He was more recognizably Hawkin now, though still the Walker in age. Will felt that he was looking at two men in one. Hawkin was dressed still in his green velvet coat; it seemed still fresh, with the touch of white lace at the neck. But the figure within the coat was no longer neat and lithe, it was smaller, bent and shrunk by age. And the face was lined and battered beneath long, wisping grey hair; the centuries that had beaten at Hawkin had left only his sharp bright eyes unchanged. Those eyes looked at Will now with cold hostility, across the mounded snow.

'Your sister is here,' Hawkin said.

Will could not stop himself from glancing quickly round the island. But it was empty as before. He said coldly: 'She is not here. You're not going to catch me with a silly trick like that.'

The eyes narrowed. 'You are arrogant,' Hawkin hissed. 'You do not see all that is to be known in the world, Old One with the gift, and nor do your masters. Your sister Mary is here, in this place, though she is not to be seen by you. This is a meeting for the only bargain that my lord the Rider will make. Your sister for the Signs. You scarcely have much choice. You people are good at risking the lives of others' – the bitter old mouth curved up in a sneer – 'but I do not think Will Stanton would enjoy watching his sister die.'

Will said, 'I can't see her. I still don't believe she's here.'

Staring at him, Hawkin said to the empty air, 'Master?' And at once the high, wordless singing began again, catching Will back into the slow contemplation that was warm and relaxing as the summer sun, but at the same time horrible in its soft clutch of the mind. It changed him, while he was listening; made him forget the tension of fighting for the Light; submerged him, this time, in watching the way the shadows and hollows made patterns on a patch of snow near his feet. He stood there loose and relaxed, gazing at a point of white ice here, a hollow of darkness there, and the singing whined in his ears like the wind through chinks in a crumbling house.

And then again it stopped, and there was nothing, and Will saw with a shock like sudden cold that he was staring not at a pattern of mere shadows on snow, but at the lines and curves of his sister Mary's face. There she lay on the snow, in the clothes she had worn when he last saw her; alive and unharmed, but gazing blankly up at him without any sign that she recognized him or knew where she was. Indeed, Will thought unhappily, he did not know where she was either, for although he was being shown the appearance of her, it was most unlikely that she was really there lying on the snow. He moved to touch her, and as he expected she vanished completely away, and only the shadows lay on the snow as before.

'You see,' said Hawkin, unmoving beside the beech tree. 'There are some things that the Dark can do, many things, over which you and your masters have no control at all.'

'That's pretty obvious,' Will said. 'Otherwise there wouldn't be such a thing as the Dark, would there? We could just tell it to go away.'

Hawkin smiled, unruffled. He said softly, 'But it will never go away. Once it comes, it breaks all resistance into nothing. And the Dark will always come, my young friend, and always win. As you see, we have your sister. Now you will give me the Signs.'

'Give them to you?' Will said with scorn. 'To a worm who crawled to the other side? Never!'

He saw the fists clench briefly at the cuffs of the green velvet jacket. But this was an old, old Hawkin, not to be drawn; he had himself under control now that he was no longer the wandering Walker but part of the Dark. There was only a small catch of fury in the voice. 'You would do well to deal with the messenger of the Dark, boy. If you will not, you may call up more than you will wish to see.'

The sky flickered and rumbled, bringing a brief, bright light to the dark roaring water all round, the great tree peaking the tiny island, the bowed green-jacketed figure beside its trunk. Will said, 'You are a creature of the Dark. You chose betrayal. You are nothing. I will not deal with you.'

Hawkin's face twisted as he stared venomously at him; then he looked towards the dark empty Common and called: 'Master!' Then again, an angry shriek this time: '*Master!*'

Will stood, tranquil, waiting. On the edge of the island he saw the white mare of the Light, almost invisible against the snow, raise her head and sniff the air, snorting softly. She looked once towards Will as if in communication; then wheeled round in the direction from which they had come, and galloped away.

Within seconds, something came. There was no sound, still, but the rushing river and the grumbling, looming storm. The thing that came was utterly silent. It was huge, a column of black mist like a tornado, whirling at enormous speed upright between the land and the sky. At either end it seemed broad and solid, but the centre wavered, grew slender and then thicker again; it wove to and fro as it came, in a kind of macabre dance. It was a hole in the world, this whirling black spectre; a piece of the eternal emptiness of the Dark made visible. As it came closer and closer to the island, bending and weaving, Will could not help backing away; every part of him shouted silently in alarm.

The black pillar swayed before him, covering the whole island. Its whirling, silent mist did not change, but parted, and standing within it was the Black Rider. He stood with the mist wreathing round his hands and head, and smiled at Will: a cold, mirthless smile, with the heavy bars of eyebrows furrowed and ominous above. He was all in black again, but the clothes were unexpectedly modern; he wore a heavy black donkey-jacket and rough, dark denim trousers.

Without a flicker in the chill smile he moved aside a little, and out of the snaking black mist of the column came his horse, the great black beast with fiery eyes, and on its back sat Mary.

'Hallo, Will,' Mary said cheerfully.

Will looked at her. 'Hallo.'

'I suppose you were looking for me,' Mary said. 'I hope nobody got worried. I only went for a little ride, just for a minute or two. I mean, when I went look-ing for Max, and then I met Mr Mitothin and found Dad had sent him to look for me, well, obviously it was all right. I had a lovely ride. It's a super horse . . . and such a lovely day now . . .'

The thunder rumbled, behind the massing grey-black cloud. Will shifted unhappily. The Rider, watching him, said loudly, 'Here's some sugar for the horse, Mary. I think he deserves it, don't you?' And he held out his hand, empty.

'Oh, thank you,' Mary said eagerly. She leaned forward over the horse's neck and took the imaginary sugar from the Rider's hand. Then she reached down beside the stallion's mouth, and the animal licked briefly at her palm. Mary beamed. 'There,' she said. 'Is that good?'

The Black Rider still gazed at Will, his smile widening a little. He opened his palm in mockery of Mary, and lying in it Will saw a small white box, made of an icy translucent glass, with lines of runic symbols engraved on the lid.

'Here I have her, Old One,' said the Rider, his nasal, accented voice softly triumphant. 'Caught by the marks of the Old Spell of Lir, that was written long ago on a certain ring and then lost. You should have looked more closely at your mother's ring, you and that simple craftsman your father, and Lyon your careless master. Careless . . . Under that spell I have your sister bound by totem magic, and yourself bound too, powerless to rescue her. See!'

He flicked the little box open, and Will saw lying in it a round, delicately-carved piece of wood, wound about with a fragile gold thread. With dismay he remembered the only ornament that had been missing from the Christmas collection carved by Farmer Dawson for the Stanton family, and the golden hair that Mr Mitothin, his father's visitor, had with casual courtesy flicked away from Mary's sleeve.

'A birth-sign and a hair of the head are excellent totems,' the Rider said. 'In the old days when we were all less sophisticated, you could, of course, work the magic even through the ground a man's foot had trod.'

'Or where his shadow had passed,' Will said.

'But the Dark casts no shadow,' the Rider said softly.

'And an Old One has no birth-sign,' said Will.

He saw uncertainty flicker over the intent white face. The Rider shut the white box and slipped it into his pocket. 'Nonsense,' he said curtly.

Will looked at him thoughtfully. He said, 'The masters of the Light do nothing without reason, Rider. Even though the reason may not be known for years and years. Eleven years ago Farmer Dawson of the Light carved a certain sign for me at my birth – and if he had made the sign with the letter of my name, as the tradition was, then perhaps you could have used it to trap me into your power. But he made it in the sign of the Light, a circle cut by a cross. And as you know well, the Dark can use nothing of that shape for its own purpose. It is forbidden.'

He looked up at the Rider. He said, 'I think you are trying to bluff me again, Mr Mitothin. Mr Mitothin, Black Rider of the black horse.'

The Rider scowled. 'Yet still you are powerless,' he said. 'For I have your sister. And you cannot save her except by giving me the Signs.' Malignance glittered again in his eyes. 'Your great and noble Book may have told you that I cannot harm those who are of the same blood as an Old One – but look at her. She will do anything that I suggest she should do. Even jump into this swollen Thames. There are parts of the craft that you people neglect, you know. It is so simple to persuade folk into situations where they bring accidents upon themselves. Like your mother, for instance, so clumsy.'

He smiled again at Will. Will stared back, hating him; then he looked at Mary's happy sleeping-waking face and ached that she should be in such a place. He thought: and all because she's my sister. All because of me.

But a silent voice said into his mind: 'Not because of you. Because of the Light. Because of all that must always happen, to keep the Dark from rising.' And with a surge of joy Will knew that he was no longer alone; that because the Rider was abroad, Merriman was near by again too, free to give help if need be.

The Rider put out his hand. 'This is the time for your bargain, Will Stanton. Give me the Signs.'

Will took the deepest breath of his life, and let it out slowly. He said, 'No.'

Astonishment was an emotion that the Black

Rider had forgotten long ago. The piercing blue eyes stared at Will in total disbelief. 'But you know what I shall do?'

'Yes,' Will said. 'I know. But I will not give you the Signs.'

For a long moment the Rider looked at him, out of the vast black pillar of swirling mist in which he stood; in his face incredulity and rage were mingled with a kind of evil respect. Then he swung round to the black horse and to Mary and called aloud some words in a language that Will guessed, from the chill they put into his bones, must be the spell-speech of the Dark, seldom used aloud. The great horse tossed his head, white teeth flashing, and bounded forward, with happy witless Mary clutching his mane and gurgling with laughter. He came to the overhanging snowbank that bordered the river, and paused.

Will clenched the Signs on his belt, agonized by the risk he was taking, and with all his might summoned the power of the Light to come to his aid.

The black horse gave a shrill, shrieking whinny and leapt high into the air over the Thames. Halfway through his leap he twisted strangely, bucking in the air, and Mary screamed in terror, grabbing wildly at his neck. But her balance was gone, and she fell.

Will thought he would faint as she turned through the air, his risk bursting into disaster; but instead of splashing into the river, she fell into the soft wet snow at its brink. The Black Rider cursed savagely, lunging forward. He never reached her. Before he was in mid-stride, a great arrow of lightning came from the storm amassed now almost overhead, and a gigantic crack of thunder, and out of the flash and the roar a blazing white streak rushed over the island towards Mary, catching her up so that in an instant she was gone, seized away, safe. Will hardly managed to get a glimpse of Merriman's lean form, cloaked and hooded, on the white mare of the Light, with Mary's blonde hair flying where he held her. Then the storm broke, and the whole world whirled flaming round his head.

The earth rocked. He saw for an instant Windsor Castle outlined black against a white sky. Lightning seared his eyes, thunder beat at his head. Then through the singing in his dazed ears he heard a strange creaking and crackling close by. He swung round. Behind him, the great beech tree was cleft down the middle, blazing with great flames, and he realized with amazement that the eager current of the island's four streams was growing less and less, dwindling down to nothing. He looked up fearfully for the black column of the Dark, but it was nowhere to be seen in the raging storm, and the strangeness of all else that was happening drove the thought of it out of Will's head.

For it was not only the tree that had been split and broken. The island itself was changing, breaking open, sinking towards the river. Will stared speechless, standing now on an edge of snow-mounded land left by the vanished streams, while around him snow and land slid and crumpled into the roaring Thames. Above him, he saw the strangest thing of all. Something was emerging out of the island, as the land and snow fell away. There came first, from what had been the taller end of the island, the roughly shaped head of a stag, antlers held high. It was golden, glinting even in that dim light. More came into sight; Will could see the whole stag now, a beautiful golden image, prancing. Then came a curious curved pedestal on which it stood, as if to leap away; then behind this a long, long horizontal shape, as long as the island, rising again at the other end to another high, gold-glinting point, tipped this time by a kind of scroll. And suddenly Will realized that he was looking at a ship. The pedestal was its high curving prow, and the stag its figurehead.

Astounded, he moved towards it, and

imperceptibly the river moved after him, until there was nothing left of the island but the long-ship on a last circle of land, with a last rearing snowdrift all around it. Will stood staring. He had never seen such a ship. The long timbers of which it was built overlapped one another like the boards of a fence, heavy and broad; they looked like oak. He could see no mast. Instead there were places for row upon row of oarsmen, up and down the whole length of the vessel. In the centre was a kind of deckhouse that made the ship look almost like a Noah's Ark. It was not a closed structure; its sides seemed to have been cut away, leaving the corner beams and roof like a canopy. And inside, beneath the canopy, a king lay.

Will drew back a little at the sight of him. The mailed figure lay very still, with sword and shield at his side, and treasure piled round him in glittering mounds. He wore no crown. Instead a great engraved helmet covered the head and most of the face, crested by a heavy silver image of a long-snouted animal that Will thought must be a wild boar. But even without a crown this was clearly the body of a king. No lesser man could have merited the silver dishes and jewelled purses, the great shield of bronze and iron, the ornate scabbard, the gold-rimmed drinking-horns, and the heaps of ornaments. On an impulse Will knelt down in the snow and bowed his head in respect. As he looked up again, rising, he saw over the gunwale of the ship something he had not noticed before.

The king was holding something in his hands, where they lay tranquilly folded on his breast. It was another ornament, small and glittering. And as Will saw it more closely, he stood still as stone, gripping the high, oaken edge of the ship. The ornament in the quiet hands of the long-ship king was shaped as a circle, quartered by a cross. It was wrought of iridescent glass, engraved with serpents and eels and fishes, waves and clouds and things of the sea. It called silently to Will. It was without any question the Sign of Water: the last of the Six Great Signs.

Will scrambled over the side of the great ship and approached the king. He had to take care where his feet moved, or he would have crushed fine work of engraved leather and woven robes, and jewellery of enamels and cloisonné and filigree gold. He stood looking down for a moment at the white face half-hidden by the ornate helmet, and then he reached reverently across to take the Sign. But first he had to touch the hand of the dead king, and it was colder than any stone. Will flinched and drew back, hesitating.

Merriman's voice said softly, from close by, 'Do not fear him.'

Will swallowed. 'But – he's dead.'

'He has lain here in his burial-ground for fifteen hundred years, waiting. On any other night of the year he would not be here at all, he would be dust. Yes, Will, this appearance of him is dead. The rest of him has gone out beyond Time, long since.'

'But it's wrong to take tribute away from the dead.'

'It is the Sign. If it had not been the Sign, and destined for you the Sign-seeker, he would not be here to give it to you. Take it.'

So Will leaned across the bier and took the Sign of Water from the loose grip of the dead cold hands, and from somewhere far off a murmur of his music whispered in his ears and then was gone. He turned to the side of the ship. There beside it was Merriman, sitting on the white mare; he was cloaked in dark blue, with his wild white hair uncovered; the hollows of his bony face were dark with strain, but delight gleamed in his eyes.

'It was well done, Will,' he said.

Will was gazing at the Sign in his hands. The sheen over it was the iridescence of all mother-of-pearl, all rainbows; the light danced on it as it danced on water, 'It's beautiful,' he said. Rather reluctantly he loosened the end of the belt and slipped the Sign of Water on, to lie next to the glimmering Sign of Fire.

'It is one of the oldest,' Merriman said. 'And the most powerful. Now that you have it, they lose their power over Mary for ever – that spell is dead. Come, we must go.'

Concern sharpened his voice; he had seen Will grasp hastily at a beam as the long ship, suddenly, unexpectedly lurched to one side. It rose upright, swayed a little, then tipped in the opposite direction. Will saw, scrambling for the side, that the Thames had risen still further while he was not watching. Water lapped round the great ship, and had it almost afloat. Not for long now would the dead king rest on the land that had once been an island.

The mare wheeled towards him, snuffling a greeting, and in the same enchanted, music-haunted moment as before Will was up on the white horse of the Light, sitting in front of Merriman. The ship tilted and swung, fully afloat now and the white horse wheeled out of its way to stand near by, watching, the river-water foaming round its sturdy legs.

Creaking and rattling, the long ship gave itself to the rush of the swollen Thames. It was too large a vessel to be overwhelmed; its weight kept it steady even on that swirling water, once it had found a balance. So the mysterious dead king lay in dignity still, among his weapons and gleaming tribute, and Will had a last glimpse of the mask-like white face as the great ship moved away downstream.

He said over his shoulder, 'Who was he?'

There was grave respect on Merriman's face as he watched the long-ship go. 'An English king, of the Dark Ages. I think we will not use his name. The Dark Ages were rightly named, a shadowy time for the world, when the Black Riders rode un-hindered over all our land. Only the Old Ones and a few noble brave men like this one kept the Light alive.'

'And he was buried in a ship, like the Vikings.' Will was watching the light glimmer on the golden stag of the prow.

'He was part Viking himself,' Merriman said. 'There were three great ship-burials near this Thames of yours, in days past. One was dug up in the last century near Taplow, and destroyed in the process. One was this ship of the Light, not destined ever to be found by men. And one was the greatest ship, of the greatest king of all, and this they have not found and perhaps never will. It lies in peace.' He stopped abruptly, and at a movement of his hand the white horse turned, ready to leap away from the river to the south.

But Will was still straining to watch the long-ship, and something of his tension seemed to infect both horse and master. They paused. In that moment, an extraordinary streak of blue light came hurtling out of the east, not from the thundering sky but from somewhere across the Common. It struck the ship. A great silent rush of flame burst there, over the broad river and its craggy white banks, and from prow to stern the king's ship was outlined by leaping fire. Will gave a choking wordless cry, and the white horse stirred uneasily, pawing at the snow.

Behind Will, Merriman's strong deep voice said, 'They vent their spite, because they know they are too late. Very easy it is, now and again, to predict what the Dark will do.'

Will said, 'But the king, and all his beautiful things—'

'If the Rider paused for thought, Will, he would have known that his outburst of malice has done no more than create a right and proper ending for this great ship. When this king's father died, he was laid in a ship in the same way, with all his most splendid possessions round him, but the ship was not buried.

That was not the way. The king's men set fire to it and sent it off burning alone over the sea, a tremendous sailing pyre. And that, look, is what our King of the Last Sign is doing now: sailing in fire and water to his long rest, down the greatest river of England, towards the sea.'

'And good rest to him,' Will said softly, turning his eyes at last from the leaping flames. But for a long time afterwards, wherever they went, they could see the glow from the blazing long-ship whitening a part of the storm-dark sky.

The Hunt Rides

'Come,' Merriman said, 'we must lose no more time!' And the white mare wheeled them round away from the river and rose into the air, skimming the foaming water, crossing the Thames to the side that is the end of Buckinghamshire, the beginning of Berkshire. She leapt with desperate speed, yet still Merriman urged her on. Will knew why. He had glimpsed, through the flowing folds of Merriman's blue cloak, the great black tornado-column ofthe Dark gathered again even larger than before, bridging earth and sky, whirling silently in the glow of the burning ship. It was following them, and it was moving very fast.

A wind came up out of the east and lashed at them; the cloak blew forward round Will, enfolding him, as if he and Merriman were shut in a great blue tent.

'This is the peak of it all,' Merriman shouted into

his ear, shouting his loudest, but still scarcely to be heard over the rising howl of the wind. 'You have the Six Signs, but they are not yet joined. If the Dark can take you now, they take all that they need to rise to power. Now they will try hardest of all.'

On they galloped, past houses and shops and unwitting people fighting the floods; past roofs and chimneys, over hedges, across fields, through trees, never far from the ground. The great black column pursued them, rushing on the wind, and in it and through it rode the Black Rider on his fire-jawed black horse, spurring after them, with the Lords of the Dark riding at his shoulder like a spinning dark cloud themselves.

The white mare rose again, and Will looked down. Trees were everywhere below them now; great single spreading oaks and beeches in open fields, and then tight-growing woods split by long straight avenues. Surely they were galloping down one such avenue now, past brooding snow-weighed fir trees, and out again into open land . . . Lightning flashed at his left side, leaping in the depths of a huge cloud, and in its light he saw the dark mass of Windsor Castle looming high and close. He thought: if that's the castle, we must be in the Great Park.

He began to feel, too, that they were no longer

alone. Twice already he had heard again that strange, high yelping in the sky, but now there was more. Beings of his own kind were about here, somewhere, in the tree-thronged Park. And he felt, too, that the grey-massed sky was no longer empty of life, but peopled with creatures neither of the Dark nor of the Light, moving to and fro, clustering and separating, holding great power . . . The white mare was down in the snow again now, the hooves pounding over drift and slush and icy paths, more deliberately than before. All at once Will realized that she was not responding to Merriman, as he had thought, but following some profound impulse of her own.

Lightning flickered again round them, and the sky roared. Merriman said beside his ear: 'Do you know Herne's Oak?'

'Yes, of course,' Will said at once. He had known the local legend all his life. 'Is that where we are? The big oak tree in the Great Park where—'

He swallowed. How could he not have thought of it? Why had Gramarye taught him everything but this? He went on, slowly, '—where Herne the Hunter is supposed to ride on the eve of Twelfth Night?' Then he looked round fearfully at Merriman. 'Herne?'

'*I go to gather the Hunt,*' Old George had said.

Merriman said, 'Of course. Tonight the Hunt rides. And because you have played your part well, tonight for the first time in more than a thousand years the Hunt will have a quarry.'

The white mare slowed, sniffing the air. Winds were breaking the sky apart; a half-moon sailed high through the clouds, then vanished again. Lightning danced in six places at once, the clouds roared and growled. The black pillar of the Dark came hurtling towards them, then paused, spinning and undulating, hovering between land and sky. Merriman said, 'An Old Way rings the Great Park, the way through Hunter's Combe. They will take a little while to find their path past that.'

Will was straining to see ahead through the murk. In the intermittent light he could make out the shape of a solitary oak tree, spreading great arms from its short tremendous trunk. Unlike most other trees in sight, it bore not the smallest remnant of snow; and a shadow stood beside its trunk, the size of a man.

The white mare saw the shadow at the same time. She blew hard through her nose, and pawed the ground.

Will said to himself, very softly, '*The white horse must go to the Hunter . . .*' Merriman touched him on the shoulder, and with swift enchanted ease they slid down to the ground. The mare bent her head to them, and Will laid his hand on the tough-smooth white neck. 'Go, my friend,' Merriman said, and the horse swung about and trotted eagerly towards the huge, solitary oak tree and the mysterious shadow motionless beneath. The creature who owned that shadow was of immense power; Will flinched before the sense of it. The moon went behind the clouds again; for a while there was no lightning; in the gloom they could see nothing move beneath the tree. One sound came through the darkness: a whinny of greeting from the white mare.

As if in counterpoint, a deeper, snuffling whinny came out of the trees beside them; as Will swung round, the moon sailed clear of cloud again, and he saw the huge silhouette of Pollux, the shire horse from Dawsons' Farm, with Old George high on his back.

'Your sister is at home, boy,' Old George said. 'She got lost, you know, and fell asleep in an old barn, and had such a curious dream that she is already forgetting . . .'

Will nodded gratefully and smiled; but he was gazing at a curious rounded shape, muffled by wrapping, that George held before him. 'What's that?' His neck was tingling even from being close to it, whatever it was.

Old George did not answer; he leant down to Merriman. 'Is all well?'

'All goes well,' Merriman said. He shivered, and drew his long cloak round him. 'Give it to the boy.'

He looked hard at Will out of his inscrutable deepset eyes, and Will, wondering, went towards the cart-horse and stood at George's knee, looking up. With a quick mirthless grin that seemed to mask great strain, the old man lowered the shadowed burden towards him. It was half as large as Will himself, though not heavy; it was wrapped in sacking. As he laid hands on it, Will knew instantly what it was. It can't be, he thought incredulously; what would be the point?

Thunder rumbled again, all around.

Merriman's voice said, deep in the shadows behind him, 'But of course it is. The water brought it, in safety. Then the Old Ones took it from the water at the proper time.'

'And now,' Old George said, from his place high on patient Pollux, 'you must take it to the Hunter, young Old One.'

Will swallowed nervously. An Old One had nothing in the world to fear, nothing. Yet there had been something so strange and awesome about that shadowy figure beneath the giant oak, something that made one feel unnecessary, insignificant, small . . .

He straightened. Unnecessary was the wrong word, at any rate; he had a task to perform. Raising his burden like a standard, he pulled away its covering, and the bright, eerie carnival head that was half-man, half-beast emerged as smooth and gay as if it had just arrived from its distant island. The antlers stood up proudly; he saw that they were exactly the shape of those on the golden stag, the figurehead to the dead king's ship. Holding the mask before him, he walked firmly towards the deep shadow of the broad-spreading oak. At its edge, he paused. He could see a glimmer of white from the mare, moving gently in recognition; he could see that the mare had a rider. But that was all.

The figure on the horse bent down towards him. He did not see the face, but only felt the mask lifted from his hands – and his hands fell back as if they had been relieved of a great weight, even though the head had from the beginning seemed so light. He backed away. The moon came sailing suddenly out from behind a cloud, and for a moment his eyes dazzled as he looked full into its cold white light;

then it was gone again, and the white horse was moving out of the shadow, with the figure on its back changed in outline against the dim-lit sky. The rider had a head now that was bigger than the head of a man and horned with the antlers of a stag. And the white mare, bearing this monstrous stag-man, was moving inexorably towards Will.

He stood, waiting, until the great horse came close; its nose gently touched his shoulder, once, for the last time. The figure of the Hunter towered over him. The moonlight now glimmered clear on his head, and Will found himself gazing up into strange tawny eyes, yellow-gold, unfathomable, like the eyes of some huge bird. He gazed into the Hunter's eyes, and he heard in the sky that strange high yelping begin again; with the difficulty of escaping an enchantment, he dragged his gaze aside to look properly at the head, the great horned mask that he had given the Hunter to put on.

But the head was real.

The golden eyes blinked, feather-fringed and round, with the deliberate blink of an owl's strong eyelids; the man's face in which they were set was turned full on Will, and the firm-carved mouth above the soft beard parted in a quick smile. That mouth troubled Will; it was not the mouth of an Old

One. It could smile in friendship, but there were other lines round it as well. Where Merriman's face was marked with lines of sadness and anger, the Hunter's told instead of cruelty, and a pitiless impulse to revenge. Indeed he was half-beast. The dark branches of Herne's antlers curved up over Will, the moonlight glinting on their velvety sheen, and the Hunter laughed softly. He looked down at Will out of his yellow eyes, in the face that was no longer a mask but living, and he spoke in a voice like a tenor bell. 'The Signs, Old One,' he said. 'Show me the Signs.'

Without taking his eyes from the towering figure, Will fumbled with his buckle and held the six quartered circles high in the moonlight. The Hunter looked at them and bent his head. When he raised it again, slowly, the soft voice was half-singing, half-chanting words that Will had heard before.

'When the Dark comes rising, six shall turn it back;
Three from the circle, three from the track;
Wood, bronze, iron; water, fire, stone;
Five will return, and one go alone.

Iron for the birthday, bronze carried long;
Wood from the burning, Stone out of song;

Fire in the candle-ring, water from the thaw;
Six Signs the circle, and the grail gone before.'

But he too did not end where Will expected him
to; he went on.

'Fire on the mountain shall find the harp of gold
Played to wake the Sleepers, oldest at of the old;
Power from the green witch, lost beneath the sea;
All shall find the light at last, silver on the tree.'

The yellow eyes looked at Will again, but they
did not see him now; they had grown cold,
abstracted, a chill fire mounting in them that
brought the cruel lines back to the face. But Will saw
the cruelty now as the fierce inevitability of nature. It
was not from malice that the Light and the servants
of the Light would ever hound the Dark, but from
the nature of things.

Herne the Hunter wheeled round on the great
white horse, away from Will and the single oak tree,
until his fearsome silhouette was in the open, under
the moon and the still-lowering stormclouds. He
raised his head, and he made to the sky a call that
was like the halloo blown by a huntsman on the horn
to call up hounds. The hunting horn of his voice

seemed to grow and grow, and to fill the sky and come from a thousand throats at once.

And Will saw that this it did, for from every point of the Park, behind every shadow or tree and out of every cloud, leaping round the ground and through the air, came an endless pack of hounds, sounding, belling as hunting dogs do when they are starting after a scent. They were huge white animals, ghostly in the half-light, loping and jostling and bounding together; they paid not the least attention to the Old Ones or to anything but Herne on his white horse. Their ears were red, their eyes were red; they were ugly creatures. Will drew back involuntarily as they passed, and one great silvery dog broke stride to glance at him with as casual a curiosity as if he had been a fallen branch. The red eyes in the white head were like flames, and the red ears stood taut upright with a dreadful eagerness, so that Will tried not to imagine what it would be like to be hunted by such dogs.

Round Herne and the white mare they bayed and belled, a heaving sea of red-flecked foam; then all at once the antlered man stiffened, his great horns pointing as a hunting dog points, and he called the hounds together with the rapid urgent collecting-call, the *menée*, that sends a pack after blood. A bedlam of yelping urgency rose from the milling white dogs, filling the sky, and at the same moment the full strength of the thunderstorm erupted. Clouds split roaring into bright, jagged lightning as Herne and the white horse leapt exultantly up into the arena of the sky, with the red-eyed hounds pouring up into the stormy air after them in a great white flood.

But then a sudden terrible silence like suffocation came, blotting out all sound of the storm. In the moment of its last desperate chance, breaking across the barrier that had been holding it at bay, the Dark came for Will. Shutting out the sky and the earth, the deadly spinning pillar came at him, dreadful in its furious whirling energy and utter quiet. There was no time for fear. Will stood alone. And the towering black column rushed to engulf him with all the monstrous forces of the Dark arrayed in its writhing mist, and at its centre the great foam-mouthed black stallion reared up with the Black Rider, his eyes two brilliant points of blue fire. Will called vainly on every spell of defence at his command, yet knew that his hands were powerless to move to the Signs for help. He stood where he was, despairing, and closed his eyes.

But into the dead, world-muffling silence

enwrapping him, one small sound came. It was the same strange high whickering far up in the sky, like the passing of many migrant geese on an autumn night, that he had heard three times that day. Nearer, louder it grew, opening his eyes. And he saw then a scene like nothing he had ever seen before, nor ever saw again. Half the sky was thick and dreadful with the silent raging of the Dark and its whirling tornado power; but now riding down towards it, out of the west with the speed of dropping stones, came Herne and the Wild Hunt. At the peak of their power now, in full cry, they came roaring out of the great dark thundercloud, through streaking lightning and grey-purple clouds, riding on the storm. The yellow-eyed antlered man rode laughing dreadfully, crying out the *avaunt* that rallies hounds on the full chase, and his brilliant, white-gold horse flung forward with mane and tail flying.

And around them and endlessly behind them like a broad white river poured the Yell Hounds, the Yelpers, the Hounds of Doom, their red eyes burning with a thousand warning flames. The sky was white with them; they filled the western horizon; and still they came, unending. At the sound of their hell-like, thousand-tongued yelping, the magnificence of the Dark flinched and swayed and seemed to tremble. Will caught sight of the Black Rider once more, high in the dark mist; his face was twisted in fury and dread and frozen malevolence, and behind these the awareness of defeat. He spun his horse so fiercely round that the lithe black stallion tottered and almost fell. As he jerked at the rein, the Rider seemed to cast something impatiently from his saddle, a small dark object that fell limp and loose to the ground, and lay there like a discarded cloak.

Then the storm and the rushing Wild Hunt were upon the Rider. He rode up into his whirling black refuge. The fantastic tornado-pillar of the Dark curved and twisted, lashed like a snake in agony, until finally there was a great shriek in the heavens, and it began rushing at furious speed northward. Over the Park and the Common and Hunter's Combe it fled, and after it went Herne and the Hunt in full cry, a long white crest on the surge of the storm.

The yelping of the hounds died with distance, fading last of all the sounds of the chase, and above Herne's Oak the silver half-moon was left floating in a sky flecked with small ragged remnants of cloud.

Will drew a long breath, and looked round. Merriman stood exactly as he had last seen him, tall and straight, hooded, a dark featureless statue. Old George had drawn Pollux back into the trees, for no normal animal could have faced the Hunt so close and survived.

Will said, 'Is it over?'

'More or less,' Merriman said, faceless under the hood.

'The Dark – is—' He dared not bring out the words.

'The Dark is vanquished, at last, in this encounter. Nothing may outface the Wild Hunt. And Herne and his hounds hunt their quarry as far as they may, to the very ends of the earth. So at the ends of the earth the Lords of the Dark must skulk now, awaiting their next time of chance. But for the next time, we are this much stronger, by the completed Circle and the Six Signs and the Gift of Gramarye. We are made stronger by your completed quest, Will Stanton, and closer to gaining the last victory, at the very end.' He pushed back his broad hood, the wild white hair glinting in the moonlight, and for a moment the shadowed eyes looked into Will's with a communication of pride that made Will's face warm with pleasure. Then Merriman looked out across the dappled, snow-mounded grassland of the Great Park.

'There is left only the joining of the Signs,' he said. 'But before that, one – small – thing.'

A curious jerkiness caught at his voice. Will followed, puzzled, as he strode forward close to Herne's Oak. Then he saw on the snow, at the edge of the tree's shadow, the crumpled cloak that the Black Rider had let fall as he turned to flee. Merriman stooped, then knelt down beside it in the snow. Still wondering, Will peered closer, and saw with a shock that the dark heap was not a cloak, but a man. The figure lay face upward, twisted at a terrible angle. It was the Walker; it was Hawkin.

Merriman said, his voice deep and expressionless, 'Those who ride high with the Lord of the Dark must expect to fall. And men do not fall easily from such heights. I think his back is broken.'

It occurred to Will, looking at the small still face, that this time he had forgotten that Hawkin was no more than an ordinary man. Not ordinary perhaps – that was not the word for a man who had been used by both Light and Dark, and sent many ways through Time, to become at the last the Walker battered by wandering through six hundred years. But a man nonetheless, and mortal. The white face flickered, and the eyes opened. Pain came into them, and the shadow of a different, remembered pain.

'He threw me down,' Hawkin said.

Merriman looked at him, but said nothing.

'Yes,' Hawkin whispered bitterly. 'You knew it would happen.' He gasped with pain as he tried to move his head; then panic came into his eyes. 'Only my head . . . I feel my head, because of the pain. But my arms, my legs, they are . . . not there . . .'

There was a dreadful, desolate hopelessness in the lined face now. Hawkin looked full at Merriman. 'I am lost,' he said. 'I know it. Will you make me live on, with the worst suffering of all now come? The last right of a man is to die. You prevented it all this time; you made me live on through the centuries when often I longed for death. And all for a betrayal that I fell into because I had not the wit of an Old One . . .' The grief and longing in his voice were intolerable; Will turned his head away.

But Merriman said, 'You were Hawkin, my foster-son and liege man, who betrayed your lord and the Light. So you became the Walker, to walk the earth for as long as the Light required it. And so you lived on, indeed. But we have not kept you since then, my friend. Once the Walker's task was done, you were free, and you could have had rest for ever. Instead you chose to listen to the promises of the Dark and to betray the Light a second time . . . I gave you the freedom to choose, Hawkin, and I did not take it away. I may not. It is still yours. No power of the Dark or of the Light can make a man more than a man, once any supernatural role he may have had to play comes to an end. But no power of the Dark or the Light may take away his rights as a man, either. If the Black Rider told you so, he lied.'

The twisted face gazed up at him in agonized near-belief. 'I may have rest? There can be an end, and rest, if I choose?'

'All your choices have been your own,' said Merriman sadly.

Hawkin nodded his head; a spasm of pain flashed across his face and was gone. But the eyes that looked up at them then were the bright, lively eyes of the beginning, of the small, neat man in the green velvet coat. They turned to Will. Hawkin said softly, 'Use the gift well, Old One.'

Then he looked back at Merriman, a long unfathomable private look, and he said almost inaudibly: 'Master . . .'

Then the light went out behind the bright eyes, and there was no longer anyone there.

The Joining of the Signs

In the low-roofed smithy Will stood with his back to the entrance, staring into the fire. Orange and red and fierce yellow-white it burned, as John Smith pushed at the long bellows-arm; the warmth made Will feel comfortable for the first time that day. There was no great harm in an Old One being fish-wet in an icy river, but he was glad to feel warm in his bones again. And the fire lit his spirits, as it lit the whole room.

Yet it did not properly light the room, for nothing that Will could see appeared solid. There was a quivering in the air. Only the fire seemed real; the rest might have been a mirage.

He saw Merriman watching him with a half-smile.

'It's that half-world feeling again,' Will said, baffled. 'The same as that day in the Manor when we were in two kinds of Time at once.'

'It is. Just the same. And so we are.'

'But we're in the time of the smithy,' Will said. 'We went through the Doors.'

So they had; he and Merriman, Old George, and the huge horse Pollux. Out on the wet, dark Common, when the Wild Hunt had driven the Dark away over the sky, they had gone through the Doors into the time six centuries earlier from which Hawkin had once come, and into which Will had walked on the still, snowy morning of his birthday. They had brought Hawkin back to his century for the last time, home on Pollux's broad back; when they were all come through the Doors, Old George had taken the horse away, bearing Hawkin's body in the direction of the church. And Will knew that in his own time, somewhere in the village churchyard, covered either by more recent burials or by a stone crumbling into illegibility now, there would be the grave of a man named Hawkin, who had died some time in the thirteenth century and lain there in peace ever since.

Merriman drew him to the front of the smithy, where it faced the narrow hard-earth track through Hunter's Combe, the Old Way. 'Listen,' he said.

Will looked at the bumpy track, the dense trees on the other side, the cold grey strip of almost-morning sky. 'I can hear the river!' he said, puzzled.

'Ah,' Merriman said.

'But the river's miles away, the other side of the Common.'

Merriman cocked his head to the rushing, rippling sound of water. It had the sound of a river that is full but not in flood, a river running after much rain. 'What we are hearing,' he said, 'is not the Thames, but the sound of the twentieth century. You see, Will, the Signs must be joined by John Wayland Smith in this smithy, in this time – for not long after this the smithy was destroyed. Yet the Signs were not brought together until your quest, which has been within your own time. So the joining must be done in a bubble of Time between the two, from which the eyes and ears of an Old One may perceive both. That's not a real river we hear. It is the water running in your time down Huntercombe Lane, from the melting of the snow.'

Will thought of the snow and of his family beset by floods, and suddenly he was a small boy wanting very much to be at home. Merriman's dark eyes looked at him compassionately. 'Not long,' he said.

A hammering sound came from behind them; they turned. John Smith had finished pumping the bellows at his red-white fire; he was working at the anvil instead, while the long tongs waited ready before the fire's glow. He was not using his usual heavy hammer, but another that looked ridiculously small in his broad fist; a delicate tool more like those Will saw his father use for jewellery. But then, the object on which he was working was far more delicate than horseshoes; a golden chain, broad-linked, from which the Six Signs would hang. The links lay in a row beside John's hand.

He looked up, his face flushed red by the fire. 'I am almost ready.'

'Very well, then.' Merriman left them and stalked out to the road. He stood there alone, tall and imposing in the long blue cloak, the hood pushed back so that his thick white hair glinted like snow. But there was no snow here, and even through the sound of the water that Will could still hear rushing, no water either . . .

Then the change began. Merriman seemed not to have moved. He stood there with his back to them, his hands loose at his sides, very still, without the least movement. But all around him, the world was beginning to move. The air shivered and quaked, the outlines of trees and earth and sky trembled, blurred, and all things visible seemed to swim and intermingle. Will stood looking at this wavering world, feeling a little giddy, and gradually he began to hear over the sound of the unseen, rushing river-road the murmur of many voices. Like a place seen through a shimmering haze of heat, the trembling world began to resolve itself into outlines of visible things, and he saw that a great indistinct throng of people filled the road and the spaces between all the trees and all the open yard before the smithy. They seemed not quite real, not quite firm; they had a ghostly quality as if they might disappear when touched. They smiled at Merriman, greeting him where he stood, his face turned away still from Will. Thronging round him, they gazed eagerly ahead at the smithy like an audience about to watch a play, but as yet none of them seemed to see Will and the smith.

There was an endless variety of faces – gay, sombre, old, young, paper-white, jet-black, and every shade and gradation of pink and brown between, vaguely recognizable, or totally strange. Will thought he recognized faces from the party at Miss Greythorne's manor, the party in a nineteenth-century Christmas that had led Hawkin to disaster and himself to the Book of Gramarye – and then he knew. All these people, this endless throng that

Merriman had somehow summoned, were the Old
Ones. From every land, from every part of the world,
here they were, to witness the joining of the Signs.
Will was all at once terrified, longing to sink into the
ground and escape the gaze of this his great new
enchanted world.

He thought: these are my people. This is my
family, in the same way as my real family. The Old
Ones. Every one of us is linked, for the greatest
purpose in the world. Then he saw a stir in the
crowd, running like a ripple along the road, and
some began to shift and move as if to make way. And
he heard the music: the piping, thrumming sound,
almost comical in its simplicity, of the fifes and
drums he had heard in his dream that might not
have been a dream. He stood stiffly with his hands
clenched, waiting, and Merriman swung round and
strode to stand beside him, as out of the crowd
towards them came the little procession just as it had
been before.

Through the thronging figures, and curiously
seeming more solid than any, came the little procession of boys: the same boys in their rough,
unfamiliar tunics and leggings, shoulder-length hair,
and strange bunched caps. Again those at the front
carried sticks and bundles of birch twigs, while those

at the back played their single repeated melancholy tune, on pipes and drums. Again between these two groups came six boys carrying on their shoulders a bier woven of branches and reeds with a bunch of holly at each corner.

Merriman said, very softly, 'First on St Stephen's Day, the day after Christmas. Then on Twelfth Night. Twice in the year, if it is a particular year, comes the Hunting of the Wren.'

But now Will could see the bier plainly, and even at the beginning, this time, there was no wren. Instead, that other delicate form lay there, the old lady, robed in blue, with a great rose-coloured ring on one hand. And the boys marched up to the smithy and very gently laid the bier down on the ground. Merriman bent over it, holding out his hand, and the Lady opened her eyes and smiled. He helped her to her feet. Moving forward towards Will, she took both his hands in hers. 'Well done, Will Stanton,' she said, and through all the crowd of Old Ones thronging the track, a murmur of approval went up like the wind singing in the trees.

The Lady turned to face the smithy, where John stood waiting. She said, 'On oak and on iron, let the Signs be joined.'

'Come, Will,' said John Smith. Together they

moved to the anvil. Will laid down the belt that had borne the Signs through all their seeking. 'On oak and on iron?' he whispered.

'Iron for the anvil,' said the smith softly. 'Oak for its foot. This big wooden base of the anvil is always oak – the root of an oak, strongest part of the tree. Have I not heard someone telling you the nature of the wood a while ago?' His blue eyes twinkled at Will, and then he turned to his work. One by one he took the Signs and joined them with rings of gold. In the centre he set the Signs of Fire and Water; on one side of them the Signs of Iron and Bronze, and on the other, the Signs of Wood and Stone. At each end he fastened a length of the sturdy gold chain. He worked swiftly and delicately, while Will gazed. Outside, the great crowd of Old Ones was still as growing grass. Behind the tapping of the smith's hammer and the occasional hiss of the bellows, there was no sound anywhere but the running water of the invisible river-road, centuries away in the future and yet close at hand.

'It is done,' said John at last.

Ceremonially he handed Will the glittering chain of linked Signs, and Will gasped at the beauty of them. Holding the Signs now, he felt from them suddenly a strange fierce sensation like an electric shock: a strong, arrogant reassurance of power. Will was puzzled: danger was past, the Dark was fled, what purpose had this? He walked to the Lady, still wondering, put the Signs into her hands, and knelt down before her.

She said, 'But it's for the future, Will, don't you see? That is what the Signs are for. They are the second of the four Things of Power, that have slept these many centuries, and they are a great part of our strength. Each of the Things of Power was made at a different point in Time by a different craftsman of the Light, to await the day when it would be needed. There is a golden chalice, called a grail; there is the Circle of Signs; there is a sword of crystal, and a harp of gold. The grail, like the Signs, is safely found. The other two we must yet achieve, other quests for other times. But once we have added those to these, then when the Dark comes rising for its final and most dreadful attempt on the world, we shall have hope and assurance that we can overcome.'

She raised her head, looking out over the unnumbered ghostly crowd of the Old Ones. '*When the Dark comes rising*,' she said, expressionless, and the many voices answered her in a soft, ominous rumble '*six shall drive it back*.'

Then she looked down again at Will, the lines

around her ageless eyes creasing in affection. 'Sign-seeker,' she said, 'by your birth and your birthday you came into your own, and the circle of the Old Ones was complete, for now and for ever. And by your good use of the Gift of Gramarye, you achieved a great quest and proved yourself stronger than the testing. Until we meet again, as meet we shall, we remember you with pride.'

The far-stretching crowd murmured again, a different, warm response, and with her thin small hands, the great rose ring glimmering, the Lady bent down and set the chain of the linked Signs around Will's neck. Then she kissed him lightly on the forehead, the gentle brushing-by of a bird's wing. 'Farewell, Will Stanton,' she said.

The murmur of the voices rose, and the world spun round Will in a flurry of trees and flame, and rising over it all was the bell-like haunting phrase of his music, louder and more joyful now than ever before. It chimed and rang in his head, filling him with such delight that he closed his eyes and floated in its beauty; it was, he knew for a crack of a second, the spirit and essence of the Light, this music. But then it began gradually to fade, to grow distant and beckoning and a little melancholy, as it always had been before, fading into nothing, fading, fading, with the sound of running water rising to take its place. Will cried out in sorrow, and opened his eyes.

And he was kneeling on the cold beaten snow in the grey dead light of early morning, in a place he did not recognize beside Huntercombe Lane. Bare trees rose out of pitted, wet snow on the other side of the road. Though the Lane itself was once more a clear paved road, water ran furiously in each of its gutters with a sound like a stream, or even a river . . . The road was empty; no one was anywhere to be seen among the trees. Will could have wept with the sense of loss; all that warm crowd of friends, the brightness and light and celebration, and the Lady: all gone, all fled, leaving him alone.

He put his hand to his neck. The Signs were still there.

Behind him, Merriman's deep voice said, 'Time to go home, Will.'

'Oh,' Will said unhappily, without turning round. 'I'm glad you're still there.'

'You sound most glad,' Merriman said dryly. 'Restrain your ecstasy, I pray you.'

Sitting back on his heels, Will looked at him over his shoulder. Merriman gazed down at him with immense solemnity, his dark eyes owlish, and suddenly the emotions that were drawn into a tight, unbearable knot inside Will cracked and broke, and he dissolved into laughter. Merriman's mouth twitched slightly. He put out his hand, and Will scrambled to his feet, still spluttering.

'It was just—' Will said, and stopped, not quite sure yet whether he was laughing or crying.

'It was – an alteration,' Merriman said gently. 'Can you walk now?'

'Of course I can walk,' said Will indignantly. He stared about him. Where the smithy had been, there was a battered brick building like a garage, and around it he could see traces of cold-frames and vegetable beds through the melting snow. He looked quickly up and saw the outline of a familiar house. 'It's the Manor!' he said.

'The back entrance,' Merriman said. 'Near the village. Used mainly by tradesmen – and butlers.' He smiled at Will.

'This really is where the old smithy used to be?'

'In the plans of the old house it is called Smith's Gate,' Merriman said. 'Buckinghamshire historians writing about Huntercombe are very fond of speculating on the reason. They're always wrong.'

Will stared through the trees at the Manor's tall Tudor chimneys and gabled roofs. 'Is Miss Greythorne there?'

'Yes, she is, now. But didn't you see her in the crowd?'

'The crowd?' Will became aware that his mouth was foolishly gaping, and shut it. Conflicting images chased one another through his head. 'You mean she is one of the Old Ones?'

Merriman raised an eyebrow. 'Come now, Will, your senses told you that long ago.'

'Well . . . yes, they did. But I never knew quite which Miss Greythorne it was who belonged to us, the one from today or from the Christmas party. Well. Well, yes, I suppose I knew that too.' He looked up tentatively at Merriman. 'They're the same, aren't they?'

'That's better,' Merriman said. 'And Miss Greythorne gave me, while you and Wayland Smith were intent on your work, two gifts for Twelfth Night. One is for your brother Paul, and one is for you.' He showed Will two shapeless, small packages wrapped in what looked like silk; then drew them again under his cloak. 'Paul's is a normal present, I think. More or less. Yours is something to be used only in the future, at some point when your judgement tells you you may need it.'

'Twelfth Night,' Will said. 'Is that tonight?' He looked up at the grey early-morning sky. 'Merriman, how have you stopped my family wondering where I've been? Is my mother truly all right?'

'Of course she is,' Merriman said. 'And you have spent the night at the Manor, asleep . . . Come now, these are small things. I know all the questions. You will have all the answers, when you are once at home, and in any case really you know them already.' He turned his head down towards Will and the deep dark eyes stared compelling as a basilisk. 'Come, Old One,' he said softly, 'remember yourself. You are no longer a small boy.'

'No,' said Will. 'I know.'

Merriman said, 'But sometimes, you feel how very much more agreeable life would be if you were.'

'Sometimes,' Will said. He grinned. 'But not always.'

They turned and strode over the little edge-stream of the road to walk together towards the Stantons' house along Huntercombe Lane.

The day grew brighter, and light began to infuse the edge of the sky before them, where the sun would soon come up. A thin mist hung over the snow on both sides of the road, wreathing round the bare trees and the little streams. It was a morning full of promise, with a hazy, cloudless sky tinged faintly with blue, the kind of sky that Huntercombe had not seen for many days. They walked as old friends walk, without often speaking, sharing the kind of silence that is not so much silence as a kind of still communication. Their footsteps rang out on the bare wet road, making the only sound anywhere in the village except the song of a blackbird and, somewhere further off, the sound of someone shovelling. Trees loomed black and leafless over the road on one side, and Will saw that they were at the corner that passed Rooks' Wood. He stared upwards. Not a sound came out of the trees, or the untidy great nests high up there in the misted branches.

'The rooks are very quiet,' he said.

Merriman said, 'They are not there.'

'Not there? Why not? Where are they?'

Merriman smiled, a small grim smile. 'When the Yell Hounds are hunting across the sky, no animal or bird may stay within sight of them and not be driven wild by terror. All through this kingdom, along the path of Herne and the Hunt, masters will not be able to find any creature that was loose last night. It was better known in older days. Countrymen everywhere used to lock up their animals on Twelfth Night Eve, in case the Hunt should ride.'

'But what happens? Are they killed?' Will found

that in spite of all the rooks had done for the Dark, he did not want to think of them all destroyed.

'Oh, no,' Merriman said. 'Scattered. Driven willy-nilly across the sky for as long as the nearest hound chooses to drive them. The Hounds of Doom are not of a species that kills living creatures or eats flesh . . . The rooks will come back eventually. One by one, bedraggled, weary, sorry for themselves. Wiser birds who had no dealings with the Dark would have hidden themselves away last night, beneath branches or house-eaves, out of sight. Those who did are still here, unharmed. But it will take a while for our friends the rooks to recover themselves. I think you will have no trouble with them again, Will, though I would never quite trust one if I were you.'

'Look,' Will said, pointing ahead. 'There are two to trust.' Pride came thick into his voice, as down the road towards them came rushing and bounding the two Stanton dogs, Raq and Ci. They leapt at him, barking and whining with delight, licking his hands in a greeting as gigantic as if he had been gone for a month. Will stooped to speak to them and was enveloped in waving tails and warm panting heads and large wet feet. 'Get off, you idiots,' he said happily.

Merriman said, very softly: 'Gently, now.' Instantly the dogs calmed and were still, only their tails enthusiastically waving; both turned to Merriman and looked up at him for a moment, and then they were trotting amiably in silence at Will's side. Then the Stanton driveway was ahead, and the noise of shovels grew loud, and round the corner they found Paul and Mr Stanton, wrapped against the cold, clearing wet snow and leaves and twigs away from a drain.

'Well, well,' said Mr Stanton, and stood leaning on his shovel.

'Hallo, Dad,' said Will cheerfully, and ran and hugged him.

Merriman said: 'Good morning.'

'Old George said you'd be about early,' said Mr Stanton, 'but I didn't think he meant quite this early. However did you manage to wake him up?'

'I woke myself up,' Will said. 'Yah. I turned over a new leaf for the New Year. What are you doing?'

'Turning over old leaves,' Paul said.

'Ho, ho, ho.'

'We are, though. The thaw came so suddenly that the ground was still frozen, and nothing would drain away. And now that the drains are beginning to thaw as well, the flood's got everything jammed up with washed-away rubbish. Like this.' He lifted a dripping bundle.

Will said, 'I'll get another spade, and help.'

'Wouldn't you like some breakfast first?' Paul said. 'Mary's getting us some, believe it or not. There's a lot of leaf-turning going on here, while the year's still new.'

Will suddenly realized that it was a long time since he had last eaten, and felt a gigantic hunger. 'Mmmm,' he said.

'Come on in and have some breakfast or a cup of tea or something,' said Mr Stanton to Merriman. 'It's a chilly walk from the Manor this time of the morning. I really am extremely grateful to you for delivering him, not to mention looking after him last night.'

Merriman shook his head, smiling, and pulled up the collar of what Will saw had now again subtly changed from a cloak to a heavy twentieth-century overcoat. 'Thank you. But I'll be getting back.'

'Will!' a voice shrilled, and Mary came flying up the drive. Will went to meet her, and she skidded into him and punched him in the stomach. 'Was it fun at the Manor? Did you sleep in a four-poster?'

'Not exactly,' Will said. 'Are you all right?'

'Well, of course. I had a super ride on old

George's horse, it was one of Mr Dawson's huge ones, the show horses. He picked me up in the Lane, quite soon after I'd gone out. Seems ages ago, not last night.' She looked at Will rather sheepishly. 'I suppose I shouldn't have gone out after Max like that, but everything was happening so quickly, and I was worried about Mum not having help——'

'Is she really all right?'

'She'll be fine, the doctor says. It was a sprain, not a broken leg. She did knock herself out, though, so she has to rest for a week or two. But she's as cheerful as can be, you'll see.'

Will looked up the drive. Paul, Merriman, and his father were talking and laughing together. He thought perhaps his father had decided that Lyon the butler was a good chap after all, not merely a manorial prop.

Mary said, 'Sorry about you getting lost in the wood. It was all my fault. You and Paul must have been very close behind me actually. Good job Old George ended up knowing where everyone was. Poor Paul, worrying about both of us being lost, instead of just me.' She giggled, then tried to look penitent, without great effort.

'Will!' Paul swung away from the group, excited, running towards them. 'Just look! Miss Greythorne calls it a permanent loan, bless her – look!' His face was flushed with pleasure. He held out the bundle Merriman had been carrying, now open, and Will saw lying on it the old flute from the Manor.

Feeling his face break into a long, slow smile, he looked up at Merriman. The dark eyes looked down at him gravely, and Merriman held out the second package. 'This, the Lady of the Manor sent for you.'

Will opened it. Inside lay a small hunting horn, gleaming, thin with age. His gaze flicked more briefly to Merriman, and down again.

Mary hopped about, giggling. 'Go on, Will, blow it. You could make a noise all the way to Windsor. Go on!'

'Later,' Will said. 'I have to learn how. Will you thank her for me very much?' he said to Merriman.

Merriman inclined his head. 'Now I must go,' he said.

Roger Stanton said, 'I can't tell you how grateful we've been for all your help. With everything, through this mad weather – and the children – you really have been most tremendously—' he lost his words, but thrust out his arm and pumped Merriman's hand up and down with such warmth that Will thought he would never stop.

The craggy, fierce-carved face softened;

Merriman looked pleased and a little surprised. He smiled and nodded, but said nothing. Paul shook hands with him, and Mary. Then Will's hand was in the strong grasp, and there was a quick pressure and a brief intent look from the deep, dark eyes. Merriman said, '*Au revoir*, Will.'

He raised his hand to them all and strode off down the Lane. Will drifted after him. Mary said, skipping at his side, 'Did you hear the wild geese last night?'

'Geese?' Will said gruffly. He was not really listening. 'Geese? In all that storm?'

'What storm?' said Mary, and went on before he could blink. 'Wild geese, there must have been thousands of them. Migrating, I suppose. We didn't see them – there was just this gorgeous noise, first of all a lot of cackling from those daft rooks in the wood, and then a long, long sort of yelping noise across the sky, very high up. It was thrilling.'

'Yes,' said Will. 'Yes, it must have been.'

'I don't think you're more than half awake,' Mary said in disgust, and she went hopping ahead to the end of the drive-way. Then she stopped suddenly and stood very still. 'My goodness! Will! Look!'

She was peering at something behind a tree, hidden by the remnants of a snowbank. Will came to look, and saw, lying among the wet undergrowth, the great carnival head with the eyes of an owl, the face of a man, the antlers of a deer. He stared and stared without a word in his throat. The head was crisp and bright and dry, as it had always been and always would be. It looked like the outline of Herne the Hunter that he had seen against the sky, and yet not like.

Still he stared, and said nothing.

'Well, I never,' said Mary brightly. 'Aren't you lucky it got stuck there? Mum will be pleased. She was awake by then, it was when the floods came up all of a sudden. You weren't there of course; the water came in all over the ground floor and quite a lot of things got washed out of the living-room before we realized. That head was one of them – Mum was all upset because she knew you'd be. Well, look at that, fancy that—'

She peered closer at the head, still prattling gaily, but Will was no longer listening. The head lay very close to the garden wall, which was still buried in snow but beginning to break through the drifts at either side. And on the drift at the outer edge, covering the verge of the road and overhanging the running stream in the gutter, there were a number of marks. They were hoofprints, made by a horse stopping and pivoting and leaping away over the snow. But none of them was in the shape of a horse-shoe. They were circles quartered by a cross: the prints of the shoes that John Wayland Smith, once at the beginning, had put on the white mare of the Light.

Will looked at the prints, and at the carnival head, and swallowed hard. He walked a few paces to the end of the driveway and looked down Huntercombe Lane; he could see Merriman's back still, as the tall, dark-clad figure strode away. And then his hair prickled and his pulses stood still, for from behind him came a sound sweeter than seemed possible in the raw air of the cold grey morning. It was the soft, beautiful yearning tone of the old flute from the Manor; Paul, irresistibly drawn, must have put the instrument together to try it out. He was playing 'Greensleeves' once more. The eerie, enchanted lilt floated out through the morning on the still air; Will saw Merriman raise his wild white head as he heard it, though he did not break his stride.

As he looked down the road still, with the music singing in his ears, Will saw that out beyond Merriman the trees and the mist and the stretch of the road were shaking, shivering, in a way that he knew well. And then gradually, out there, he saw the great Doors take shape. There they stood, as he had seen them on the open hillside and in the Manor: the tall carved doors that led out of Time, standing alone and upright in the Old Way that was known now as Huntercombe Lane. Very slowly, they began to open. Somewhere behind Will the music of 'Greensleeves' broke off, with a laugh and some muffled words from Paul; but there was no break in the music that was in Will's head, for now it had changed into that haunting, bell-like phrase that came always with the opening of the Doors or any great change that might alter the lives of the Old Ones. Will clenched his fists as he listened, yearning towards the sweet beckoning sound that was the space between waking and dreaming, yesterday and tomorrow, memory and imagining. It floated lovingly in his mind, then gradually grew distant, fading, as out on the Old Way Merriman's tall figure, swirled round again now by a blue cloak, passed through the open Doors. Behind him, the towering slabs of heavy carved oak swung slowly together, together, until silently they shut. Then as the last echo of the enchanted music died, they disappeared.

And in a great blaze of yellow-white light, the sun rose over Hunter's Combe and the valley of the Thames.